the rest is silence

the rest is
silence

a novel

scott fotheringham

GOOSE LANE

Edited by Bethany Gibson.
Cover illustration: morguefile.com.
Cover and page design by Julie Scriver.
Printed in Canada.
10 9 8 7 6 5 4 3 2 1

Library and Archives Canada Cataloguing in Publication

Fotheringham, Scott, 1961-
   The rest is silence / Scott Fotheringham.

Issued also in electronic format.
ISBN 978-0-86492-656-2
   I. Title.

PS8611.O797R48 2012   C813'.6   C2011-907592-X

Goose Lane Editions acknowledges the financial support of the Canada Council for the Arts, the Government of Canada through the Canada Book Fund (CBF), and the Government of New Brunswick through the Department of Wellness, Culture, and Sport.

The author and publisher recognize the support of the Province of Nova Scotia through the Department of Communities, Culture and Heritage.

Goose Lane Editions
500 Beaverbrook Court, Suite 330
Fredericton, New Brunswick
CANADA E3B 5X4
www.gooselane.com

for
Alexa Macleod Fotheringham

But the effect of her being on those around her was incalculably diffusive: for the growing good of the world is partly dependent on unhistoric acts; and that things are not so ill with you and me as they might have been, is half owing to the number who lived faithfully a hidden life, and rest in unvisited tombs.

— *Middlemarch*, George Eliot

Annie
We landed on the same branch.

It is my judgment in these things that when you see something that is technically sweet, you go ahead and do it and you argue about what to do about it only after you have had your technical success. That is the way it was with the atomic bomb.

—J. Robert Oppenheimer

A farmer's is a very healthy happy life; and the least hurtful, or rather the most beneficial profession of any.

—*Frankenstein,* Mary Shelley

*Best of any song
is bird song
in the quiet, but first
you must have the quiet.*

—*A Timbered Choir: The Sabbath Poems, 1979-1999,* Wendell Berry

This is what I've lost.

I was seven, growing up in a neighbourhood that had space for me to run. On an October afternoon, the air dry and cool, I was playing touch football in my backyard with my friends. Ripe pumpkins lay in our garden under the cloudless blue sky. Mom was at the kitchen window watching birds land on the feeder that she and I kept filled for them. The plenitude of summer had passed, easing us into the cold. That winter we would build the skating rink on the grass that was covered now with a collage of red and yellow leaves. Despite the end of things it was a dreamy time for a kid like me, for whom death was still an unexplored abstraction.

It was all so clean and clear, pure in its changing. I loved being in the world and the world loved me in October. How else to explain the smell of a forest full of crinkly leaves underfoot, the skeletal fingers of trees scratching against the sky, and the cold air on my ears hinting at frost in the nighttime? How else to explain the V of geese flying south over our house, all of us stopping mid-game to look heavenward, Mom rushing outside onto the lawn to come see? They were honking and flapping, saying goodbye to us, saying goodbye to what we had known of summer.

When they were a distant line, we could still hear their faint clamour. Then even that was gone and, not long after, her voice with it. I was left with an emptiness I hadn't known before, an emptiness I was certain would stay with me forever.

That childhood innocence and the freedom to play are not all I've lost. I have lived to see parts of the world I loved as a kid ruined.

We learn from the mistakes we make, not those we avoid because someone warned us of them. We discover our own faith, unwrap what we believe and how we worship life, not by following age-old rituals out of duty but by asking questions about our suffering. The faith we discover and the choices we make have a large impact on who we become. Usually their impact on the rest of the world is small, but there are exceptions.

Take a scientist like Oppenheimer. When he and his colleagues were constructing the atom bomb at Los Alamos, they worried that the chain reaction that it depended on might use whatever it came in contact with as fuel—a perpetual-motion machine that would turn the Earth into a nuclear furnace like the sun. They guessed that the gun was not loaded, crossed their fingers, and played Russian roulette with the planet.

Humans are no good at shelving ideas. We insist that our inventions be used without much thought as to whether they will benefit us. Scientists have made some big errors, unleashing technologies we can't control. We are paying for their mistakes.

I am an active member of this meddling species, compulsive and insistent, and I believe that technology can also be used to remedy what ails us. Perhaps this is only a justification for the mistakes I have made.

In the beginning was the word. Out of the void an idea is voiced, and for no other reason than being spoken, it inevitably becomes manifest. As the power of the split atom, once it was discovered, had to be acted upon; as we created GMOs once we were capable of genetic engineering; as human cloning is now possible, not because we need it, but because the technology exists: energy becomes matter, word becomes deed, the unmanifest is brought forth as form.

Don't voice your ideas if you don't want them realized.

1

Lily Lake Road
North Mountain, Nova Scotia

Islands of quiet remain, where we can hear birdsong and the air smells sweet, but they are shrinking. I have found one in the woods where I feel safe.

One way to get here is by the lone highway, curving through spruce forests like a scar, which connects this land to the harried continent at its back. You can trace the scar from New York all the way to Maine, through New Brunswick over marsh and by tidal rivers whose banks are slick red mud when the water is low. You will scream past the trees and the dead porcupines with their streaming guts on the side of the road to get where you think you need to be. And when you get to this point of land, surrounded by the sea assaulting its rocky shores, you have only two choices: stay and make it home or visit a while, then turn around and go back the way you came. For this is Nova Scotia, and Nova Scotia is the edge of the world.

Or else you can fly, over ages of trees and lakes and rock. Flap your wings and look upon the carpet of spruce and balsam fir colouring the land green from shore to shore.

Fly until you see the broad valley with the apple orchards, a few vineyards on its slopes, and the river winding through it. Running along the northern edge of that valley, between it and the bay with the high tides, is an ancient mountain range made of volcanic rock. These mountains have been ground down over millennia by the winds off the salt water, by ice sheets advancing and retreating, by the rains from November to May, so that they now stand a mere nine hundred feet above the sea.

Atop this mountain ridge is a small clearing in the forest, low-lying and wet. If it's winter you'll see a skating rink, its edges curvy, interrupted by small islands bumping out of the ground on which birch and maple grow. The snow glistens on the spruce boughs in the bright sun. When you see this you can land and stay. Then you are home.

I am living on two hundred and fifty acres of forest on the crest of the North Mountain. I bought it from a local logging company that had taken everything here that was worth a dollar. The trees and stumps they left behind were of no value to anybody but me and the coyotes, deer, and songbirds. I love this place like nowhere else I've lived because nobody else wants it, and because of the tranquility of living alone in the woods, a half-mile from my nearest neighbour. A few thousand dollars and a piece of lawyer's paper say I own this land, but I know it's not mine and never will be. My tent, which I tucked under some white spruce, is surrounded on three sides by woods. Twenty feet from my tent I built an outdoor kitchen where I make all my meals, even in the rain and snow. I have an apartment-sized propane stove on an oak pallet. Where I hammered nails into the spruce to hold a pot and a frying pan, thick yellow sap creeps down the bark and hardens, not letting me forget the wound. My cutlery sits in a red enamel mug on a beaten-up table my neighbour Martin was throwing away. My drinking water, which comes from his well, is stored in one-gallon glass pickle jars I was lucky to find at a yard sale. From the kitchen there are paths worn to my tent and to the garden, and from the garden to the dirt road. I grow vegetables in no more than a couple feet of soil resting between outcroppings of bedrock. Even when I'm wet and cold there are days I am happier here than I remember being since I was a kid.

When I was twenty-eight I came here seeking anonymity, a cipher lost to the world I'd known as well as to this new one I've chosen to inhabit. I am an orphan, determined to leave behind those who are gone — dead and otherwise — from my life. My main purpose here, now that the world seems to be falling apart, is to learn to grow my own food and put down roots in this thin soil.

I woke this morning to another sunny day. It hasn't rained once this hot August. After lunch I go for a tramp in the woods. The woods are thick behind my tent, even if the loggers have taken the big trees, and I want to visit the grove of white pine they missed. A light breeze blows along the mountain ridge. Cattle low to the east. It's an eerie sound, disembodied, like ghosts floating between the trees, reaching me as I leave the clearing. I start on the rough road, walking in the ruts the skidders left behind. It's a moss-covered logging road that has fir seedlings a foot tall growing out of it, one of which would make a lovely Christmas tree if I had a room to put it in. There are mushrooms dotting the route and carpets of crackerberry with white dogwood flowers. I see the occasional delicate balloon of a moccasin flower rising plump and pink above the forest floor. When I come to the marsh with its abundance of bulrushes and wild rhododendron, a pileated woodpecker raps on the tallest spruce for insects. A white-throated sparrow sings nearby and a trio of crows pass overhead. I spend days when birds are my only companions, and I am grateful for it.

When I first moved to New York I was mesmerized by things like the stream of red taillights heading up First Avenue, the surge of pedestrians everywhere I went, and the constant hum of voices, traffic, and construction. This contrast to the natural beauty I'd seen with my dad on our annual camping trips might have repelled me if I hadn't been twenty-four. I was in awe for the first year, but the feeling wore off and the sirens and honking cabs grated instead of thrilled. After that I was a rat in a cage.

I find the pine grove and lie on the needles laid out for me like a russet mattress in the tree shadows. Soon I fall asleep. When I wake it is early evening. I start for home, but within a few minutes I have no idea where I am. Nothing is recognizable. The light between the trees darkens and there is no moon to light the way. I crash through the underbrush like a rutting bull moose, rushing from tree to tree until I can no longer see their trunks. I find one with my hand, fall to my knees, and rest my back against it, panting. It makes no difference whether I close my eyes, it is that dark.

Coyotes sound more real when you're in their home than they do when you're inside your own. There must be a dozen of them yipping in the blackness. It doesn't calm me when they stop because I think they are sneaking up on me. I search on my hands and knees for a large stick, but all I find are branches that snap or crumble when I bend them.

I open my eyes at the crunch of boots snapping dry twigs. The shadowy light of false dawn brings tree branches into relief against the sky. Coming toward me is a man in a plaid hunting jacket, an orange cap, and leather work boots. I crouch behind the tree. The barrel of his rifle is aimed at the ground. I have yet to confront the hunters I know use this land each fall. Martin told me that the "No Hunting" signs I have painted and nailed to trees by the road might dissuade polite hunters, but already the signs have been shot up or torn down, and deer season doesn't begin until October. Once the hunter is close enough for me to see, I recognize a man I met once but don't much like. I stand up. He remembers me.

"You're up early."

"I slept out here."

He looks at me, then smiles.

"You got lost, eh?"

He points into the forest. His hand is big like my father's were, and all of a sudden I am small, standing at Dad's side. A robin has hit our kitchen window so hard that it leaves feathers on the glass and we are sure it has broken its neck. We rush outside to find the bird lying on the patio beneath the window. Dad picks it up and confines it in his cupped hands, slowing its racing heart and keeping it warm. After a couple of minutes Dad opens his hands. The robin stands, shits onto his palm, and, with a jump, flies into the branch of a tree, where it regales us with a song I am certain is of thanks as much as of freedom.

"Your place is through there."

Art starts walking and I follow him. We are at my tent site in less than five minutes. I offer to make him a cup of tea.

"You buy this place from Ernie Bent?"

I nod, then change the subject. "Did you shoot anything?"

"I forgot my shells. No matter. I like to walk these woods as much as hunt in them these days."

"You've hunted here before?"

He laughs. "Son, my pop showed me how to shoot a .22 back here when I was this high." He puts his hand by his hip. "I had a trapline running through these woods. Rabbits mostly. The occasional squirrel. It went from my place over this mountain and down into the valley."

"You don't trap anymore?"

"I had my fill of rabbit meat. I did it then 'cause I was young enough to enjoy it. That and I had to help out some way at home. I sold the rabbits Mother didn't cook to folks for a quarter the pair. Some years there wasn't much meat besides what I trapped."

"I thought deer season doesn't open till late October."

"There's more'n enough deer in these woods to go around. Besides, there's no good meat in town."

The shortage of plastic means that less food is being shipped. The food we do get is all packaged in glass or tin. I wonder if Art would teach me to hunt. I can only stomach so much creamed corn and applesauce. A bit of deer meat would taste good.

"Do me a favour? Let me know when you're coming up here to hunt. I'm not big on surprises."

He nods. I relax a bit.

"Ever see any water in these woods? A stream or a spring?"

"Nope. Dry as a preacher's bone back here in the summer. In winter there's all the water a fella could want, and then some."

"Tell me about it."

He looks me up and down. "You want some work?"

"Maybe." I do, though. I'm not getting much food off my land this first year, and as much as I am growing to hate it, creamed corn in a can still requires cash. I have little money left.

"I need some digging done at my place. I'd get a backhoe, but it's a fiddly situation. I bet I could still dig better than a lanky guy like you, but my body's just not what it used to be."

"I know what you mean."

He glares at me from under his bushy eyebrows, long hairs sprouting in all directions.

"Come by my place Saturday morning. Early. I'm in Margaretsville, third driveway after the restaurant on the shore side."

2

Lily Lake Road

I moved here because this was far from the rest of civilization—from Boston, New York, Toronto—and I had grown weary of a world that didn't make sense. We compliment ourselves on being a rational species and an advanced civilization, denigrating dumb animals and primitive cultures, but everything I saw in that difficult world suggested that our self-congratulation is misplaced. By the end of my time in the city I just wanted to go for a long walk. I wound up here because my dad was born in Middleton and had brought me here as a kid. If I was going to escape, I figured this might feel like coming home.

I spent the first winter in Halifax washing bacon and sausage grease off dishes in a diner downtown. I rented an apartment in a creaky wooden building. The rent was cheap, and my bedroom window, with its flaking white paint, looked out on the restaurant I worked in halfway down Grafton Street. Mixed blessing, that. I had a short walk to work, but when someone called in sick I was the go-to guy. I did some prep there too. I got along with the kitchen staff but didn't make any friends. I think of one thing when I remember that restaurant. I pulled a head of romaine, wrapped in plastic, out of the cold room. As I cleaned it I found a white moth between two leaves, fluttering as the warm kitchen air hit it. Its wings pressed uselessly against its body, vibrating back and forth rapidly in an attempt to escape. As a larva it had led a secure life, munching voraciously, slumbering as a pupa, then hatching as a winged chrysalis into an enclosed plastic world. Cold, damp, dark, with no freedom to fly, that moth waited until I ripped open the bag and peeled back a leaf. The rush of warm air, light, and room to stretch its wings were a rapid reversal of its fortune. It flew to the window above my dish pit, where it stayed for a few days, then disappeared.

There were bars on every downtown street. When they closed, crowds converged at Pizza Corner. Three of its corners housed pizza shops and my room was above one of them. On the fourth corner was a large stone church, into and out of which I never saw a person venture. In the wee hours when I was awake, often because of the noise on the street, I sat in a chair in front of the window overlooking that church and wished all sorts of nastiness on the drunks below.

On the coldest nights the walls of my room came alive, winter winds pushing through fissures and, one February morning, frosting the sill by my pillow. I was by myself except at work and even then I was lonely. On my days off I'd go to the public library a block away and look at *New Yorker* cartoons or old issues of *Harrowsmith* to dream about the gardening and building I longed to do far from the city. When the library was closed on Mondays I went to the medical library at Dalhousie to look stuff up.

The following spring I left the city and worked on organic farms around the province. The best place I stayed was Martin and Jen's ten-acre homestead next door. For a year before I bought my land I lived with them, working in their organic gardens and on construction projects with Martin. In return for my work I was given a bed in a nook off the kitchen and all the lettuce, carrots, potatoes, tomatoes, beans, raspberries, and garlic I could eat. It was the best food I'd ever tasted, and I liked living with Martin and Jen because they didn't ask a lot of personal questions. They had four cats patrolling the gardens and woods around their homestead. The cats left daily deposits of squirrel heads, writhing mice, and bird feathers on the front doorstep. One of them ate entire adult rabbits. I woke once to the crunching of bones underneath my bed.

My friends have a steady supply of labour, eager people who want to learn how to live off the land. Like me, these visitors want to grow food, build houses, and forge community. The ones I've met are idealists. Most are young and full of a naïveté that can be both uplifting and heartbreaking. The few older people tend to be cynical when they arrive but invariably recover a hope for the world that they had thought irretrievable. It makes me think that what Martin and Jenifer are doing on a small scale is the kind of thing that might just save us.

While I stayed with them I went for walks in the forest next door. The "For Sale" signs along the road intrigued me and late that fall I bought all these trees and rocks and solitude. I stayed at their place the rest of that winter, then moved here this past spring.

At the end of April I put up my tent and began the long process of clearing the ground of fallen branches and small trees that had been felled and left to decay. It was a near-impenetrable tangle of brush. I removed rotting stumps. I yanked on spruce roots, some of which snaked through the thin topsoil for twenty feet before snapping off. I dragged all this debris to the crest and dumped it in a pile that grew to eight feet tall and thirty feet long. Later that summer birds and snakes and mice made it home. But this was April in Nova Scotia and all the smart animals were still south or underground, knowing what came next.

April may be the cruellest month where T.S. came from, but it was May in Nova Scotia that broke my heart. I was ready for the blossoms and the bees, the spring rain stirring dull roots, and instead it snowed on the ninth. When I woke that morning my sleeping bag was cold and clammy and a pool of water had collected in the corner of the tent by my feet. I zipped open the flap to see blowing white globules splattering the canvas. I spent that day digging stumps in the wet ground to stay warm. Clumps of earth stuck to the shovel and my rubber boots. By mid-afternoon I was soaked through and muddy. I retreated to Martin and Jen's and sat in their warm, dry house with an orange cat in my lap while we watched TV. Martin drank beer, Jen knitted, and I scratched Charlie behind the ears. Domestic bliss.

Within a week, despite the cold, I was ready to plant peas. I depend on three gardening books: *The Good Life* by Helen and Scott Nearing, which I'd brought with me from New York; *The New Organic Grower* by Eliot Coleman; and *How to Grow More Vegetables* by John Jeavons. The first bed went in among the wild grasses and the previous year's dead plants. I swung the mattock to remove sod, rocks, and roots in a foot-wide row the length of the garden. There were more spruce roots between the basalt bedrock and the surface.

I yanked on them and carried them to the brush wall. The bed ended up being a wonky shape that curved around stumps I couldn't get out. I held a palmful of crinkled peas that the cold and muddy fingers of my other hand struggled to grab. I pushed a seed into the soil every three inches among the stones and clods of wet earth. A Canada jay flitted from the ground nearby onto the brush wall. Even the discomfort of being cold and wet couldn't dampen my joy of putting life in the ground.

I struggled with loneliness, with missing my friends and family. I was excited by the challenge to survive, to carve a life out of the forest, but I wasn't finding enjoyment in much else. I had always liked my own company until then, but what was the point of growing my own food, of making it on my own, if there was nobody to share it with? I wanted a woman in my life, but it seemed that there was no room in this world for love anymore. Everyone looked sick with worry, heads down, plodding into an uncertain future. And what woman would be willing to live in a tent and plant peas in this weather? As much as I was glad to be free of my life in Manhattan, with all its complications, I wondered if I would be able to last in the woods in these difficult times.

After the snow and the pea sowing came warm weather. It brought out the fiery buds of the red maples, bumblebees, and green shoots; it also brought blackflies from one of the rings of hell. Between periods of windmilling my arms to shoo the pesky bastards, I found a trio of wood ticks on my pants. Blackflies have been wed to this geography forever, but a decade ago nobody around here even knew what a tick was. People speculate that they arrived in Yarmouth with a shipment of Florida oranges or cheap American beef, or on the pant leg of a tourist from Maine. Jenifer, who is gentle with her cats and whom I've seen stop her car to help a turtle safely cross the road, is brutal with the eight-legged bloodsuckers. She insists on cutting in two any tick she finds with a pair of nail clippers she carries for that purpose. It's the exceptional trait that makes her goodness human, the flaw we search for in one we admire that makes us like them better. Even if I wanted to kill ticks, doing so one at a time would never get rid of them. We might be moving into an age when all that will survive the environmental onslaught are the small and numerous. I flick ticks into the grass like an arachnid god. Be fruitful and multiply. It drives Jenifer nuts.

Soon I had another bed prepared and sowed with bunching onion seed, trenches planted with fifty pounds of Century russet seed potatoes, and more rows of peas. I piled the sods I'd removed from the beds with the grass facing down, then mixed manure with soil, shovelled it into the hollowed-out centre of each pile, and covered the whole thing with straw. Once the soil in the centre warmed up, I planted scarlet runners in it. Later, when the days were hot, I sowed squash and corn seed around the bean shoots.

The clouds of blackflies grew thicker as May progressed. I was O.K. as long as I was moving. They found me when I was sowing or weeding, zigzagging in front of my face. They got stuck in my ears and buzzed, biting the delicate skin. They landed on my wrists, drawing blood that dried in crusts on the elasticized cuffs of my jacket. I burned branches and grass, hoping to smudge the flies out. After gardening for a few minutes, I'd jog over to the smouldering fire, hold my breath, and let the smoke surrounding my head drive the buggers away. As soon as I went back to work they rediscovered my bare neck and ears and made life miserable. On the worst days, when it was still and hot, their persistence was greater than mine and I cut my workday short, opting for a brisk walk in the woods or reading *The Good Life* in my tent for inspiration on how to be a homesteader. It is a softcover book with a photo of the authors on the front. A man standing with an axe looking at the camera and a woman sitting on the rocks looking up at him in admiration. It was bought at Books & Co. on Madison Avenue a long time ago.

I needed to buy a screen veil for my head, oil for my bike chain, and a bike helmet. On a Saturday near the end of April I glided down the mountain on my bike. The air breezed through my hair as I picked up speed. I loved the speed and kept my hands off the brakes. I learned to ride when I was five by leaning my bike against a tree by the driveway in our front yard. I kept pushing away and stumbling. After two days of this, when Dad came home from the high school where he taught math, I was ready to push away from the tree, pedal, and stay upright. I moved jubilantly and liberated along the grass.

Middleton is four miles down the mountain in the valley. I passed a field of Herefords destined for the table. They were docile, unlike the feisty Holsteins farther down the road. When I got off my bike, those black-and-white beasts came up to the fence.

Hello, biped. Got any corn for us?

The sweet scent on the soft breeze reminded me that my father loved the smell of manure on a farmer's field. I inhaled deeply. My father moved from here as an infant with his mother and sister. He grew up in dairy country not unlike this, around silos, big red barns, and mixed herds of Holsteins and Jerseys. I am prone to confuse his memories with my own, since I spent time where he had been a boy when we visited my grandmother in Williamstown and because he often told me stories of what it had been like. The newly mown hayfields on the edge of town; the bread baked by his neighbour, slices slathered with butter and jam; roller skating down the steep hill in front of the house with no way to brake. It's as if I did these things.

The cows trotted beside me for a while when I remounted my bike to continue down the hill. I passed a few farmhouses that a green sign said was "Spa Springs." It's another of the communities whose residents have melted into the city. The Mi'kmaq are said to have used the spring as healing waters. The British spooked, starved, and scalped them off their land and then, in the nineteenth century, put up a hotel and a spa that hosted thousands of European guests. The hotel burned down and was never rebuilt. In the 1970s a German consortium got provincial promise-us-you'll-make-a-couple-of-jobs-for-locals funding to build a water bottling plant. They took the money, built the plant, but never opened it. All that is left of Spa Springs is six houses.

I passed a few more farms, coasted under the highway overpass, and cycled into town. Middleton, population 1,745, closes up tight between Saturday noon and Monday morning. I got to the bakery as Norm was getting ready to lock the door.

"Any chance for a butter tart?" I asked.

He held the door for me. "Are you still living with Martin?"

"No, I bought the land down the road from them."

"Don't know it."

"You wouldn't. Nobody's ever lived there."

He saw me eyeing the tarts and pushed the plate toward me. I took one and continued talking with half of it in my mouth.

"It's tough land to grow on."

"Dad and I planted last weekend. Seeded our beans, carrots, onions, potatoes, turnips, and beets."

His farm was like many of the older farms nearby. Their hundred-plus acres ran in a narrow band from the river, through the valley, and up the side of the mountain. They had lumber and firewood standing at their backs while they plowed. The soil was sandy and fertile, and if there was enough rain, it was so hot down there that the crops grew while you watched.

"You're lucky to have the river so close for the cattle," I said.

He shook his head. "You kidding? I wouldn't let them drink that. There's all that runoff from the farms upstream. Last time we let them drink from it our vet bills went way up. Antibiotics and such. No, I'd trade some of our land for the good water you've got up on the mountain."

"I keep hearing about that water." I smiled. "Wish some of it was flowing on my land."

I asked for five more butter tarts to take with me.

"I hope a paper bag's all right by you."

"I don't have much choice, do I?"

I walked my bike through town. It looked like it hadn't changed much since Dad and I were there seventeen years before. There was a new Baptist church on Commercial Street, and the train tracks had been torn up. Other than that it struck me as sleepy and quaint, as if it belonged to another era. I went to the SaveEasy, hoping for something fresh from the produce section. I didn't know whether to laugh or cry. A few dried-up bunches of spinach from Quebec, some local carrots and lettuce. There were, amazingly, a few avocados. I bought them all, as well as a bunch of kale and some snow peas from a farm in Paradise, downstream from Middleton. I went down every aisle. An old man, a farmer whose family had probably lived here since 1800, pushed his cart through the near-empty store. He was skinny, with concave cheeks and bony hands. He wore a ratty ski hat despite the warmth. He stopped in front of a shelf of soup, pulled a single can, and put it in his cart. He reached for a second and held it, as if weighing the can. He was looking at the price. He put it back on the shelf. We are too far off the beaten track to get much of the new plastic packaging, and from what I hear on late-night radio coming out of Boston and Portland, there are shortages even in the major cities. The store did its best to hide the gaps on the shelves by spreading out what boxes, jars, and cans they had.

But then, at the front of the store by the checkout, there was a display of plastic bottles of soda and water. Behind them, a large, youthful face on a piece of cardboard beamed at us. In large red letters she said, "They're here! In non-biodegradable bottles!" I pulled a bottle of water from the display and squeezed it. It was flexible, like the plastic it had replaced. The label read:

> NuForm Plastix® bottles are made exclusively with PolyOx® technology. They are guaranteed never to biodegrade. All NuForm products pass stringent FDA regulations and are safe to drink

from, and safe to re-use, over and over. For optimal
use please keep your NuForm Plastix® product
out of direct sunlight.

I had heard about these. They were made by EcoPlast, a
chemical company that had made its name manufacturing
environmentally friendly plastics. When plastics became
susceptible to bacterial digestion, EcoPlast was one of the
manufacturers that scrambled to solve the problem. They
found a temporary solution by joining the hydrocarbon chains
in their plastics with heavy metals. When these new plastics
were eaten by the genetically engineered bacteria, they released
mercury, arsenic, and lead, killing the microbes immediately.
EcoPlast had received special dispensation from the FDA,
through emergency legislation rushed through Congress to
bypass the normal safety testing, though everyone guessed
that the heavy metals would leach into the contents of the
bottles like bisphenol A does.

I placed my box of oats, the produce and avocados, and
the cans of corn on the checkout counter. The girl in the
green smock, who looked sixteen with her strawberry blond
hair tied back in a ponytail, was trying her best. She smiled
and asked how I was. Had she lived in a more salubrious
era, when most of the country's population lived on family
farms, she would have been a wholesome farm girl wearing
gingham and laughing a lot. She had a pasty complexion and
flaky patches of eczema at her hairline. She asked me what
the green, egg-shaped thingies were.

"Avocados."

"What do you do with them?"

I asked her if she'd ever had guacamole. She shook her head. She had probably never left the Annapolis Valley.

On the way home I biked past a dairy farm with three fields. The precision and uniformity of those fields was appealing. Their square edges, the green of the triple-mix hay, the lighter rye grass, and the parallel rows of sprouting corn. Those fields were the only beautiful thing about that farm. Holstein calves taken from their mothers and awaiting vealization were housed in tiny pens the size of outhouses. Dozens of old tires held down gigantic sheets of shredded plastic covering a manure pile, the ammoniac stench of which crossed the road as I pedalled slowly up the hill. My heart thumped against my ribs and I was panting with the effort. Farther along, past the herds of Holsteins and Herefords, pasture gave way to woodlots. I got off the bike and walked it up the hill at the foot of Lily Lake Road.

By the time I got home, my shirt was damp and blackflies were stuck in the sweat on my neck. I had elevated a small barrel seven feet off the ground atop a platform made of short logs laid logcabin style. The water in the barrel had been heated by a black rubber hose coiled on the side facing the sun. I stood beside the barrel on an oak pallet and opened the spigot. The warm water felt refreshing as it hit my skin and cooled in the air. It takes surprisingly little water to clean the sweat and dirt off my skin. As there was nobody to see me, I walked naked in the luscious warmth of the late-afternoon sun and air-dried my body and hair.

3

Lily Lake Road

On Saturday I coast downhill on my bike to work at Art's house. Toward the Bay of Fundy, weaving across the median from one side of the road to the other, relishing the sun on my back. In the twenty minutes it takes, only three cars pass. The drivers wave as if we know each other. I come into fog at Margaretsville as it streams off the bay and up the slope at my back. The temperature drops ten degrees. The sharp curve takes me to the right, past the takeout place that sells haddock fish 'n' chips. All along the high bluffs worn by Fundy's tides are old houses and summer cottages owned by people from away: Americans, Germans, and what the locals call Upper Canadians. Jenifer described Art's place to me, a big, white house almost hidden from the road by trees. When I turn in to his gravel driveway a border collie runs at me with a foaming mouthful of teeth. I jump from my bike and stand as still as a heron fishing in the shallows as the dog circles around me, figures I am harmless, and trots back to the house.

"I see you met Lucy." Art is smiling by the side of his house. It is the first time I've seen him without a hat. His hair is silver, wavy and thick like the wolf pelt I recall raking my fingers through when I was a kid and my class was on a field trip at a museum. If I have hair like his when I'm eighty, I'm never going to wear a hat. He is good-looking, though I'll be damned to say so out loud after the embarrassment at the fire hall when we first met. I catch up and walk beside him. He leads me around the side of the house. Rose bushes are growing wild against the house between the cultivated flower beds. I stick my nose into a pink flower and inhale its scent.

"Salt air makes them big and pungent. The septic tank should be here."

He scuffs the ground with his boot. "Or over here a bit. My brother, Joshua, kept track of that sort of thing. All the drains are backed up and the house smells bad. One of the pipes is blocked and we need to find it. According to the map Joshua drew forty years ago, the pipe runs along here." I follow his hand with my eye to a half-dozen trees on the edge of the cliff that drops into the bay. "The outlet is between those two trees."

The outlet? The crazy bugger is flushing his raw shit onto the beach.

"Just like in Halifax, huh?"

My voice sounds harsh, but it makes me sad to see how the city treats its harbour like a giant toilet bowl. Piss, shit, and toilet paper, bleach, paint, used motor oil, battery acid: one big cesspool. The tides come twice each day, out-in, out-in, but don't flush it out. There are snails in the harbour that can't decide whether they are male or female, their indeterminate sex the result of who-knows-what synthetic hormones flowing out of sewage pipes.

"No, no, no." He laughs. "The outlet pipe is a hundred feet from the edge of the cliff."

I'm relieved.

"If you dig here, you should find the connection. I'm going to the woods for a bit," he says. "I've got a log that's hung up in another tree."

A mattock and shovel lie on the ground near us. Digging holes by the shore is no easier than in my so-called garden. The shovel hits rock after rock, the shocks reverberating along my forearms. I straighten my back for a rest and lean on the shovel. Trees rim the clearing in front of me. The spruce and firs are blasted by the cold winds off the sea in winter and stunted by the cool fogs of summer. They might be a hundred years old, but none is so tall that I couldn't throw a stone over it. From my right, beyond where the trickle of the pipe overflows onto the grass, comes the sound of waves licking the cliffs along the shore. Art walks through the clearing wearing an orange helmet and face guard and carrying a chainsaw and a couple of orange plastic wedges. His gait is stiff but purposeful. Soon, the crashing of the waves is interrupted by the whine of his saw.

I go back to digging, bending down with each shovelful to remove the stones that impede my progress. It is almost an hour before I make it down three feet and feel the *click-click* of the shovel on the clay pipe we are looking for. Shit, it stinks out here. I dig a wider hole to locate the suspect connection, see that the outlet of the pipe is shattered, and begin to clear the soil from around and under it so it can be replaced. The lines on my fingers are traced with soil, like mini tattoos, and there is a dark rim under each of my chipped nails. My hands are never clean since I moved here.

I think back over this first summer, all the hard work I've done alone, and I remember meeting Art a month ago. I had spent the afternoon in the sun weeding Martin's carrot beds. He gave me a dozen lush tomato transplants when I was done. Jen invited me to go with her to a dance at the fire hall in Margaretsville that night. I was eager to get out and have some company. Martin doesn't like to dance and didn't want to go with his wife. I was glad he wasn't coming. He's always crapping on me for not being practical enough, and I suspect he's jealous of the friendship I have with Jen. At that point it had been so long since I'd been in a city or heard live music that I would have listened to a marching band of accordions and kazoos.

I went home and put the tomato plants in the ground late enough in the day that they wouldn't be shocked by the sun and watered them. Then I watered myself.

Jen drove us down the winding road to the Margaretsville fire hall in her Lada. She had cleaned the dash with lavender so it smelled nice, but there was no hope for the seats. They were covered with cat fur. I never tire of that stretch of road running downhill from Victoria Vale to Margaretsville, especially when it opens up out of the trees and beyond the fields of hay the water and sky are separated from each other by the wide ribbon of land on the other shore. I was in a good mood and sat sideways so I could watch Jenifer drive while I teased her about the cat hair on the seats. She has a lovely face and is thoughtful and fun, and I was attracted to her that night.

The dance took place in a large room beside the garage that housed the fire trucks. Most of the picnic tables set up at the back of the room were filled with people drinking beer or coffee. In front of the heavy woman at the canteen counter lay brownies, date squares, and cookies covered with Smarties. I gave the woman two loonies for a date square and a cup of strong black tea.

The fiddler was a leathery man who played jigs and reels that made it impossible to sit still. He sat stiff-backed in a wooden chair, one foot tapping the rhythm on the stage. I danced with Jen. Between sets, canned music played through the speakers. Jen didn't want to stop dancing, so I twirled her around as best I could. I felt dozens of pairs of eyes watching us, wondering who the new guy with Jenifer was, dancing like a flustered chicken. A slow song came on and we kept dancing. Jen is almost my height and I was relishing how good it was to have a woman in my arms again when I felt a tap on my shoulder.

"I'm cutting in," a deep voice said.

I pulled my cheek away from the softness of Jen's hair and turned to see the creased face of the fiddler, the bill of his John Deere cap aimed at my nose. I looked at her as we separated, then reached for his hands. He shoved me away.

"Not you, you fairy," he said. "I wanna dance with her."

I snorted, pretending I'd been joking, and found a picnic table at the back of the hall. If it hadn't been such a long walk uphill in the dark, I would have started right then for home. When the song ended Jen came and joined me. I didn't look at her.

"So now you've met Art."

"Lucky me."

"He's blunt but really quite sweet."

I grunted like a caveman. The rest of the dance was ruined for me. All I could think of was that everyone had seen me reach for his hands.

—

The screen door at the back of the house slams shut and I am woken from my daydream. Lucy comes running around the corner wagging her tail and sneezing the way border collies do when they like you. She is followed by a young woman whose motion is the opposite of Art's: fluid, graceful, lithe. There is no wagging, no sneezing, but her eyes make up for that. Their irises are black, and huge, as she stares at me and says nothing. Unnerved, I put my head back down and poke around the pipe.

"I've got a strange request."

Her voice is soft like water running through my cupped hands. I look up.

"Will you sit for me while I sketch you?"

"Your grandfather seems to think it's important that I get to the bottom of this hole."

She laughs. She smells of geraniums. "Art won't mind if I borrow you for half an hour. I'll pay you for your time."

I lay the shovel beside the hole. "They don't call them odd jobs for nothing."

I reach out to introduce myself. She eyes the dirt on my fingers suspiciously.

"It's only soil. I haven't had to deal with the pipe yet."

"I'm Lina."

Her hand is cool and has the rough skin and strong grip of someone who could be digging the hole instead of me. It's as if I'm clasping the handle of a whip that runs up her arm, coils through her core, and whose tips end in the black centres of her eyes.

She turns toward the house and I follow the thick, dark braid that flows like a tail down her back. The scarlet ribbon

tied at the end, near her sacrum, sways from side to side as if
flicking flies off her hips. Her studio is in the northwest corner
of the house, facing the water. It smells of oil paints, turpentine,
and books mouldering from the damp sea air. The spines
on the shelves are discoloured from sunlight. It is a strange
collection. Poetry by Hopkins and Hardy, a thirty-volume
set by Trollope, and three works by Krishnamurti. Portraits
are hung on the high white wall opposite the windows. The
features in each one look like they are made of melted wax.
Out of the top of each head emerges the clear and precise
image of a bird, its wings outstretched in liftoff.

Lina motions for me to sit in a chair facing the row of
windows and moves to her easel. I rest my hands on my thighs.
My shoulders and forearms relax after their exertion. I reach
up to remove my hat, with its floppy, dirty-white brim.

"Oh, leave it on. It's what made me want to sketch your
head. That and your nose."

"It's the hat that becomes the bird?"

"Sometimes."

"What bird will this become?"

"Can't say yet."

She is quiet while she draws. She wears loose, paint-
splattered jeans and a white T-shirt that hugs her breasts
and accentuates the darkness of her skin. I focus on her eyes
while she is intent on my portrait. Even when she looks up
from the easel she ignores me, as if she is a surgeon and I am
her patient etherized upon the table. When she looks back
at the paper, her irises are iridescent, like the glossy purple
head of a grackle. She looks up again, this time into my eyes,
and smiles. Her smile is subtle, lips pressed together, corners
curving up slightly. I wait for another. Her pencil scratches are

punctuated by the scream of Art's chainsaw coming through the open windows.

"Where are you from?" I ask.

"Quebec."

"And where's your family from?"

She guesses what I'm wondering and, in a minute, says, "My mother's Wendat."

"Wendat?"

"Huron. I grew up on the Wendake reserve in Quebec City."

I don't interrupt her concentration again. Instead I imagine what she is drawing coming out of my head. Based on my hat it could be a gull or tern. A few minutes pass, and she puts down her pencil and sighs.

"Can I see it?"

"It didn't work."

"I don't get to have a pileated woodpecker pounding on my head?"

"Not today, I'm afraid."

She walks me to the door. I stand, awkward and quiet, wanting her to say more, wanting her to keep me from leaving. I want her hand in mine again.

"Let me get your money." She turns back into the room.

"Forget it. The rest was good."

I leave the house.

"By the way," she says as I stand on the grass below her. "He's not my grandfather."

Lucy follows me back to the hole and lies nearby while I finish digging. When Art comes back I show him where the pipe is broken.

"I called down to Home Hardware," he says. "They stopped

ordering PVC pipe a month ago. Everybody's afraid it's gonna fall apart like the rest."

"It won't. It's different plastic."

"I have a length of the old clay stuff in the shed."

It is suppertime when we finish, fill the hole, and stomp the ground back into place. Art helps me put the tools back in the shed.

"Will you stay for supper?"

The smell of sewage is stuck in my nostrils if not on my clothes. I look at my pants and shirt sleeves, covered in dirt, and then at him.

"To hell with that." He waves a thick hand in the air. "I've smelled a lot worse."

I wash my hands, then stick my head under the tap, revelling in the warmth and volume of water. I grab a towel from the rack and rub my hair. The towel smells like Lina. On the shelf above the toilet is a bottle of geranium essential oil. I consider putting a drop of it on my wrist but think better of it. In the kitchen, I sit on a stool at the counter where Art cuts vegetables for a one-pot chicken casserole. He pulls two bottles of homemade beer from the fridge and puts one in front of me. The cap flips off the stubby brown bottle and rolls in a spiral in front of me.

"To shit staying underground," he says as he raises his bottle.

Our bottles click and he raises his to take a sip.

"You want a glass?"

I shake my head and tip the bottle to my lips, pretending to drink it. The pine floorboards creak at the back of the house. Lina comes into the kitchen and washes her hands at the sink.

"I was telling our friend here that you don't care much for the sludge at the bottom of my beer." He winks at me.

"And I told you, Art, it has nothing to do with your sludge."

Her back is to us. I could lift that braid, feel its heft, coil it around my neck like a heavy scarf. She dries her hands on a dish towel and pours a glass of tap water. She comes to sit on the stool beside me. She smells, not only of flowers, but of laundry hung out in the sun, and when she smiles, I take a small step toward feeling human again, as if there is more to life than splitting firewood and hauling water.

"I tried to draw him while you were in the woods, but it didn't work out."

"He'd make a good hawk with a nose like that," Art says.

"His nose wasn't the issue. Some days I can draw and some I can't."

"On the days you can't, you might as well lay your pencil down and take up a hoe." He turns to me. "Lina's here to look after Louise's gardens for me. I can do the rough work, but it takes a feminine touch to make the flower beds look like they used to."

"Your wife?" I say.

"She's living in a home in Bridgetown. Her memory's all shot to hell."

"I'm sorry."

He waves me off with a snort. "How can you be sorry? You never knew her." He continues chopping the onions and carrots. "I hate this time of day. She called it *entre chien et loup*. Soon after Louise and I married, Joshua sold us this land at the edge of the farm he and I grew up on. There was an old house here with its roof caving in. Louise and I were up there together, into November, with the rain beating down on our backs, repairing it. She passed me boards and I'd nail them in place. We shingled the whole thing too."

He is staring through the window. It's dusk, and though I can see his reflection, he's looking far beyond it as though he were expecting his wife to return from the garden, a spectre holding a hoe and her gardening gloves, mind intact.

After supper, while I help Lina do the dishes, Art gets out his fiddle and plays a melancholy tune. His mood has infected me, and, given Lina's reticence, she and I say little, listening to the plaintive singing of the sheep-gut strings under his bow. She hands me a heavy pottery plate, handmade, and our hands touch for the second time. Her tapered fingers return to the sudsy water and massage the sponge against a cup. When she hands it to me and meets my gaze I realize I've been staring. I look down and go back to wiping the plate.

Before it gets dark, I get on my bike for the long, slow ride uphill. Half an hour later I climb into my tent. The air is hot and the sweaty skin of my legs and back sticks to the nylon of my sleeping bag. I close my eyes, see Lina's, and can't sleep. I turn on the AM radio and tune in stations from the States. The baseball game from Boston, music, evangelists spouting their apocalyptic gibberish. Then, farther along the dial, a news report that makes me question if it is gibberish after all.

> ... the lack of plastic containers of many kinds has
> fuelled a drastic shortage of blood for surgeries in
> most hospitals. Authorities attribute this primarily
> to the loss of plastic collection bags and tubing.
> The dissolution of these and many other plastics
> has authorities baffled, but new evidence confirms

the spread of a strain, or strains, of genetically engineered bacteria.

Blackouts continue to plague most cities as the coating on high-voltage power lines is dissolving or being eaten. The nylon in gas tanks is being digested from the outside and people are finding their cars standing in puddles of gas.

And while most computers continue to be susceptible as key components disintegrate, one company's products appear to be immune to this biological threat. Horus Computers' sales have skyrocketed. Company spokespeople say they simply can't keep pace with the demand even with the influx of money from the U.S. and Chinese governments to expand production.

It's only a matter of time before all this reaches out here. It's perverse, I know, but listening to this soothes me to sleep.

*

I am in a lake sinking and wanting to touch bottom. I empty my lungs and move my arms upwards to propel me down. Down, down to the soft bottom, where the muck oozes between my toes. My body feels weightless as I crouch, then push off, now hoping for the surface. The lack of air makes my skinny body less buoyant. I ought to feel like I am flying, but the movement is too slow, the leaden-footed escape from nightmare monsters. I am made of stone. My muscles ache for oxygen as I struggle for the surface. It is right there, the partition between water and air. The blue sky and the sun's orange shimmering down to me. At last I burst through this limen, open my mouth, and gasp in breath after grateful breath.

It is early morning, and I have been sleeping on my back again. My sleeping bag is unzipped and covers one leg. There is the sound of rain hitting the leaves outside my tent. These drowning dreams began soon after my father killed himself. What if I did not wake up, if I continued to sink and couldn't open my mouth no matter how I craved to inhale? That is a scab I am in the habit of picking and won't let heal. Scabs are reminders that something's gone wrong. In bed, I try to piece together what that something is, breathing in, out.

One night when I was a child, waking from a nightmare, I called to my father, and though my voice was hushed out of fear that the fox in my dream would get me, Dad heard and came to comfort me.

"Hey, bud, try to fall asleep on your side, O.K.? I have nightmares too when I sleep on my back."

He sat on the edge of my bed and calmed me by rubbing my back until I fell asleep again. In the morning the daylight allowed me to wonder how I could ever have been afraid.

After he died, after he left without so much as a note explaining why, I felt him near me as a presence. For months after he died, whenever I was home from school, I'd open the door to his closet, run my fingers over his pants and his suit, and bury my face in his shirts. I slept with one of his shirts on my pillow. Over time, as I fell back into my routine at school, I was surprised when I noticed that I had a few minutes or part of an hour when I hadn't thought of him. And then his scent faded. I couldn't tell if he was leaving slowly or if I was pulling away from him by continuing to live. His presence dimmed as I ate and slept and lived without him, but there continue to be times, mostly at night, mostly when I dream, when he comes back.

I think of Art and the way he said he finds that Louise's physical presence has been replaced by silence. His memories can't keep that silence from roaring across the bay, through his woods, over the roof they repaired and shingled together, and on up the mountain. Something almost clicks into place for me — the sense of drowning, suffocation, people leaving without saying goodbye — and I roll that something into a ball and hold it in my head for another breath, trying to make sense of it. I exhale all of it hoping it will go where it needs to go and I can be done with it.

I open the tent door. The sound of the zipper is all there is besides the rain. But, hey, what's this? Sunshine. Again. The flutter of poplar leaves has fooled me into welcoming rain that still has not come. I pull on my shorts and a T-shirt. I don't need to garden today. The garlic bulbs I've harvested, gleaming white and tied in bunches, are hanging to dry from the branches under the canvas tarp of my outdoor kitchen.

I cook oats on the stove and carry them into the garden, picking blueberries as I go and dropping them in the pot. The crunch of the dry grass under my bare feet sounds like the crackling fire I have most nights in front of my tent. The garden craves rain and the road needs rain and the leaves of the dusty poplars lining that road beg for rain. All that dust has been churned up by the pickups, tractors, hay wagons, and manure spreaders that use Lily Lake Road as a shortcut. I can do nothing about the lack of rain, but I can wash the dust off my skin in the pond down the hill. I leave the empty bowl by the stove.

At the base of the steep hill Lily Lake Road becomes paved and crosses the main road connecting Margaretsville to the town of Middleton. Then there is a small, fenced cemetery next to Phinney's Pond. A man who once owned my land is buried there among the dandelions and dry grass, the candy wrappers and broken glass. Phineas Bent was descended from a New England Planter, Elijah Bent, who received a land grant in 1760 from the governor of Nova Scotia following the expulsion of the Acadians. Elijah moved his family from Sudbury, Massachusetts, to twelve hundred acres of fertile land straddling the Annapolis River and running up the North Mountain. Generations of Bents made their home in the Annapolis Valley, including Phineas, and with each new batch of sons, parcels were carved off the family grant until all that remained was the fraction of rock and trees and blackflies I bought. As far as I know neither Phineas nor any of the Bents lived on what is now my land. There's a rotting door hanging from the trunk of a balsam fir not far from my tent, and I found one high-heeled shoe deep in the woods. But that's it for evidence of habitation.

Some of the gravestones have eroded, their archaic lettering unreadable. A few have toppled or broken. Phineas is buried off to one side. He was an RCAF officer who died in 1942. The lettering on his marble stone has sharp edges.

Beloved in life
Cherished in memory
He liveth and was cut down like a flower.

Despite the poetry on some of the stones, I don't go in the graveyard anymore and am glad it's fenced. I don't need to have Phineas haunting me. I'm not sure that memory is something to cherish. It may be a blessing, but nostalgia is a curse, and the line between them is thin. I'm tripping over it too often these days.

You're supposed to pay a quarter to use the beach since it's part of a private campground, but it is rare that anyone is present at the canteen to collect my change, and there's nobody here today. This is the distilled essence of my experience of rural Nova Scotia: a canteen with ice cream cones and potato chips, change rooms that double as outhouses, the twenty-five-cent swim. What can you get for a quarter anywhere else these days? It's as if I travelled thirty years back in time when I came here. I change into my running shorts in a rank outhouse and choose to think that the damp on the soles of my bare feet is condensation from the plywood floor. On the way to the shore of the pond I wipe my feet across the dry grass, then on the coarse sand of the beach. I wish I could strip on the shore and swim naked, but getting caught once was enough. The morning that happened, I had believed it was early enough that nobody would be around. The man who surprised me took one look and turned away without saying a word. He looked at least as embarrassed as I was. I can't afford to be ostracized, and the locals already have me pegged as strange, even though they are polite. They drive by me as I'm riding my ratty old bike, my long hair flowing out of my Blue Jays cap, and must wonder what a Come From Away thinks he's doing buying a chunk of rocky forest, living in a tent, and trying to grow peas and carrots in bedrock.

Dad and I used to walk over to Crystal Lake and swim off the public dock when I was a kid. I always found it hard to jump into cold water. I would count out loud, one, two, three, and run off the end. I had to talk myself into jumping, though I knew it was inevitable.

There's no dock here, so I walk into the pond and do the breast stroke with my head out of the water. There is a small island some sixty feet out, and though there are signs prohibiting it, I always swim beyond the roped-off area and do a lap around it. Unlike in those drowning dreams, when I am awake and swimming it feels like I'm flying. It's as if my bones are hollow, like a bird's, filling with air each time I reach forward, making me float.

There are frogs sunning in the reeds along the shore. Martin tells me we should be saying goodbye to any frog we see since something is finishing them off. It may be the lack of ozone, he says, all that UV getting through and damaging their DNA. If they survive the mutations from that they have to leap the gauntlet of acid rain, global warming, and pesticides in the river from agricultural runoff. The worst thing for them is the estrogen that leaches into the waterways from all those pissed-out birth control pills and estrogen-mimicking BPA. He's seen frogs on the banks of the Annapolis River downstream from the sewage treatment plant in Kentville with extra limbs and males with female genitals. I say goodbye to the frogs.

I am cold by the time I swim around that island once. Back when I carried twenty more pounds only fatigue could have stopped me. I leave the pond and sit in the sun on the grass. UV be damned.

I climb back up the hill and am sweating by the time I reach the top. The path from the road to my garden weaves among poplar saplings and passes between two large white ash that create a natural gate. It opens into the one-acre clearing where

I am building my garden. When I moved here the clearing was covered with branches and other brush from the trees felled by the logging company that sold it to me. Most of the forests in Nova Scotia are, like this one, sad and small. They are recovering from being clear-cut at least three times. This land was cleared during World War II, when the spruce and fir were harvested to make pit logs for coal mines in Cape Breton to keep the land from caving in. It was cleared again for lumber and pulp. Now the woods are jammed with scrawny birch, alder, maple, ash, and willow. The trees have trouble remembering what it means to grow tall; before they reach their potential they are turned into two-by-fours, newsprint, or toilet paper.

Late September. I've been hauling rough lumber from the road to the site where I'm building an outhouse, downhill and downwind from my tent. I've got the last of the two-by-fours on my shoulder. Even with a rolled-up towel under them they bounce with each step and are bruising the bone. A vehicle stops on the road. Its engine is turned off and a door opens, then slams shut. There is no reason for a car to stop on the road unless someone is coming to visit or hunt. I don't get visitors. Other than Martin and Jenifer, whom I might talk to when I get water, I don't see anyone. I crouch behind some brush to spy on whoever it is. She is almost beside me when I recognize her, and it's too late for me to stand up without startling her.

"Yiyy!" Lina says, jumping back.

"Sorry, sorry."

"Why are you hiding?"

She laughs at me and I have to laugh too. Then she opens her arms to hug me. When she does I am enveloped, not only in the softness of her embrace, her breasts pressing against my chest, but by a faint smell of curry, earthy and warm. She is wearing a tank top, a skirt, and flip-flops.

I show her the vegetable beds and the growing pile of firewood I've sawn and split from the birches surrounding the clearing. She picks some apple mint and yarrow and offers to make me a bitter tea. At my outdoor kitchen I boil water. When the tea is ready, we sit on the straw bales I use as chairs. She says nothing for the longest time and I wait for her to speak first.

"You know, I've got farming in my blood. My mother's ancestors were the first farmers in Canada."

"In Quebec?"

"Ontario. By Georgian Bay. We once had villages and farming, a whole culture that was wiped out by missionaries and smallpox. Some of my people went south to Kansas three hundred and fifty years ago. Others fled to Quebec."

I don't know the geography, so she picks up a stick and begins to draw a map of Georgian Bay on the ground at our feet. I lean over with her to watch. Her hair, brushing my cheek, feels like the feathers from the belly of a crow. I smell her again and long to run my fingers over the warmth of her bare shoulder. She points to a place on her map.

"It was quite a small area."

I am enjoying the closeness of our faces, and then she sits up.

"It was small, but they did some amazing things. They grew enough—corn, beans, sunflowers, squash, tobacco—to feed themselves and to trade for meat and iron tools." She looks around at my little clearing. "Their gardens were something like this. A clearing carved out of the woods. Plantings between stumps. Forest gardening."

I've bought a chunk of land that is too wet in the winter, probably too dry in the summer, and infested with blackflies and ticks. The trees are stunted, there is little topsoil, no electricity or running water, and it's in the middle of nowhere on a dirt road. All this has made me question my sanity. What she says fills me with pride for what I am doing.

"It's so peaceful here," she says. "Have you got good water?"

"I hope so. There's a healing spring directly below here in the valley. For now I haul water in jars from the neighbours'. I'm going to get a well drilled next spring."

"I could see living here."

Those five words are better than a cord of wood, enough to fuel a winter's worth of dreaming. I take her comment, and her whole visit, as an invitation. It's heartening that Lina sees what I am doing as hopeful, not as an escape. I miss love, and she makes me optimistic for its return.

After we finish the tea we walk in the woods to the pine grove, the ground spongy with decades of fallen needles. She climbs one of the six tall white pines that weren't cut down, hoping to see the Bay of Fundy. She can't, but she pretends she can see Art in his yard. Too soon we are back at her pickup and she gives me another hug before she drives away.

4

Lily Lake Road

A week after Lina's visit the rain is splattering mud out of puddles onto the canvas of my tent. I have no interest in gardening, no desire to read my homesteading books. My tent is small, damp, and gloomy. A hurricane is racing up the Atlantic coast and threatens to come ashore. I put on my rain gear and coast on my bike down to Art's.

I knock on the glass door that opens into his kitchen at the back. The CBC is on loud and he's doing push-ups on the carpet. I admire him for hopeful stunts like that, an old man making the effort to stay in shape. Without hope we're nothing but a sorry sack of bones, waking regretfully each day, mulling over a list of woes, then falling heavily and gratefully into sleep, TV, alcohol—whatever it takes. I'd better not lose my hope.

He can't hear me knocking. I wander through his yard on top of the leaves thrown to the ground before their time by the rain and wind. A fishing boat struggles in the waves on the bay. The gusts keep shifting direction, churning the surface of the dark mass of the water into white foam. The wind whipping the treetops behind me is exhilarating, but it is hard to enjoy it, seeing the boat being made sport of. My hair is wet from the rain blown under my hood. The damp sleeves of my shirt cling to my forearms. The sound of the radio gets louder and Art is standing in the open door. Lucy barks and comes running toward me, wagging her tail.

"Get your foolish keester in here," he yells.

I take off my rubber boots and hang the dripping raincoat and pants on hooks in his mud room.

"Nova Scotia ain't for sissies. What the hell brings you down here in this weather?"

"I figured you and Lina wouldn't be doing much on a day like this."

"I drove her to the bus yesterday."

My face betrays my disappointment.

"I see why you're here now," he said, laughing. "But you'll have to keep your pecker in your pants till she shows up again next spring."

He tells me that they had spent the week bucking logs, trying to beat the storm, before she left for Quebec. I sit in his kitchen all morning, listening to him talk. He speaks of his life with Louise, of what it had been like to grow up in rural isolation. Any little thing I say sets him off on another story from his past. At one point I ask if there used to be a lot of white pine on my land.

"Sure. There were two-hundred-year-old pine all through the Maritimes till the Royal Navy needed masts. They took the tallest, straightest ones. Every single one that was any good. They should never have cut 'em like they did. You never take the tallest tree."

"Why not?"

"Your sons will never know how tall a forest ought to be."

"How many sons do you have?"

"This branch of the Mosher clan ends when I kick the can." He stops. "You look like you seen a ghost."

I force a laugh. "Do you have any relatives around here?"

He laughs hard at that. "Son, there's a spot down the road called Mosher's Corner. We've been here for seven generations."

I laugh too, hoping he will go on talking.

"No sons, but Louise and I had two daughters. Neither of them wants to take over the farm."

His family always had beef cattle, a few Jerseys for milk, a couple of sows, gardens large enough to put fruit and vegetables by two winters in advance, and the woodlot for firewood, lumber, and maple sugar. It must have been a hard life if my approximation of it is anything to go by. At least I can bike to Middleton if I have a hankering for a butter tart, and I always know Martin and Jenifer's place, with its lights and bathtub, is next door. Over the generations, chunks on the edges of his family's farm ablated like ice off the Antarctic ice sheet each time an eldest son wed. Art's older brother, Joshua, moved into the original farmhouse when their mother died. Art and Louise lived within sight of the smoke from the farmhouse chimney. When Joshua died of stomach cancer, Art and Louise moved into the farmhouse. Their daughters had moved away by then. When Alzheimer's took Louise to Bridgetown, the house was more than Art wanted to handle by himself, and he returned to the familiar memories of the smaller house they had repaired together. Over the years, the subdivided pieces had all been sold to vacationing Americans and Germans, and Art was the sole Mosher on the stump of what had been the original farm.

"If you cut the tallest tree," he goes on, "the woods get shorter and shorter. Young folks nowadays see the forest and think that's what it should look like. Their inheritance has been squandered."

"There's a small pine grove on my land."

"I used to wonder why they left those trees. I suppose they're not the straightest sticks on the ice."

"They're not, but they must be a hundred and fifty years old."

"I used to climb 'em with Emmett Whitman. We thought we'd be able to see the bay from up there, but we could never get high enough."

He sits silently for a while, then goes on.

"For some reason we got it in our heads to join the navy. Two farm boys like us on the ocean. Can you imagine? The first day we puked till we thought we was gonna die. Then we looked at each other and laughed. 'I'd prefer blackflies and a kick in the nuts to this shit,' he says to me. 'Why'd we ever sign up for the fuckin' navy?' But we got our sea legs soon enough. The last place I saw him we was landing in Sicily."

He swirls the cold coffee in his mug and stares at the wall as if I'm not there.

"Real quiet and still day. But hot. I was standing on deck with Emmett. His mother sent three boys to that war and only one came back. And that one was crippled in the head for life from what he seen. It was in July, when we was transporting soldiers to invade Italy. There wasn't a wave that morning but the ones we made on our way to the beach. Out of that stillness came a hum from the horizon, sounding like a hive of bees you hear off in the distance before you register what they are. But we knew, and I doubt there wasn't one of those boys who didn't feel the sick, empty feeling Emmett and I felt. We saw the Stuka bombers flying toward us over the water. I've never known anything like that before or since. You're standing on the deck feeling as naked as the day you was born, with nothing between you and those bastards but your prayers, and you've got all your fingers and toes crossed. There's nothing else to do. You can't run for cover or hope they won't see you.

"We see the bombs, little specks that grow big, like raindrops coming toward us. Some drop in the water. Then I see one hovering over our ship and my body does what it needs to do. I dive into the hold and fall twenty-five feet. I land on my back between two tanks. The bomb hits and destroys the decks. When I come back Emmett is lying on the deck all smashed up. He's burned real bad and his jaw is hanging off his face. I can't do a blasted thing for him. I talk to him, but he isn't all there. His eyes are looking at the angel of death, or his mama, I dunno."

Art stops talking.

"Did he die then?"

He shakes his head. "I pull my Enfield out of the holster and point the barrel at his temple. Emmett closes his eyes and nods." Art goes quiet again and bows his head. "I couldn't do it." His eyes are watery. He wipes them on his sleeve and exhales. "Emmett lay like that for an hour until a medic knelt beside him with a needle of morphine and gave him the whole thing."

Small explosions in the wood stove punctuate the quiet in the room. I had intended to be home by now, but I find myself watching the thick clouds sail over the sea toward New Brunswick and soon enough it is dark. I eat supper at Art's table, not talking. His story is still rolling over us like the wake from their ship washing the beach. He must be thinking of Emmett, and my mind is elsewhere. I'm remembering my dad, my mom, the people I knew in New York. You'd think it would be silence they left behind, but there's a chatter in my head, voices insisting on being heard.

When I rise to go home, the wind has picked up, but the rain has stopped.

"You sure you wanna bike home in this weather?" he says.

I do. I need the wind to clear my head. "Can I borrow a flashlight?"

He pulls one off the shelf by the door and hands it to me. He smiles and I see the man that his wife must have fallen in love with.

"I knew someone named Mosher when I lived in New York," I say. "Sometime I'll tell you her story."

"Fair enough. You must be tired of hearing an old man crow."

"Art?"

"What?"

"You did the right thing."

"I tell you, if I could do it over, I'd pull that trigger. Too bad we're not given second chances in this life."

As I leave the driveway, the flashlight I grip to the handlebar shines on his mailbox. "Arthur Mosher," hand painted in the same green as the trim of his house. I must have been distracted when Lucy came barking at me. I begin the ride up the back side of the mountain. All I want is to be in my sleeping bag in my tent. The wind is loud and the flashlight casts crazy shadows off the leaves and small branches that litter the pavement, as if things are lunging at me from the bushes lining the ditch.

I lie sleepless on the ground that night with the tent flap open. The treetops swirl against the black sky as if they are trying to get away from the wind chasing them. I can't get Benny out of my head. She is responsible for this loss of plastic. I don't know how to tell the story to Art.

A long way from here, I could start, *there's a graduate school on the Upper East Side of Manhattan. There are no tall trees on those streets, no cattle lowing in a valley below.*

Art was born within a rifle shot of the house he currently lives in, has spent much of his life in the woods, married an Acadian woman from Pointe-de-l'Église down the shore, and except for that war experience, has travelled no farther than Halifax. I don't know if I can tell him at all.

Raindrops patter against my tent. I zip the vents closed. Soon it is raining hard again. I feel no better protected than the birds that are somewhere out in that storm. Gusts of wind slap the tent walls, pressing moisture through the canvas onto my face, as if some imp is outside intermittently throwing buckets of water against the tent. Any time I float off, I am startled by the pop of canvas and a spray of water on my face. At some point the wind dies down a bit and I fall asleep.

5

The calendar said that summer had ended, but waves of heat rose from the pavement of York Avenue anyway, enveloping Benny as she walked home from her grad school lab. It was late on a Friday afternoon in September. Voices echoed into the air-conditioned lobby of her building on East 70th Street from a room at the back. She made her way through the dim light and cool air toward the ground-floor lounge. It was an open room, with vinyl tiles and orange plastic chairs. Bottles of beer, gin, and scotch and two-litre bottles of cola, ginger ale, and tonic water sat on a table beside cups and bags of chips. The first-year med students had a cocktail party every Friday afternoon during their first term, paid for out of their student fees.

A thin man leaned against the door jamb in front of Benny, watching a short woman with dirty-blond hair and bangs cut straight across her forehead. She was in conversation with two other freshmen students, tall and clean-cut men who were undoubtedly from Harvard or Yale or Princeton, like most of the college grads who made up the med class. They were peppering her with questions. When one of the men went to get her a drink, she looked over toward the door, rolled her eyes at the man in front of Benny, and smirked.

"Is that your girlfriend?" Benny said.

"I wish," he said.

"Be careful what you wish for, Leroy." Benny passed her arm through his. "Let's sit down."

She led him to two chairs by the drinks table and turned them to face each other. She poured ginger ale into the porcelain mug she'd brought from her room. Leroy reached for the bottle of gin and poured another drink into his plastic cup.

"This one's a little more g and a lot less t," he said.

Benny took a sip of her soda as Leroy sat down.

"Next week, if you want, I'll bring you a glass from my room so you don't have to drink out of that plastic shit."

"Saves washing it."

She shrugged. Leroy looked over her shoulder, probably searching for his would-be girlfriend. Benny turned to follow his gaze. The woman had moved across the room and was in another animated conversation, this time with a woman.

"She's cute."

He nodded and took a sip.

"Now you know why I'm here with all these med students. What's your excuse?"

"I heard the noise on my way home. Then I saw you." She paused. "I hope I didn't offend you when I came into your room."

"How?"

"My rant about clubbing seals."

Leroy laughed.

"Want to know why I'm really here?"

"Happy Hour?"

She shook her head. "Grad school."

"Sure. Then let's go out for dinner."

"What about the cute doctor?"

He shrugged and shook his head. "What are you studying?"

"I came to this school to learn how to rid the planet of plastic," Benny said. "When our grandparents were kids there were no plastic bags. No yogourt containers, no six-pack rings. Nothing."

"They were plastic virgins, eh?"

She smiled. "There were some synthetic resins produced back then. Bakelite pot handles and telephones. But that was like holding hands for plastic virgins."

"They had yet to be screwed by plastic."

She liked that. "Then, before World War II, the Germans invented polystyrene and polyvinyl chloride. DuPont followed with nylon. Then acrylics, polyethylene, polyurethane. During the war the British made polyethylene terephthalate. It's used to make these." She tapped the back of a fingernail on the ginger ale bottle on the table. "Now we have polypropylene underwear and fleece jackets made out of recycled bottles. Our birthright is seventy pounds of plastic garbage, hanging around our necks. We drink water poisoned with effluent, breathe noxious fumes from incineration, and little boys are growing tits from bisphenol A poisoning."

Leroy looked at his chest.

"You're a strange bird, Benny," he said.

"I do my best."

"Is there anything else you're passionate about?"

"Did you just wink at me?"

"I was trying for coy."

"Talk to me about passion when you're sober."

As he fiddled with the empty cup in his lap, she wondered why she had to be like that. He was good-looking and seemed to like her, and here she was blowing it.

They had met a few days earlier. Benny was at the desk in her room on the fifteenth floor, looking south, on the evening before Labour Day, ostensibly reading a paper on oncogenes for a course. Her reading lamp cast a cone of light onto the paper in front of her. Beyond that light was darkness. It was still muggy, though the sun was long gone, and she couldn't read. What she would have liked to do was go for a swim.

The city's thick, sweet air pushed its way into the room and surrounded her. The smell of that breeze reminded her of time spent at the lake near her house. The photo above her desk was taken by that lake when she was a little girl. Her father was wearing shorts and no shirt, laughing as he held her over the water. She was squealing, trusting his strong arms to keep her suspended above the danger.

She got up from her chair and left her apartment. The door to the apartment across the hall was propped open. A fellow student sat by the open window reading a journal paper of his own. She knocked.

"Studying?"

"Daydreaming, actually. Come in."

She strode over to his desk with her left hand outstretched.

"I'm Benny."

He was staring when he reached across to shake her hand, stood partially, and struck his knee on the corner of the desk.

"Shit!" he said, plopping back down in the wooden chair.

He was bent over with his right hand on his left knee. For some reason he continued to hold her hand as though they were playing Twister. He was grimacing.

"You look like a pretzel. Here, have your hand back."

She let go and he put his hand on top of the one that was already on his knee.

"I'm Leroy."

Shadows cast by the light on his desk hid his eyes but emphasized the pronounced cheekbones jutting below them. He was trying to smile.

"You look so tall hovering over me," he said.

"Well, I am, Leroy. Five-ten and a bit, to be exact. Where are you from?"

"Toronto."

"A Canadian among us. How exotic."

He said nothing.

"The land of lakes and trees and snow."

He smiled.

"Clubbing baby seals, hunting moose in the backwoods."

Shut up, she told herself, shut up while he's still smiling.

"Not a lot of seals in Toronto," he said. "Are you a med student?"

"Nope. Grad student, like you." She bit her lower lip.

"What makes you think I'm a grad student?"

"The hair, Nature Boy." She pointed at her own hair and raised her eyebrows. "We don't need to look respectable."

He laughed. The drone of traffic came through the open window, regularly interrupted by taxi horns and sirens heading down 70th to the hospital's emergency department. They heard shouting on the street and Benny went to the window to look out. Leroy joined her and they stuck their heads out the screenless window, side by side, fifteen floors above the street. A homeless man was berating an invisible passerby. When they brought their heads back into the room, they faced each other.

"Where'd you get the scar?" he asked.

She had a strong nose and a sharp chin and thought they made her face harsh. Someone once told her that her face was saved by her smile. They also said that the inch-long scar under her right eye made her look vulnerable.

"Bashed my face on the side of a pool when I was a kid. You?"

He hesitated. She reached up to touch his forehead.

"Oh, that one. I fell on cement stairs at a rink when I was watching my mom play hockey."

Benny smiled. She knew she was wrong about the seals and the moose, but this was wonderful: a hockey-playing mother! "It's been a pleasure chatting with you. I'd love to shake your hand again, but we seem to be accident-prone. I'll leave you to your daydreaming." She bowed instead, turned, and walked toward the door.

"Benny." She turned. "One day you and I will be living in Canada," he said. "With our children."

She gave him a look, half smile, half question mark. Sometimes she was stunned by the things people could say.

"Nice image, Nature Boy," she said. "But far from possible."

"You don't want children?" He was grinning.

She hesitated, then laughed. "I can't imagine living in Canada. Good night, Leroy." Then she turned again and left.

The crowd in the lounge was starting to disperse, leaving in groups to go out for dinner. Benny would have to leave soon too if she wanted to get a run in before going back to the lab.

"Turn it over," Benny said.

Leroy was picking at the rim of his plastic cup.

"What?"

"Look at the bottom." She grasped his hands and guided them to turn the cup upside down. A drop of his drink landed on the thigh of his pants. "See that? Six. Polystyrene. It'll disappear. And this bottle—" She reached over to the table, grabbed the bottle of ginger ale, and turned it over. "One. PETE. Polyethylene terephthalate. It'll be the first to go."

"How?"

"There are bacteria that eat plastic."

She told him of the Japanese researchers who found *Pseudomonas* downstream of a nylon manufacturing plant that was dumping its waste into the river. The bacteria were using by-products from the plant as their only source of carbon and nitrogen. They had adapted to survive on the waste from the plant.

"I've seen hundreds of tampon applicators, like pink snail shells, washed up on beaches where sewage has been pumped into the water. Nylon fishing rope, busted-up bleach jugs, coffee cup lids. You name it, the beaches are covered with it. Then there's the grocery bags flapping in trees, syringes in Tompkins Square Park. They say it's a social problem that recycling can solve. But that's not the right tack. It's a technical problem. No matter how much we recycle or landfill, burn or bury, more plastic will be made. So, instead we'll soon have microbes capable of digesting plastic. They'll eat their way through all that crap." She patted Leroy on the knee. "Well, my inebriated friend, I'm going for a run in the park."

"What about dinner?"

"I need to get back to the lab."

"You just arrived last week. What could you have going so soon?"

She stood up and ran her hands down her legs to loosen her jeans where they had bunched up around her thighs. "I'll show you sometime."

He put his cup on the floor.

"See you around," she said and left the room.

6

Lily Lake Road

A tree crashing behind my tent wakes me from an apocalyptic dream. The wind has picked up again. There is no point in moving. I am already wet, and if a tree has my number, well, there must be worse ways to die than being crushed in a tent in the middle of a storm.

The hurricane hits hardest southeast of here, toward Halifax. When the air finally grows still that afternoon, I go for a walk to assess the damage. Spruce have toppled across the roads and taken power lines with them. Their root systems, planar from growing in the thin soil, offer themselves up like dinner plates to the sky. The power is out at Martin and Jenifer's. There is something comforting about seeing that Mother Nature is still in control, that our juggernaut can be stopped by a storm.

You'd think I'd hate camping by now. It seems like every time I get in a tent the weather turns sour.

It was August 1978, and I was a week shy of my third birthday when my father took us on a tour of New England. He told me the story of that trip enough times that it's my memory now, vivid as it could not possibly be given my age then, given that, according to him, I slept most of the time we were in the car.

He sat behind the steering wheel of his 1972 Buick LeSabre, a powder-blue convertible, blasting *Who's Next* from the eight-track tape player. He sang along to *Music from Big Pink* and *Blue* all the way across Massachusetts, with the top rolled down, the wind blowing my mother's hair back, and me lying on a blanket in the back seat. We drove through little towns in Vermont, past white clapboard houses and fire hydrants painted with stars and stripes, chipped now, to celebrate the Bicentennial. We pulled into the campground near Bennington in the dark.

Across a stream my parents found our site as raindrops began to splatter the windshield. It rained for a week. Dad took me exploring in the woods, the two of us coming back soaked despite our rain gear. I wasn't bothered by the rain, or so he told me. Mom stayed in the lean-to, reading, playing solitaire, and cooking. We went to bed as soon as the sky began to get darker after supper. On the fifth day Dad walked in the deluge to the canteen to buy the local paper. When he came back, Mom's good humour had evaporated. She wanted to go home.

Before they were done packing, a ranger came by our site to tell them that the stream by the gate had flooded its banks and the road. They weren't letting any vehicles cross it.

"We can't leave?" Mom's voice cracked.

He told them they hoped the water would recede soon and we'd be able to leave. When it didn't recede by the next day, the rangers brought in two girders to span the rushing flow, laying them on top of the road. Anyone leaving would have to drive carefully with the wheels of their car in the grooves of the girders. My parents packed up in a hurry and we joined the line of cars and tent-trailers waiting to cross the crude bridge. The rain had finally eased, but the stream continued to flow across the road, carrying branches, leaves, and plastic bags with it. I sat in my mother's lap. When it came our turn to go, Dad turned to her.

"Don't squeeze so tight."

"Let me out," my mother said.

"You think I'm going to drive across that with the two of you in the car?"

My mother huddled with me under her slicker, watching as Dad negotiated the girders and crawled across the bridge. He got out and hurried back to help us walk across. All I remember of that trip is clinging to her neck as the silver water rushed over the tops of the rusty girders and around her black rubber boots. And one more thing: I was happy in her arms.

When we got home she vowed she would never camp again.

I clean up the fallen branches on the paths and in the garden beds. When it gets sunny I hang my clothes and sleeping bag to dry.

As daunting as it can be to be caught in a storm, I find it thrilling. When it ends, the elation is unlike any feeling I know, and I have a renewed faith that something is looking after me. Somehow I know it won't be a storm that kills me.

The last few days have been gorgeous, and it's easy to forget the discomfort when it's sunny and warm. It's as if the summer sky's fire has licked the branches of the maples and birches, burning their leaves yellow, orange, red. The full moon last night brought the first fall frost. Today I am harvesting potatoes, carrots, and turnips. I loosen the soil along each row with a digging fork. Then I press my hands into the ground and pull them out. The potatoes, Century russets I planted in May, are my buried treasure. I lay the huge bakers in piles beside each row to dry in the sun. Once they are dry, I rub each potato between my palms to loosen the dirt. They fill a feed bag, more than fifty pounds. It turns out I have had less success with the carrots and turnips. The carrots are hairy and small, hardly worth saving. The turnips didn't like the rocky, shallow soil and are the size of malformed baseballs. I take them all next door and put them in Martin and Jen's root cellar anyway.

Deer season has opened and sporadic gunshots resound in the woods behind my tent. I walk along Lily Lake Road in the gloaming to find an apple for my dessert. There is an old wild tree growing in the ditch by the road, gnarled and twisty, but replete with large green apples. I shake a low branch and half a dozen apples thump to the ground around me. I stroll farther along to the stream that passes beneath the road, and there, not more than twenty feet into the woods in front of me, a coyote is huddled over a carcass. It crouches as if to pull another bite off the bones. Coyotes are usually shy, and they run if they see me. This one doesn't budge. It is the size of Lucy, with short grey-brown fur and a menacing gaze. Its hackles are raised as it stares back at me, and mine, if I can call them hackles, are raised too. I jog home along the dirt road, looking over my shoulder as I go.

I light a fire in the evening light and cook my dinner in the outdoor kitchen. I sit down to eat rice and beans when something comes out of the woods toward me. I stand, heart pounding. A silhouette is holding a rifle by its barrel. It walks into the clearing and is lit by the glow of flames.

"Shit, don't sneak up on me like that," I say. Art rests his rifle against the big spruce to which my tent is tied. "You're lucky I don't have a gun of my own."

"You should have one," Art says, "living up here all by yourself." He sits on a straw bale and stares into the light.

I tell him about the coyote. He nods toward the gun.

"Want me to go get it?"

"No. Any luck in the woods?"

"With this hip clicking I suspect they hear me coming from a mile away."

"Tea?"

"You got anything stronger?"

I don't. When your father's an alcoholic you have to make a tough choice. You can either embrace the bottle or turn away. When your father is an alcoholic who kills himself, then you learn that if you want to survive there is really only one choice to make. After a couple of years, when it seemed like I might be willing to follow his lead, I made it. I have not had a drink since I left New York.

I walk beyond the light thrown by the fire into the shadows of the kitchen. My eyes adjust and I strike a match and turn on one of the gas burners. The propane hisses until I touch the match to it, when it pops blue into life. I move the full kettle on top of the flame and return to the fire.

"I've been thinking of you up here," Art says, "by yourself. What you want is a good woman to keep you warm at night."

"If you hadn't scared Lina off so fast."

When the kettle begins its high-pitched whistle I rise to

get it. I pull two Earl Grey bags from the jar on the stove and drop them into the teapot. Its ceramic spout is chipped. I'm seeing my life through Art's eyes now, imagining what he must think. There is food crusted on the stovetop, I make my meals standing under a spruce, and my dining-room furniture consists of two straw bales. I don't see other people making life hard for themselves on purpose. I pour the boiling water over the tea bags. We let the tea steep, and then I pour some into his cup.

"You got any milk?"

"I don't drink it."

"I've been getting it fresh from Reagh's Jerseys since they stopped selling bags at the SaveEasy. It ain't convenient, but it tastes better, that's for sure."

Harold Reagh lives along the Shore Road not far from Art. He's the one I bought lumber from to build my outhouse. It's his equipment—manure spreader, tractors, a hay wagon—that is responsible for churning up the dust in front of my property as it rattles over the potholes and gullies of Lily Lake Road. Sticks in the fire crackle and burn, sending up sparks into the night air.

"How'd Louise fare in the hurricane?"

He shakes himself like a bear. "What? Oh. She did O.K. Their power was out for a few days like the rest of us." Sparks explode up with the flames. "Sorry, I'm not much company tonight. I've got memories rattling around in my head like change in a can."

"Tell me about it. Makes it hard to fall asleep, huh?"

"A young guy like you can't have much to forget." He pokes at the fire for a bit before he seems to realize something and stares at me. "What're you doing up here all alone, anyway?"

"I'm not alone. I've got the coyotes."

"I see how much you like having them around."

Then it strikes me that tonight his rifle is a prop. "Why'd you come here tonight?"

He stares into the flames, saying nothing. Then: "You told me you had a story for me."

7

New York City

Benny woke at six and prepared to head into the dark for her morning run. She laced her shoes and pulled her sweatshirt over her head. Once she was on the sidewalk, the cool morning air felt fresh. Underneath that, however, was a warmth that told her she'd be pulling off the sweatshirt once she got to the park. It was a straight run west, then down one block to the entrance at 69th Street, at which point her pace became steady. There were no cars on the park road. Some of the men she passed checked her out. If they smiled, she smiled in return, content, from the limber way her legs felt, that it was a good day. She increased her pace. Today she could run forever.

Back at her apartment she showered, and she was heading for the lab by 8:30. Her calf muscles were sore in that way that reminded her of her run with each step. She walked down York Avenue to the entrance of the art deco building that housed both the hospital and her school. Her breath flowed without effort, like pulling a silk ribbon gently through the palm of your hand. Her mind was clear. Time stopped and she thought she might never again feel as healthy, fit, and complete as she did in that golden moment.

The glass doors at the entrance were emblazoned with the university's seal. She showed her ID and smiled at the security guards, two sullen men who had no doubt seen too many medical students with their white lab coats and their entitled airs, and refused, on principle or from ennui, to smile back. Her lab was on the third floor, and she took the stairs two at a time. The Department of Microbiology was adjacent to some pathology labs, and over the years the smell of formaldehyde had wafted throughout and soaked into the walls. She opened the doors to a corridor that was thirty feet long, lit with the sickly hue of fluorescent bulbs. On her left was a room housing caged mice. Beyond that was an equipment room filled with centrifuges the size of commercial washing machines, incubators, and scintillation counters. On the right was a lounge for the grad students and post-docs to eat lunch and drink coffee, as well as the offices belonging to the principal investigators of the two labs, Gabriel Nawthorn and Melvin Leach.

As Benny walked down the corridor she was met by a fellow grad student who also worked in Leach's lab, on his second pet project: the search for new antibiotics to fight staph infections. Jonathan Yovkov was an MD/PhD student, the son of a Bulgarian refugee who had slipped out from under the watchful eye of the USSR in 1971. Father and son had made their way to New York, leaving behind Jon's mother and two sisters. Jonathan was serious about science, insofar as it was his stepping-stone to getting rich. He shared Leach's assessment that, given the emergence of antibiotic-resistant strains of

Staphylococcus, any new antibiotic would be exceptionably valuable to its discoverers. He and Leach had apprised what the other was worth to his career and interacted accordingly. What Leach offered was a lab that was creating commercial products and, with them, the opportunity to make a business out of science. Jon brought his intellect to the lab and, with it, a nascent business acumen. Jon's book outlining the process of successfully applying to medical school was in its third printing. The royalties from that book financed the bulk of his education. His publisher was asking him to write a second guide, this time for young investors.

Jon moved as though he had a private stash of time, gaining interest as he strolled from bench to desk to library. When Benny had first joined the lab, she assumed he lacked ambition. She was wrong. She had wanted to befriend him, knowing they might be working together for the next four or five years, but they kept grinding against each other. Instead of wearing down to something smooth, the edges of their relationship became sharp and treacherous. This morning he grinned when he saw Benny, as if he was telling himself a joke at her expense.

Leach's lab at the end of the corridor smelled of growing bacterial cultures—musty, earthy—and the complicated smell of organic compounds mingling in the air. She was alone in the room among the metal and glass, desktop centrifuges, microscopes, and bottles of reagents ranged on the open shelves above each black bench. The benches were covered in bottles and stacked petri plates, some of them new and sterile and ready to be inoculated with bacteria. Others had yellow agar medium and bacterial colonies growing on them. For her this was a room full of promise.

She had been led to this lab by a confluence of events. The first occurred while she was reading the text for her Intro to Plastics course, *Plastics: Their Chemistry and Uses,* at the library at the University of Massachusetts. The chapter on nylon held a brief section on plastic dissolution and degradation with the following reference.

Kinoshita, S., et al., 1975. Utilization of a cyclic dimer and linear oligomers of e-aminocapronoic acid by *Pseudomonas* sp. K172. Agric. Biol. Chem. 39(6): 1219-1223.

She closed the book and went looking for the article in the grey subterranean stacks. Marine bacteria had been discovered feeding off the effluent from a nylon manufacturing plant flushed into a Japanese river. Ridding the planet of plastic wasn't a social problem, she knew that. But here was a technological fix. What they needed were efficient plastic-digesting bacteria. She pictured the recycling symbol, with its three arrows encircling the number 1, as a triad of snakes eating each other's tails. The circle they made shrunk until it disappeared. Perhaps she could engineer them.

Until that point she had been assuming she was headed for an R&D job at one of the many plastics manufacturing companies in Lowell. Before she read that article, the only environmental solution to the problem of plastic pollution she had envisaged, other than recycling, was the creation of biodegradable plastics. The problem with these — plastics made of polylactic acid and cellulose acetate—was that nobody could afford to make them.

Then Melvin Leach came to her college to deliver a seminar,

and her path was set. Leach gave his lecture early on a cold February morning in an auditorium. Benny's class had been encouraged to attend by the prof who taught them a short course on the degradation of plastics. She had needed no other encouragement than the poster advertising the seminar:

The Potential Use of Micro-organisms in
the Biodegradation of Xenobiotic Compounds:
Digestion of Waste Plastics
Melvin Leach, PhD
Cornell University Medical College, New York

Benny scanned the auditorium for her classmate Alicia. She wasn't there. She sat in the aisle seat, planning to save the seat next to her for her friend if she turned up. Her notebook lay open on her left knee.

Leach was introduced, then went to the lectern, smiling to the audience of drowsy students. He wore a navy suit jacket, a maroon tie, and a white shirt. His thick hair was short, receding at the edges above his temples, and would have been curly if he let it grow. A slide of a landfill site, heaped with discarded plastic bottles, bags, and Styrofoam containers filled the screen.

"This is the heritage we appear willing to leave our children," he began. The next slide showed what might be the same site, this time without any of the plastic visible. Corn and flowers grew on part of the site. "With bioremediation, this is the heritage we *will* leave them."

He stood, erect, with confidence, making eye contact with the few students who were paying attention. Benny was rapt as, slide after slide, he explained the work he was doing in his lab. He had adapted soil and water bacteria to eat some of the building blocks of plastic. The newly evolved bacterial strains had genetic changes that altered enzyme activities, allowing catalysis of these xenobiotic compounds.

When Leach ended his lecture, Benny closed her notebook and rose from her seat to jog down the stairs to the front of the lecture hall. Behind her was the noise of restless students, leaving their seats, chatting, the heavy auditorium door repeatedly opening and clicking shut. She was by herself with Dr. Leach at the lectern.

"This is thrilling work. Have you got far with the practical applications?"

"We've thought about them, certainly." He leaned with one elbow on the lectern and took off his glasses. "But the elucidation of the molecular mechanisms behind these adaptations has taken up most of our time. I hope to push the practical side of things soon."

"Couldn't you start with nylon digestion? You know, harnessing bacteria and fungi that metabolize amide bonds? Then manipulate their genomes to be more efficient?"

He arched an eyebrow. He told her there were only a few papers and that it was a wide-open field. The funding potential was limitless if they could tap into governments wanting to eliminate garbage and reduce their landfill footprints.

Benny asked if he had room for another graduate student. She told him she had a co-op placement coming up, then her final two semesters of course work. She would.be graduating in a little over a year.

"Then you have plenty of time to apply." He checked her out from head to toe. "Your youthful exuberance is appealing."

She left the lecture hall as if she were flying among the

treetops, seeing the landscape unfold beneath her on her way to the library. She found a copy of Leach's most recent article in *Science*. In the Introduction he had written:

> It may be possible, in the near future, to utilize such novel life forms as we intend to generate, to treat much of the plastic waste that ends its life in landfills. There are considerable deficits in any program aimed at the recycling of plastics. It is not possible to recycle many synthetic polymers. For others there is a limited number of times they can be recycled. For those that can be recycled, the array of materials into which they can be remoulded is also limited. These processes are energetically expensive and polluting. Finally, consumer compliance with recycling programs is abysmal.
>
> Ideally, all plastic, including that which currently ends its life in the waste stream, could be refashioned into usable products. However, since this is not possible, those plastics that remain in landfills need to be eliminated in an environmentally sound fashion. Our work is aimed at making this possible in a clean, efficient, and economical manner using novel bacteria to digest the waste into carbon dioxide and water. Biological degradation is attractive because it is energetically neutral and non-toxic, it is self-perpetuating, and it recycles nutrients into the ecosystem. We will design bacteria to break down even the most stable and noxious xenobiotic compounds into

molecules that are easily utilized by a vast array
of soil-borne micro-organisms. The key is to begin
the process of nutrient release. Nature will take
care of the rest.

She carried on her studies with renewed vigour. In the spring
she began a four-month co-op work placement at a plastics
manufacturing company in Lowell. Working at EcoPlast taught
her what she needed to know about the industry. They made
conventional plastics but were benefitting from environmental
anxiety by creating and producing biodegradable plastics as
well.

At EcoPlast she tested novel formulations for their bio-
degradability. They made polymers with bonds that were
unstable and, unlike conventional plastics, could be digested
by bacteria and fungi. Shopping bags tattered in trees because
nothing could recycle them back to the soil. EcoPlast strove
to make them attractive to microbes by inserting promoters
throughout the polymer structure that made the bonds
digestible. Benny knew that EcoPlast's claim that they fully
broke down was disingenuous. They broke wherever a
promoter was eaten, leaving non-visible pieces of plastic that
contaminated soil and water.

She came home from her job and studied textbooks from
the library: *Biology*, *Principles of Genetics*, *Molecular Biology of
the Cell*, *Microbiology*. Her knowledge of biology had been
limited to introductory courses in her freshman year. She
knew her physics and mathematics, the building blocks for
a mechanistic view of the world, and applied them to the
workings of the cell. She had studied organic chemistry,
including that of long-chain polymers such as silk protein

and its synthetic mimic, nylon. She took her GRE, then sent her transcript to Cornell.

While she waited, she studied the ways that enzymes act on natural long-chain polymers to break them down into their constituent parts so that these can be recycled within the cell. Because plastics are long-chain polymers whose structures are unrecognizable to enzymes found in nature, she would need to engineer enzymes capable of digesting the bonds in inert plastics.

She received a thin envelope from the Registrar's Office at Cornell. She turned it over in her hands. That winter, imagining the possibility of rejection, she had searched the literature for other labs, other researchers who were doing anything comparable to Leach's work. There were labs in Japan that had made some of the initial discoveries, but Leach was leading the pack by a long way. And she wasn't about to move to Japan. She tore the envelope open. The single page told her, in the language of academic bureaucracy, that she had been accepted, on a full scholarship plus stipend.

Lily Lake Road

Art rolls another smoke. After licking the paper, he picks a fleck of tobacco from his tongue with his thumb and finger. He pulls a stick from the fire and raises the glowing end to his smoke.

"Why are you telling me this?"

The fire pops and a spark shoots into the sky, one flame of orange against the millions of blue stars. After our birth and before our death we spin a web of stories so intricate that it's easy to become tangled within it. There are too many reasons and I don't want to lose the thread, so I pick one and pull it down.

"We tell stories to make sense of our lives. My dad said that we remember what we don't understand. Like you told me about getting bombed near Sicily because you haven't figured it out yet."

"Phooey. I'm only trying to forget it." He drags on his smoke, then exhales. "If you're gonna keep talking, you're sure as hell gonna have to lubricate my ears."

"With what?"

"Whisky. Canadian Club would be nice."

At least he didn't say gin. He puts his hand on my knee to help him rise from his straw bale. He wipes some chaff from his pants. His hand reaches up to straighten his hat, then grabs his rifle.

"How are you getting home?"

"My truck's parked up the road by Martin's."

Once he's gone, I piss, brush my teeth, and get into my tent. From my sleeping bag I watch the coals of the fire shimmer. This is a hard life I've chosen, but there are small things, like the freedom of living in a tent, that I love. There is nothing between me and the stars but canvas, thin enough for that orange firelight to throw shadows on it. I am being hardened off, like a tomato transplant, being made ready for whatever is to come.

*

Listening to LPs, Winter 1977
My earliest true memory, not one that I recorded from the telling and retelling by my dad: A black disc spinning, circle of purple paper in the centre, the sound of mandolin, guitars, and an organ.

Learning to skate, 1979
It was cold enough after Christmas to start making the skating rink. Dad rented a lawn roller, filled it with water, and pulled it back and forth over the snow to pack it down. After that he used a sprinkler to turn the snow to ice. Mom was out there every morning, setting up the sprinkler before I was up. After school it was Dad's turn. They did this for a week or more until it was hard enough to stand on. Then he began to flood

the ice by hand with a hose, filling the valleys with snow and water, scraping off the hills with a shovel. After two weeks it was ready for skating.

He taught me to skate when I was four, first pushing a chair as he told me Bobby Orr learned, then with a hockey stick in my hand for support. In the beginning I was such a bad skater that Dad stood in front of the net, in his boots, while I wobbled in and tried to score. He never let me get the puck past him that first winter. He poke-checked me whenever I brought the puck too close. But my skating improved, and in subsequent winters, I was good enough that he pulled out his old glove and blocker from when he played goal at teachers' college. Some afternoons the two of us would be out there for two hours after school taking shots. By the time Mom called us in for dinner we could barely see the puck.

Chasing me on the lawn, 1982
There were things he shared only with me and, now that he's gone, I can only rescue them from obscurity by writing them down. He would hold up his two fists and glower at me with feigned menace. "See this," he'd say, holding one fist higher than the other. "Sudden Death." Then he held up his other fist. "See this? Kick of a Mule." Then I ran away, squealing with delight when he caught and tickled me mercilessly.

Sam Peabody, May 1984
We didn't go camping again until I was eight. We were sitting at the dining-room table and Dad was reminiscing about our trip to Bennington. He got a gleam in his eye and looked at me. The next thing I knew we were packing the car with the tent, stove, lantern, and sleeping bags. He looked so excited,

like a little boy, that Mom couldn't have said no. And I think she must have been pleased that we were leaving her by herself for the weekend. She packed the cooler for us, my big orange towel, and my bathing suit.

It was a two-hour drive from home, and it was dark before we got there. As we approached the campground it began to pour. We sat in the car as sheets of rain washed over the windshield like we were in a car wash. It stopped as suddenly as it had begun. We set up the tent and got in our sleeping bags.

The next morning I woke to the sound of poplar and cottonwood leaves rustling in the little breeze there was, sounding like water. Waves broke on the sand dunes not far from where we lay. A bird sang into the space between the leaves, clean and pure as the blueness of the sky.

Sam Peabody, Peabody, Peabody.

Dad said it was the white-throated sparrow welcoming us. I ran up and down the beach, swam in the gentle waves. I lay on my stomach, pressing my hips and knees into the sand, enjoying the warmth of the sun on my back. The cool onshore breeze masked the intensity of the sun. This was before we learned about sunscreen and the ozone layer disappearing, and by suppertime my skin was pink. Dad said I looked like a lobster. By the time I was in my sleeping bag the itching on my back was crazy-making.

We stayed out of the sun after that and hiked in the woods. My father bought me a set of watercolours and paper, and I painted birds we saw. An oriole, seagulls by the lake, and a white-throated sparrow.

It wasn't as if we tried to exclude Mom from what we did. The inflexibility of a triangle, especially in a family like ours, meant that one of us always felt left out. More often than not it was Mom, since she wasn't interested in the things Dad and I were. She liked being inside, reading, and she painted sometimes. She had worked as an artist's assistant when she was a teenager. When I was an infant she used our den as a painting studio. I liked this because it was something she and I did together when I was young. Over time my toys filled up the space in the den, and when we got a TV for the room, her easel went into the closet and she stopped painting.

They should have had another kid. It might have saved them.

On Saturday afternoons Dad and I built things. The s   I was nine I wanted to enter the science fair at scho with an astronomy project. He bought me a telescope, and we sat on the patio at night, all the lights in the house turned off, and looked at the moon's craters and the Galilean moons of Jupiter. He helped me build a planetarium in our living room for the fair. We superimposed a star map over a piece of cardboard and poked holes at the location of all the largest stars. This was mounted on the rotor from our barbecue and a light bulb was connected behind it to project the stars onto the ceiling. He told me that this was an inversion of how Stone Age people viewed the night sky. They imagined it was an opaque dome with holes poked through it and a light shining behind it.

There is one spring morning I remember when I ran home from school for lunch. After the long winter of streets and driveways never being clear it was wonderful to be running

on dry ground. It was sunny and warm, and I wore the green
sweater Mom had knitted me, with the zipper undone. I wore
sneakers instead of clunky boots, and I was so light that I
floated as if I could fly, in love with life. I was brushed by the
warm breeze, the smell of lilacs on the breeze, and robin's
song. I glided over the grass, breathing in the fragrant air
on my way home. I ran at the fence, thrust my right foot into
the mesh, levered my left onto the top, pulled up, crouched,
and jumped to the ground on the other side. I passed lilac
bushes on the way and plucked a few purple and white sprays
to take to my mother. Our lawn was covered with dandelions.
Yellow disks everywhere on a sea of green. I picked some of
these too.

"We won't keep these," she said, separating out the dandelions and throwing them in the garbage. "They'll just wilt."

She reached into the cupboard for a drinking glass, half-
filled it with water from the kitchen tap, and put the lilacs in
it. She placed it on the windowsill above the sink.

Gardening, 1985

The days had begun their descent into the heat and humidity
of summer. Our vegetable garden was in the backyard beyond
the patch of grass we turned into a skating rink in winter. It
was bordered on three sides by Scotch pines with their scales
of bark, sharp needles, and branches growing in angled paths.
The garden was open to the south. The clay soil was heavy to
dig, sticking in clumps to the rusted blade of the shovel. The
last weekend in May was the official start to the gardening
season. There was no peace on the day Dad took our archaic
Rototiller from its resting place in the garage for its annual
senile perambulation. It was a wheezy old asthmatic, belching

blue smoke, hacking and coughing as he clutched the handles and guided it around the garden. I stood in the shade under the pines, certain that it was the sort of diseased vagrant that should not be polluting the soil and air of our garden. My dad's biceps bulged in his short-sleeved buttoned shirt and his whole torso shook from steadying the vibrating machine. Sweat dripped from his brow onto the white headband he wore. As he circled, he stopped to pull his rubber boots out of the muck and wipe his brow with a handkerchief pulled from his back pocket.

Once it was tilled—except for the asparagus patch and the raspberries—I joined him to plant the seeds. Beans, potatoes, carrots, and pumpkins. We transplanted tomatoes that had been started indoors, weeded and harvested the asparagus for dinner, and propped up the raspberry canes after cutting out the previous year's growth.

We weeded around the tulips in the triangular bed at the end of the driveway, as well as among the roses and peonies under the pines that grew along the side of our property. Once the tulips had died back, we dug them up and stored them in boxes in the garage and transplanted petunias and a clematis in the centre, to climb up the light standard.

All that summer we gardened in the mornings before it got too hot and then again after supper. Mom didn't like to weed or harvest, but she did like to cook the produce, serving us summer meals of yellow beans, new potatoes, and tomatoes. She liked to pick raspberries for our dessert but didn't eat any herself then, saying she had her dessert while she was picking.

For Dad's birthday my mother helped me buy an apple tree and we planted it near the edge of our yard, out of the way of where we built the rink. Its leaves were lush, but it had already bloomed in spring and wouldn't bear fruit that year. I like that she did that for me; one of the few memories I have of her that makes me smile.

It was that summer that Dad promised to take me to Nova Scotia.

I wake in the night. The coyotes are howling deep in the woods to the north. Perhaps I should get a rifle. Art could teach me to hunt and I might sleep better with it in the tent on nights like this. The image of the two of us, each sleeping with a rifle beside us as our only company, makes me laugh.

9

Lily Lake Road

The autumn here was gorgeous. Little rain until mid-November, lots of time to walk in the woods, put the garden to bed, and read in my tent. But the snow came before Christmas and was followed by rain. Then more snow. It's been a hard winter and it's only January 26. Jenifer was insisting that I move in with them for the winter, but I have to prove to myself that I can do this.

I haven't seen Art since that night in October and have spent most of my days alone here. Another storm has landed on us. This time there is no wind. I wake up from a good night's sleep to a hush and darkness everywhere except at the top of my tent, where wan light illuminates the canvas. I unzip the door to a wall of snow. I pull on pants over my long johns, then snow pants and the rest of my gear, and push my way out. I have gotten by this winter without a shovel but was wrong to assume my luck would continue. I trudge through thigh-deep drifts to Martin and Jen's to borrow one from them.

"Go in," Martin calls from beside the shed, where he's splitting firewood. "Jen's in the kitchen."

Their power is out again and she's cooking soup on top of the wood stove. Martin comes in, stamping snow from his boots before dumping an armload of maple and birch in the woodbox. It sounds like a house of children's blocks tumbling down. I face my palms toward the heat radiating off the cast iron.

"Caught with your pants down again, eh?"

Jen rolls her eyes at her husband.

"Can I borrow a shovel?"

"It's January! Were you going to wait until the snow in March?"

"There's an extra one hanging in the shed," Jen tells me.

"Don't take the red one," Martin yells after me once I am through the door.

I wait for my eyes to adjust to the darkness of the shed. The door opens again, then slams shut. It's Jen, wearing her green down vest and a red-and-white striped wool hat.

"You can use these too." She pulls a pair of snowshoes from a nail on the wall. "They're mine."

It takes most of the morning to dig out my tent and a path to the road. The road itself won't be plowed for days. There is nothing more to do here, and the thought of spending the day in my sleeping bag in that dark tent discourages me. I decide to visit Art and exchange some shovelling for a few hours in front of his wood stove. I strap on the snowshoes. They take some getting used to, and slogging through three feet of snow isn't the best way to learn. I am sweaty and tired by the time I arrive at Art's door two hours later.

Smoke rises straight from his chimney into the bright sky. He has shovelled a path from his door to the shed and to the chicken coop. He meets me at his side door.

"Go see if there's any eggs, will ya? It may be too early, but all this snow's thrown the old girls off their schedule."

I am glad to take the snowshoes off and be walking on the shovelled path. The henhouse is dark because of the piles of snow that cover the windows. I was in here once before, with Art, in the fall, to clip the hens' wings at night. They had been roosting and didn't fuss when we picked them up. I held the left wing out and Art clipped the ends of the primary feathers near the tip with scissors. He insisted it didn't hurt them, but the way they squawked and fluttered, I had to wonder. Just one wing each. They could fly short distances but at a wonky angle that made me laugh.

As my eyes adjust to the darkness, I make out a few of the hens standing on rails. The darkness obscures the laying boxes, and I can't tell if they're occupied. I blindly slide my hand into each one and hope not to get pecked. The hens are docile, the feathers of their warm breasts light and soft as my fingers find each egg. I collect five and leave the coop into the glare of sun on snow. A flash of red passes by in the air in front of me and lands in a white birch. It's a male cardinal, rare here even in summer, and this is the first one I've seen in winter. His stark feathers against the bark and snow make him look like a target, as if he is already wounded and bleeding.

"What do the roads look like?" Art says.

"It'll be a couple of days at least."

He shakes his head in disgust. Inside the house, I sit beside the wood stove in the kitchen while Art scrambles the eggs for us.

"Damn snow. There's no way to reach Louise's house. My phone's dead."

Louise's house. Conjures up an old woman in a cottage with a blanket across her knees, knitting. It's a half-hour drive in good weather to the nursing home in Bridgetown. Art has made that trip every day since she moved there until this storm hit.

"She always likes to go to chapel on Sundays to sing. She'll be wondering where I am."

From what he's told me she will be wondering no such thing. "They'll tell her why you aren't coming."

After ten minutes of chewing eggs and toast and slurping coffee, he raises an eyebrow and says, "Well, Mother Nature, that bitch, has given you a captive audience. If you wanna talk, go ahead."

It's true, we aren't going anywhere. There is enough firewood cut and stacked to last at least two winters, the days are as short for work as they will ever be, and the two of us are hanging on, alone at the edge of the world.

10

Now, a year and a half after receiving her acceptance to graduate school, Benny was in Leach's lab. She threw her cotton sweater over the back of the chair and grabbed her lab coat off a hook on the wall beside her desk. She put it on and rolled up each sleeve, halfway up her forearm so they wouldn't drag on the bench. On the shelf above her desk were binders of experimental notes, textbooks from her classes, the *Merck Manual* she had taken from her parents' bedroom, and the book that had got her to the lab in the first place, *Plastics: Their Chemistry and Uses*.

Her lab was joined to Nawthorn's by a swinging door she could see from her bench. It allowed the sharing of expensive equipment and reagents but did nothing to allay the tension between the two principal investigators. Nawthorn, a full professor, had come to research out of a love for experimentation and a curiosity for discovery. Deep in Leach's past there may have been a similar motivation, but it had been buried under years of striving for success. He was an associate professor trying to make his fame. It was Nawthorn who harboured the bulk of the animosity; Leach respected Nawthorn's abilities, if not his lack of business ambition. Leach, in his awkward way, was willing to be on good terms with everybody, though it turned out that not many liked him.

Benny worked all morning without distraction. Leach had asked her to begin her graduate work by investigating structural changes in genes of bacteria that had been cultured for long periods in unusual environments. His lab had published papers on the acquired ability of bacteria to digest toxic man-made compounds. He had already discovered strains of *Pseudomonas* capable of eating dioxins, chlorophenols, and the building blocks of the simplest plastics, such as nylon. He wanted to expand that list to include more complex plastics. To this end, Benny grew bacteria in liquid medium in Erlenmeyer flasks in which the only source of carbon and nitrogen were plastic polymers. Only those bacteria that mutated to become capable of metabolizing the plastics would survive. She sped up the process by exposing her bacterial cultures to mitogens to induce mutations, genomic rearrangements, and gene duplications.

In late afternoon she left the lab and bought a falafel from a Lebanese place on 70th. She took it to the corner, where she sat in the sun on a wall above the sidewalk. She peeled back the wax paper and ate while the crowd passed by. A jackhammer blitzed pavement somewhere nearby and horns announced another blocked intersection. A house sparrow hopped on the concrete near her, finding scraps of sandwiches. On her way back to her lab she met Leroy in the foyer going home for the night. They stopped in front of the bust of George Papanicolaou, the school's Nobel laureate, inventor of the Pap test. As had been the habit of hundreds of students wishing for good luck before their exams, Leroy reached down to rub his bald bronze pate. He was going out for dinner at a Spanish restaurant in their neighbourhood and invited her along.

She couldn't; she had an incubation to deal with. She wanted to purify a DNA fragment containing an amide-digesting enzyme gene.

Other than the freezers humming in the hallway, the lab was quiet. Benny was able to read at her desk while she waited on the plasmid DNA to be cleaved by the restriction endonucleases. She loaded a few millilitres of the reaction into an agarose gel and turned on the current. The electrophoresis would separate the DNA fragments according to size, allowing her to purify the one containing the enzyme gene.

When she was done she walked around the block and stopped on the sidewalk as a woman threw her lover's possessions at him from a third-floor window. He called up to her, begging her to be reasonable. Instead, the woman hurled one projectile after another, silent fluttering invective that made its way to the ground. Books, clothes, a toothbrush. A bag of his papers caught in the tree outside the window.

"How am I supposed to get that out of the tree?"

She unspooled a cassette and threw the tape out. It also caught on a branch and tangled in the tree.

"Ain't love a bitch?"

It was Leroy. He was with three friends, medical students. They were going home. She slid her arm into his.

"Come with me."

He waved to his friends, and Benny walked him back to the entrance of the school. They took an elevator that only went to the twenty-third floor. The last three flights were accessible by stairs and were empty. There were no offices, and the only sounds were mechanical, fans and water in pipes and their footsteps echoing off the walls. The floors were covered in a layer of dust, scraps of wood and paper, discarded coffee cups.

On the twenty-sixth floor they stepped out onto a tennis court and into the night. On the three sides of the court ahead of them, the walls rose five feet, like the turret of a castle. There was a net covering the court to prevent balls from flying over the parapet and down to the streets below. They walked across the empty court to the east side, where the lights of Queens shone beyond East River. A bench rested against the wall and they stepped onto it to look over the edge. Far below, a tug boat plied the river.

"Hey," Benny said, pointing at it. "It's Little Toot. *Toot, toot.*" Right on cue the tug tooted its bass horn two times as if in response. They looked at each other and laughed. She leaned her back against the wall and gazed up. A few brave stars winked at them.

"I come here every Friday night," she said.

"By yourself?"

"My roommate came up with me a couple of times when we first discovered it, but it creeps her out."

"You're not scared?"

"Of what?"

"It's dark. There's no one around."

"That's why I come up here." She pointed below them. "All those cars, and we can barely hear them." At that distance, the lights on FDR Drive moved slowly. "To see so much and barely any noise." A plastic shopping bag flapped by them on an updraft. "Low-density polyethylene."

"You're obsessed."

"It's one of the simplest polymers that exists. Once it's digested, all that's left is carbon dioxide and water. We'll make them literally evaporate."

"But if you get rid of bags what will replace them?"

"What did we use before plastic?"

They were silent then, leaning on the wall and looking out at the horizon. She seized his hand.

"There was a reason I thought you'd like it up here, and it wasn't to bore you about plastic."

She pulled him across the court to the south side of the building. There was another bench and they climbed onto it together. Spread out before them were the beautiful buildings she was in awe of. The Citicorp building on stilts with its beam of light cast heavenward. The Empire State Building, shining pinstripe blue and white in honour of the Yankees winning the ALCS that afternoon. And the one she liked best, the Chrysler Building, a corporate cathedral with its spire piercing the sky and gargoyles made of car parts. She let go of his hand and pulled herself halfway over the wall, pivoting on her hips, so that she could see the roof of a lower portion of the hospital and, through a gap between buildings, a slice of the traffic on York Avenue. She pointed down. He shook his head. She jabbed at the air again. Three floors below and built of twigs and grass on a small ledge.

"Peregrine falcons," she said. "They breed them upstate in Ithaca. This one was released on Mount Desert Island and damned if the silly bugger didn't fly here."

"They're beautiful," he said. "I remember a hawk, swooping down on the chickadees on our feeder. But I've never seen a falcon."

They descended to the street and walked home. Once in their building, Leroy headed for the elevator. She touched his arm and steered him toward the stairs. She attacked the stairs, two at a time, and was a flight ahead of him by the time he figured out what was happening. He took her charge as a challenge and caught up to her by the fourth floor. They were both winded by the time they got to their floor. They walked to the door of the apartment she shared with her roommate, Annika. He leaned in to kiss her and she turned her head so his lips landed on her cheek. He said goodnight and turned to go to his room.

11

Margaretsville

I have spent the day at Art's talking, eating lunch, bringing in firewood. He offers to let me spend the night on his couch. He pulls a sleeping bag from the cupboard, finds an extra pillow. The moon is huge and the trees drop their shadows onto the blue snow as if each of them has stepped out of a skirt that now lies around their feet. Talking aloud about Benny has tired me, and I long for the cold air to invigorate my lungs. But it's the thought of my tent, buried in white, that has kept me at Art's all day. He stands leaning against the door jamb as I unroll the sleeping bag on his couch.

"Louise loves to ski."

"They'll get the roads plowed soon."

He isn't listening.

"She's so graceful on skis. The nurses look at her and see the sparkle in her eyes. They tell me they know she's still there."

I have learned from the short time I've spent with him that it's best not to say anything. If you start asking questions or give him your opinion on the matter he either gets lost or shuts up. I know he needs to get where he wants to go with this.

"When she started to lose her memory it wasn't obvious. She'd leave one of the burners on after pulling the pot off. Or she'd go into the garden on a rainy day and leave the front door open. 'Put wood in the hole,' I'd shout after her. She had always been the one reminding me to close that door. Then she'd look at me all confused and say she was sorry, and I'd regret barking at her. Life's a bugger sometimes."

I nod.

He wipes his eyes with a thumb and forefinger, pretending he is weary. "I've gotta get some sleep."

He turns and leaves the room. The heat makes me drowsy, but I can't yet sleep. There are so many things I still can't understand.

*

My first trip to Nova Scotia, August 1985
As much as I liked gardening with my father, it took forever for the middle of August to arrive so we could go to Nova Scotia. When it did, my sleeping bag and bathing suit had been packed for three weeks by the end of my bed.

It was the peak of summer, and as we drove across Maine, the smell of freshly spread manure was everywhere. We had all four windows rolled down, the hot summer air pouring in, and the smell from the fields filling the car. Dad inhaled the rich pong of soil fertility through his nostrils. We crossed the bridge onto Mount Desert Island, under which the water was rushing out to sea, and drove to Bar Harbor. There we sailed on the *Bluenose* to Yarmouth. The first night in Nova Scotia we stayed at a campsite on the edge of a lake. I asked him why he always took the site the wardens assigned to us. We never looked around to see which site we wanted. He said that if he were a pioneer he would take the first piece of land he came to. He wouldn't keep walking over the next hill to see if it was any better.

The next day everyone started leaving the campground. Dad asked another camper why they were leaving, and she told us that a hurricane was sweeping up the coast. My father was the kind of father who looked at that as an adventure. Good thing Mom wasn't there.

The winds picked up long before the storm arrived, whipping the lake's surface into whitecaps. He put me in our small inflatable raft, tethered it to a tree onshore, and watched me ride the waves. I was laughing as the raft went up and down and spun around in the wind. We went to sleep that night anxious and excited, the tent tied to the spruce trees in the campsite. The wind pushed the trees around all night until I thought they would split, but there was little rain.

I woke first, as usual, and was looking down on him when he opened his eyes. Sunshine and the shadows of leafy branches fell on the canvas. I whispered, dramatically, "We're alive!" He loved that joke. He said it cured him of any doubt that I'd take to camping.

We drove along the coast by Digby. When Dad stopped at the side of the highway to pee a little beyond Annapolis Royal, he collected seeds from the pods of desiccated lupines to sow in our garden at home. Our destination that day was Middleton, the town Dad was born in. After his father died at Dieppe, my grandmother took him to live with her sister on a farm. He tried to find the house, but he had little information to go on. We found a museum that had genealogical archives and found a record for his father, Stuart, living on School Street. The house was one block from the museum. Dad held my hand as he looked at where he'd once lived.

We spent the night in a private campground on the banks of the Annapolis River. There was a caged raccoon by the campground office. It was pacing back and forth and it had a mangy, greasy coat. Dad told me he thought it was some sort of attraction. I cried when we left the office.

All that afternoon I could think of nothing but how to get back to that cage without getting caught. It was my birthday. At the river we swam, and I played on its muddy bank. We went to The Big Scoop for supper and I got to have a milkshake and a piece of cake. On the drive back to the campsite my arms and legs were gimpy and Dad joked that I was in a sugar coma.

That night I told Dad I had to pee and climbed out of the tent. The arc lamp by the office shone yellow light onto the grass in the field. Thousands of moths and other insects circled the light. The only sounds were the hum of the lamp and the continual ding when one of them bounced off the metal dome. I jogged across the field to the office. The building was dark. A dog growled in the yard as I unwound the wire holding the raccoon's cage door shut. The raccoon hissed at me with what strength it had left. I backed up, cajoling it in a whisper, and gradually it moved toward the opening. It scurried out and made for the nearest tree. The dog barked and came running to the end of its rattling chain. The raccoon went up the tree and clung to a branch to look down at me with its bandit eyes. I skulked into the shadow that the building threw and waited. The dog lost interest, sniffed its way back to the office porch, circled once around, and flopped down. The raccoon climbed backwards down the trunk and waddled off into the woods.

I peed on the grass and then returned to the tent.

"What took you so long?" Dad murmured.

I told him I was looking at the stars. I hated to lie to him, but I knew that nobody should find out I had let the raccoon go. I had learned that keeping a secret meant telling not even those you trust.

Dad looked puzzled when he saw the open cage the next morning as we checked out. I avoided his eyes while he paid the owner of the campground, who was annoyed that someone had let his raccoon go.

In the car Dad said, "It's true what he said. It's no different than stealing or breaking a window on purpose."

"I'm glad it was set free. What's wrong with that?"

"It's not wrong, Bean. But it's against the law. If everybody did what they thought was right, we'd be living in chaos."

"Then I'd like to be living in chaos."

He laughed and reached across to squeeze my knee until I squealed.

We drove up to Cape Breton. There were dirty-faced kids on the side of the road, begging for candy when they saw our licence plates. We camped in the Highlands and hiked in stunted spruce forests. When it came time to head south again, I didn't want to leave. This happened to me whenever we packed up our tent and headed home. I would not be able to sleep on the ground, go to bed as soon as it got dark and sleep under the stars, or listen to the creeping noises on the other side of the thin canvas walls for a whole year. That year the longing was more profound. Part of me thinks we would have done well to stay instead of driving back onto the ferry in Yarmouth.

In September I helped weed the flower bed on the south side of the house. We pulled out dandelions and grass from around the peonies and cleared an area for the lupine seeds we had brought back from Nova Scotia. Dad hoped they would sprout and grow enough before the fall to have a head start the next spring. I pushed a stake into the ground to mark the spot. In the vegetable garden there were still weeks of tomatoes and beans. We harvested the onions and potatoes late that month and stored them in a cool part of our basement. We also severed the pumpkins from their vines and put them in our garage, not only to beat the first hard frost, but to protect them from vandals.

On October 31 I hauled one of those pumpkins out of the darkness of the garage when I came home from school. Dad spread newspaper on the kitchen counter and I carved it for Halloween.

"Come here," he said.

He stood at the sink, looking out the window at the bird feeder. We kept millet and sunflower seeds in a green metal bucket in the garage, and each winter day one of us took a yogourt container out to the birds. I got up from the stool and stood behind him. A pair of cardinals was perched on the feeder. The red of him, his proud crest. She was paler, as if the red had been washed out. The male passed a sunflower seed to the female, from beak to rosy beak. When she flew off, he followed.

The next summer he and I drove to the sandy shore of Lake Ontario in Upstate New York. There were willows lining the dunes and a flat expanse of grey water all the way to the horizon. A little farther back from shore poplar leaves fluttered in the heat. I was barefoot for two weeks, pressing sand between my toes, grinding my arches and heels into it, pouring handfuls of warm sand on top of my feet as we lay in the sun. By late afternoon each day the beaches were covered for miles with silver fish rotting under the blue sky. The next morning, by the time we arrived to swim and play Frisbee, all that was left were parallel lines in the sand, as if a giant with a hundred fingers had grated the beach in the night. Dad wanted to know what happened to the fish, so we rose early one morning and went to the beach. A man was in the gentle waves soaping his torso, calling to his wife that the bar of soap floated as she had told him it would.

The alewives, six inches long, lay motionless against the sand, their eyes looking up at the sky while flies landed on them. Farm tractors descended on the beach pulling rakes behind them, dragging the fish into piles that were shovelled into garbage trucks and hauled away. It might have been one of nature's cycles that killed them; at the time I didn't know.

The banging of the poker in the wood stove wakes me. Art is piling the coals in the centre and adding some kindling to get the day's fire going. He offers me breakfast, which we eat in a hurry as he sees that the road has been plowed. He gives me a lift up the road on his way to see Louise.

Lily Lake Road has not been plowed, so I strap on the snowshoes and climb the hill. When I pass between the two ash trees into my clearing I feel as alone as I have since I arrived here.

12

Lily Lake Road

In March I get a letter from Lina, who is staying with her grandmother in Quebec. The envelope is addressed to me at "Forest Garden." She's christened the land, and I like the name. She admires me for what I'm doing and asks if she can live here for the summer. I want to contact her immediately, but that is not as simple as it used to be. It's still possible to email, phone, even take a plane on a whim, but at a cost inversely proportional to their availability. Because there are so few computers left, nobody emails anymore except under urgent circumstances. The one government e-pod in town is expensive and books a week in advance. I write her a long note, saying yes among much else, and bike through a cold rain into Middleton later that morning to mail it. At least Canada Post hasn't changed.

My winter work is done, but there is April to get through before I can plant outdoors. I'm waiting for the thaw and the blackflies. I read homesteading books and write in my journal.

*

The end of my childhood, 1989-1990

I still felt like a kid the day Dad and I left for our camping trip the summer I turned fourteen. I settled into the passenger seat, as comfortable and eager as I had been previous summers, then swivelled to wave at Mom through the rear window. She stood on the driveway by the garage, wiping her eyes. We pulled onto the street and she turned back into the house. In that moment something sleeping awoke within me. I thought, for the first time, *She doesn't really want me*. She had never seemed that interested, and I wondered if she thought something was wrong with me. I turned back to face the front. Dad's profile was expressionless, his lips set, his eyes looking forward. I put on my seatbelt.

We took two days to get to Maine. By the time we arrived at the state campground on Moosehead Lake I had more or less put aside my worries about my mother. On the night of my birthday I opened the gifts he had for me as well as the one Mom had sent with us. Hers was wrapped beautifully in orange tissue paper, with a blue ribbon tied in a bow around it. *Middlemarch*. It was a thick, softcover book, and its heft made me happy. Heavy going for a teenager, but I liked that she thought I could read it. Her inscription was a mystery though.

> *It is Dorothea Brooke that I identify with. Do not squander your intelligence and invention on a too domestic life as she did.*

After supper, we put on our bathing suits and drove to the beach on the lake. On the way, we tried to phone her from the pay phone at the check-in, but she didn't answer. At the beach, the air was cool and the sky black. The car's headlights shone on the shallow water near shore, the light disappearing into the murk in the middle of the lake. We waded in, and once we were immersed, the cool night air, by a trick of physics, my father explained, made the lake water feel warmer than it had earlier in the day. Everything was relative, he explained, and depended on its opposite for definition, as the languid sunny day we had spent fishing in the lake from a canoe contrasted with that cool night.

An onshore breeze, companion to the sheets of lightning dazzling soundlessly across the lake, thrilling and fresh, carried clean lake air and ozone toward us. My father, his face illuminated by lightning, smiling, was exhilarated to be out in the weather. He was not anxious about the storm, nor yet for our safety. We swam until the drops began to *plink! plink!* around our heads on the rippled black glass.

On the shore I wrapped myself in the huge orange towel. Dad put his arm around my shoulders as we gazed across the lake. We were lit up each time a flash of blue glowed above the trees on the far shore.

"The world is a wonderful place, Bean," he said. "You can do anything in it. Anything."

We were alone, embracing the night storm, the light on the water, the dry cloth against cold skin, the wind in our faces. We saw the storm that night, coming toward us, and were happy.

The nights were cold. Dad heated water on the gas stove and filled two empty gin bottles. I loved the yellow labels on those bottles, with the flowers running down the sides, and back then I loved the clean smell of juniper in his glass when he drank it. He wrapped the bottles in towels and pushed them to the bottom of our sleeping bags before we went to bed. I put my bare feet on the warm towel while my father talked. The Coleman lantern glowed white hanging from a pole in the roof. Once he was in his sleeping bag, Dad reached up to turn off the lantern. The light faltered and turned from white to yellow until all that was left was a soft glow on the mantle. When I could no longer see my father's face I contracted into myself, separate and uneasy. I lay still, waiting, remembering my mother not even waving as she turned to go into the house. When he spoke it was only one of his silly jokes, but it relieved me of my anxiety, at least for that night.

"Three men sat around a campfire. One man said, 'Joe, tell us a ghost story.' And Joe began, 'Three men sat around a campfire. One man said, 'Joe, tell us a ghost story.' And Joe began…'"

He quizzed me for a few square roots, then told me how you could calculate the height of a tree using trigonometry. It didn't matter to me what he said, as long as his voice went on until I glided into sleep, which I soon did.

It was still hot and sunny when Dad and I pulled into the driveway. Summer wasn't spent and the evening would stay muggy. The mailbox in the breezeway was full and the postie had left a pile of letters and flyers that didn't fit on the ground below it. Dad opened the door, and there was another pile of mail on the kitchen counter, unopened. The kitchen air was still and stale. The windows were all closed.

"Marlene?" he called. But we both knew. He wouldn't look at me. On the counter beside the stove was a note propped against a bottle of olive oil. He read it, looked dazed, and sat down by the bay window facing into our backyard. I asked him to read it to me, but he said nothing and stared out the window.

I went up to my room and waited. There was no sound downstairs. When he didn't come up, I unpacked the little I'd taken on the trip. I put *Middlemarch* on my bedside table. I took our sleeping bags outside and hung them on the clothesline to air out. I hung our sheets on the line too because they had been in that stuffy house and smelled stale. When I came back in Dad was still sitting in his chair, the crumpled note in his hands.

"Let me see the note."

He shook his head. Later, I ate a cheese sandwich alone and went to bed. The sheets from the line were crisp and smelled sweet and I loved their feel on my bare legs. I lay awake thinking and listening to him downstairs. He came to say goodnight as I was drifting off.

"Everything's going to be O.K.," he said. His speech was thick, and he staggered a bit on his way out the door.

I never got to read the note. I wish I still had that green sweater she knitted me.

We didn't hear anything from my mother for months, and then a thin envelope arrived, addressed to me and with no return address, containing the briefest explanation for why she left.

> *... There are things I want to do with my life that I have been putting off. No doubt they will sound small to you and I don't expect you to understand. I had dreams as a girl that I have been watching vanish. Maybe one day you will know what I mean. I think you must hate me right now and I don't blame you. But...*

There was not much there to hold on to but it turned out it was all I had. She never phoned, and I never saw her again. I wanted to, if only so I could gouge her eyes out.

Dad wouldn't talk about Mom and this meant neither could I, at least not to him. It was like she had vaporized, taking the uneasiness she had lived with in our home with her. But instead of lightening the mood or making life at home easier, her absence had the opposite effect. Marlene's desertion settled into my father like a weight that could only drag him down.

One morning in February I got up in the dark, put my bare feet on the chilled linoleum, and went to my window, which overlooked the backyard. It was as black as it ever got, a sprinkling of stars above the trees. It had snowed in the night and the rink was covered. I wanted to clear the ice so it'd be ready to play on as soon as I got home from school that afternoon. I put on my long johns, track pants, and a sweater and went downstairs. I turned the floodlight on and went out to shovel the rink. The neighbourhood was silent. No cars. No wind. No birds. Nothing. A gust blew flakes off the roof where they sparkled in the light like stars drifting through the gelid air. The snow was fluffy but deep, and shovelling was heavy work. I rested on the handle of the shovel and turned toward the house. Dad stood at the picture window, watching me. He waved. That wave, the cold air in my lungs, the stars, and the shovel scraping the ice: In that moment I needed nothing more.

That afternoon when he came home from work I gave him a painting I had done of the white-throated sparrow.

"Promise me you'll never leave," I said.

"You know I don't make promises, Bean. No promises, no debts."

I said nothing.

"I have no intention of going anywhere."

But it turns out there is more than one way to leave someone. A distance grew between me and Dad as we settled into our private preoccupations. For the rest of high school mine were pot and promiscuity. Most of what I did was either harmless or led to minor scars that do little more than remind me of that time. I spent a lot of evenings alone in my room then, reading, listening to music.

That fall I'd come home from school and shoot a tennis ball with my hockey stick at the net standing in front of the garage door. Slapshot after slapshot the muddy ball hit the garage door when I missed the net. When Mom was around she had made me paint the door each spring to cover the marks. Now there were hundreds of perfect brown circles on the beige door. I took specific joy in hitting a target, none more satisfying than the crossbar of the net. Again and again

I aimed for that bar, and when I hit it, as the net rocked back slightly and the ball flew off into the air and back toward me, I had the sensation of having accomplished something worthwhile.

One afternoon in early November, our neighbour Ted came by. My father was home but hadn't turned on the outdoor lights. Ted was studying engineering at university in the city. The tennis ball flew off the blade of his stick faster and harder as he wristed it at the door. He took a wrist shot against the door, and when the ball came back to him, he cradled it on the blade of his stick. He asked me if I thought the ball stopped at any point between leaving his stick and the time it returned. I couldn't see it come to rest. He picked up the ball and walked to the door. The ball came in, hit the door, was compressed, stopped, then reversed its motion. That moment of reversal could not be held. It was such a small length of time that it didn't actually exist.

I began going for walks most weeknights after dinner. Dad asked if could join me. He said he wanted to stay in shape, but I guess he saw us drifting and thought he should do something about it. Our routine was set early on. If we ate dinner together he would look at me as he rose to clear the table and say, "Walk?'" I always said yes. He'd go to the fridge, open the crisper, pull out an apple, and toss it to me. He pulled one out for himself and salted it. He had measured out a few routes in the car so we would know how far we walked. The one I liked best was three miles long and took us across the cut the trains used to get into the city, over to Crystal Lake. In my memory the pavement always looks oily in the streetlight and smells sweet and earthy. To fill the time I made up a game we called World Without, in which we imagined what the world would be like without, say, birds or cars. Other nights I walked by myself, relieved to have a silence I didn't have to try to fill.

One hot, still night we took our bathing suits on our walk to the lake. The surface was so smooth as we approached the dock that it looked like a challenge. I picked up a stone near the shore and threw it as far as I could, breaking the mirror with a splash.

We swam in the dark. He got out before me, dried himself and dressed, and asked me to hurry up. Dad had always been affectionate with me—wrapping an arm around my shoulder, hugging me goodnight—but that summer it stopped.

It's possible to live in something like happiness without even knowing it. There comes an instant when you recognize it exists. And in that moment it no longer does.

13

Forest Garden

It's my second May here and I'm going to meet Lina. She's taken the train to Halifax, and a bus from there to Middleton. It's foggy when I start down the hill to meet her. Walking gives me time to think and see things I miss when I whiz down the mountain on my bike. Dozens of Tim Hortons coffee cups and plastic lids in the ditch. Beer cans. Six-pack rings. Soda bottles and water bottles thrown from speeding car windows. Those may all be gone soon.

The sun has burned off the fog by the time I get to Spa Springs. A little girl in a field by the side of the road picks dandelions with her grandfather. She laughs as she puts them in the pot he is holding. The man smiles at me when I wave and stoops over to offer her the pot. The girl looks up from the flowers, and when she sees me, she stops and stares.

I pass the veal calves and the fields of rye and newly sprouted corn. Lina is standing by her backpack by the time I get to the motel where the bus stops. She is different than I remember, more beautiful, and she's cut her hair above her shoulders. She wears a navy blue hoodie with "Maine" written on the chest in large white letters, jeans, and hiking boots. When she sees me she shouts my name and comes running to me, her arms outstretched. We hug and then grow ill at ease by the intimacy. I throw her pack over my shoulders and fasten the straps for the hike home. She is reticent after our greeting. I am babbling beside her, telling her about the cows and the history of Spa Springs, and my garden.

She pitches her tent near mine by the fire circle. After dinner we sit by the campfire, talking late. Then she gets up to go to her tent and I long to hold her back, to keep her seated across the flames so I can watch the light throwing shadows on her face for a while longer. At least I know she is there for the summer and that there will be many more nights like this one.

The last few weeks have been glorious. I wake in my tent, and like a dog with its wet nose twitching at a beguiling scent, I know that she is on the land. There is a buzz, heightened energy I sense among the trees and birds and in the air.

We garden when the weather lets us. When it rains hard we sit in my tent, which is bigger than hers, and talk and read to each other. I read the gardening and building passages from *The Good Life* to her as she knits. Mostly, she is quiet around me. At times I am nervous and feel like a galumphing sea lion, the way I crawl about the tent and speak too loudly as if I am trying to prove something or win an argument we aren't having.

There are green-scented breezes this spring like the ones I grew up with, when the snow melted into puddles on the pavement under the warming sun and I put on my sweater and ran.

—

In early June I am swinging the mattock to get at tree roots and rocks in a new bed. Between tugging on spruce roots and lugging rocks to the wall at the top of the garden, I steal glances at her. We are both wearing bug shirts with screening covering our heads, and I can't see her face. She is rolling sod with the garden fork and piling it in mounds, ready for squash and pole bean seeds. She works with a determination I admire, jabbing the earth with the fork the same way each time. We work without speaking for an hour or so, then she straightens her back and looks over at me. She unzips her hood, pulls it back, and drinks water from a Mason jar. When she bends over to put the jar back on a stump her cleavage reveals that she is wearing nothing under her bug shirt. She brushes a wisp of her black hair away from her face with a dirty hand, leaving a smear of soil on her cheek. I want to go over, lick my finger, and wipe it off. Or, better, just lick her cheek directly.

"All this digging doesn't feel right to me. Every time I stab the land my arms shudder."

"Try holding your arms farther apart."

"I mean my arms don't want to stab the fork in the ground. I'm telling them to push and they're resisting: I want to plant without piercing the land."

I am skeptical, despite the experience she has gardening with her grandmother when she was a little girl and the flower gardening she did at Art's last summer. It didn't work for me at all last summer to plant directly in sod, but she insists on trying. The next day we buy a fifty-pound burlap bag of seed potatoes. We cut them, leaving at least one eye per piece, and place them a foot apart directly on the ground. We cover the rows with a foot of oat straw. Three weeks later, when the potatoes sprout, we pull the straw back a bit to let them reach light.

Our seed orders arrive in the mail from Vesey's and Richters. Spinach, lettuce, kale, chard, tomatoes, peppers, cucumbers, onions, some herbs. She opens the packet containing her tobacco seeds and pours some into my hand. They are like dust, smaller than poppy seeds. We plant the seeds in pots and take them to Martin and Jen's greenhouse. While they germinate she prepares a bed for the tobacco. This she has to dig as the seedlings will be small and fragile, unable to compete with the hawkweed and grass.

On one of the first days of summer, we plant beans and squash and corn in the mounds we made. It's too hot and dry to transplant our seedlings during the day, so we wait until the sun drops behind the trees and the garden beds are in shade. Then we go to Martin and Jen's greenhouse and retrieve all our potted seedlings. The air grows still after supper and is hotter and heavier than it has been all day. The gentle breeze of the early afternoon has abated, leaving conditions perfect for blackflies. Lina and I don our bug gear. It's like a greenhouse inside my bug shirt. Soon there are spots of blood on my wrists. The flies crawl through any fold into the jacket and buzz, trapped by the material. I rub my hands over each other like Lady Macbeth with OCD, but the buggers are assiduous in their hunger. Where the hood rests against my ears they bite through the cotton. My ears are hot and itchy.

"Leave me alone, you miserable pricks," I shout, slapping my hand against my hood and running to get away from them. It feels better while I do this, but they are quick to return once I kneel again. I ease each seedling from its pot, make a small space for it with my fingers, and put its roots below ground. Every dozen or so I sprinkle them from the watering can. We sing Beatles songs we both know while we work to distract ourselves from the annoyance. Occasionally, the dragonfly cavalry flies in, their wings crinkling like Chinese paper dragons, to snatch the flies that hover in front of my face. One lands on my arm to eat its prey, munching rhythmically on one of my tormentors.

We take turns having a shower-in-a-bag on the pallet. I promise her we'll have more water soon. I'm going to get a well drilled. I've had enough of hauling pails and jars of water down the road.

I bike to Middleton and withdraw two thousand dollars from my account, leaving little behind, and put the hundred-dollar bills in a Mason jar. I dig a shallow hole by my tent and bury the jar. Lina met someone named Jake who's a dowser on a land co-op in East Margaretsville who said he would show us where to drill.

As we sit on the dry ground by the fire after gardening all day, we hear scratching in the grass under the trees. The porcupines have been snuffling around our campsite before and we assume they are back. But porcupines don't meow. Into the light of the fire comes a small cat, black and white like a Holstein. She prances right up to us, meows again, and jumps into Lina's lap.

"Hello, little one. Where'd you come from?"

She isn't one of Jenifer's. She trots after Lina into her tent that night and I am jealous of that cat. As I climb into bed alone I imagine curling up around Lina's back, purring her to sleep.

*

The first cut, August 1992

It was my seventeenth birthday and, as it turned out, my last camping trip with my dad. We had been gabbing since Ellsworth because we were excited to be almost there. We were about to cross the bridge onto Mount Desert Island for the first time since I was ten and Dad asked me to guess whether the water rushing under the road meant the tide was going in or out.

"Out?"

The water was rushing off in the direction of the sea. Dad looked over at me across the front seat and smiled. I called him a sentimental old fart for remembering the last time we crossed that bridge, and when he laughed, it felt like we used to be, like things were all right.

We went to Allen's Campground near Somes Sound. We put up our tent and spent the afternoon playing in the waves at the ocean beach and renting bikes to travel the carriage paths. Dad poured himself a gin and tonic and cooked spaghetti, which we ate in front of a campfire with plates on our laps. He had bought a cake in Bangor. Now he put candles in it and sang to me in his croaky, off-key voice. After we did the dishes, we listened to the ball game while Dad drank a can of beer and lit a cigar. He only smoked when we camped. The scent of burning tobacco mingled with the smoke of the fire and dissipated on the light breeze. It smelled exotic outdoors under the spruce trees.

The next morning before my father awoke I discovered a long chain of rickety wharves stretching from shore two hundred feet into the sheltered bay. A bald eagle perched atop a tall conifer across the narrow bay. Gulls dove at it, careful to keep distance between their white wings and its beak. Stepping from one bobbing section to the next, I walked to the end of the floating wharves. Beyond the end, well into Somes Sound, a large sailboat was anchored, its mast naked, a contained and solitary island. On my way back to shore a squid, blood red, swam ten feet from the wharves. Its tentacles flapped with the grace of wings in slow motion. Suddenly, there was another pair of wings above me. A gull, its grey wings folded, dropped from the blue sky and its beak pierced the surface. It rose up above the water. The squid released ink, making the water murky as it escaped into the deeper, protective water of the sound. The gull landed on the surface and floated.

I wobbled along the docks, then kneeled down to see what was in the water. The tide was low and the water so clear that the bottom was visible, rich with life. Seaweed, mussels alive and empty-shelled, schools of little fish, tiny crabs camouflaged until they moved. I dipped my arm into the frigid water to get a blue-black mussel. They lived together, communities clinging tenaciously to one another and to the rocks on the floor, as if an inseparable geological fact. Their striped shells were covered with barnacles. I yanked a clump of them from the rocks and twisted one away from the others; the tension and grating of the threads that bound them together felt like cranking the leg joint off raw chicken. I laid the mussel on the wharf and brought my shoe down on top of it, cracking its shell to expose its flesh. When I dropped it back into the water, the shattered shell fell back and forth to the seabed like a maple leaf floating to the ground on a still day. Small crabs scuttled silently across the floor, attracted to the scent of exposed flesh. One, two, then a dozen or more came to eat the destroyed mussel. I felt bad to have killed it, but my curiosity got the best of me.

A school of minnows, no longer than my first knuckle, swam in the shallows like a disparate cloud of life, facing different directions while they fed. All of a sudden they aligned their bodies in parallel and darted away, the cloud now a plume of smoke rushing out of a chimney. Behind them a dozen or more mackerel, their backs black and gold, bulleted into the shoal after the school. The minnows broke the surface, which was roiling now. I ran back to the campsite for my fishing rod.

I tied my red devil lure with its treble hook onto the nylon line, going over and under six or more times, making up for my inept knots with a profusion of them. I found a school of minnows by the edge of the dock and dangled the lure among them. Twice mackerel shot in to catch minnows but avoided my lure. I removed the treble hook from the red-and-white disk, tied it by itself to the fishing line, and suspended it below the minnows after the mackerel had gone. They moved away as it plunked and sank. Once they grew accustomed to the treble hook and crowded above it, I jerked the rod up, snagging a minnow. The impaled minnow writhed on the hook among its schoolmates, and when they darted away from the next rush of mackerel, it was the obvious laggard to be eaten. There was a tug on the line, then an intense pull. I reeled the line in and a silver belly glittered near the surface as I pulled the sleek muscle from the water, the mackerel's silver turning to white in air. Holding the line with one hand, I slid the other over the fish's head and down its body, grasping it firmly as my dad had once shown me. I dislodged the hook as carefully as I could, the fish's one visible eye staring at its persecutor.

A motorboat pulled into the bay while I was doing this, cut its engine, and skimmed toward the dock. I knelt down to release the fish in the cold water, racing against the oil slick that floated toward me.

"Woo-hee! That's a beaut."

I cursed the approaching boat under my breath. Not only would it scare off the fish, but the noise and smell of diesel exhaust nauseated me. A few scales that had stuck to my fingers caught the light. I brought my hand to my face and smelled the fish. Sitting in the boat was a girl wearing frayed, cut-off jeans and a red shirt with "Marlboro" stencilled across it in white letters. Her blond hair hung below a Red Sox cap. She had a can of beer in her hand. I had never seen anything like her and I'm certain I was staring. She reached over the gunwale of the boat to hold on to the dock.

"No lure, huh? That's illegal, you know. Like jacking deer. If you got caught they'd take everything you own. Your fishing gear, your car, everything."

"I don't have a car," I said. "I'm only seventeen."

"Seventeen or seventy, it's still illegal. Don't worry, I won't tell the authorities." She winked at me. "Why'd you throw it back? That was a decent size fish."

"I don't like fish."

"Nothing like smoked mackerel. Ever had it?"

I shook my head.

"You should try it sometime." She leaned over the Evinrude,

pulled its cord, and shouted above the noise, "See you around, poacher."

I made sure to be on the dock the same time the next day and, when she didn't show up, the day after that. When she returned, she tied her boat to the dock and jumped out.

"I'm Katharine," she said, thrusting her hand at me. "What's with the hat?"

I could feel the blood rushing to my cheeks and reached for the floppy brim of my sun hat.

"Sun protection," I said.

"Take that silly thing off. You can wear this if you want."

She lifted the cap from her head and tossed it to me. Her wavy hair brushed her shoulders. It was thick, the colour of sand, and made me think it had seen a summer's worth of seawater and sun. My fingers wanted to bury themselves in her hair, to feel the tresses coated with salt.

We met each afternoon after that, while my father stayed at the campsite reading the paper or drinking gin and tonics with the ball game on the radio. She was two years older and that intimidated me. She smoked and laughed a lot and was beautiful and all I wanted was to hang out with her, to sit on the docks or in her boat, and talk.

Katharine took me out into the sound and all the way across to the far shore to the General Store in Somesville, where we bought ice cream. She taught me to fish in deeper water for cod and ocean perch. We talked about what school was like for us — she hated it — and the differences between life on an island and mine in the city.

On our last night, I told my dad I was going to watch the stars by the water. Katharine's boat was moored at the end of the docks. She met me at the shore and wrestled me to the ground before I knew what had happened. She sat on top of me, pinning my arms with her legs, and tickled me until I was finally able to throw her off. She flopped beside me, breathing heavily and we lay there, under some spruce, looking at the stars. As she talked I inched my hands closer to her head, as if trying to get comfortable on the stony ground. I rested the tips of my fingers against her hair, anxious that she would feel my touch, hoping, I suppose, that she might. At last, after what seemed like an hour of agony, I took a chance and rolled over to kiss her. It was by far the most electric kiss I'd ever had, but it confused both of us. It wasn't as if I hadn't been having sex back home. But the feeling I had with Katharine, just from that one kiss, showed me how meaningless all that casual sex had been. For the first time I felt what I assumed was love.

When it got late enough that my father would begin worrying about me I said goodbye to her. All I wanted was to stay with her by the water, and as I drifted through the darkness back to our campsite, I plotted how to see her again. I lay with my feet on the now-lukewarm bottle Dad had tucked into my sleeping bag hours before, imagining anything was possible as I tried to make sense of the fluttering wings in my belly. This all sounds so innocent, but for me it was anything but simple.

Dad and I left the next morning and began the drive home. I began writing a letter to her as soon as we left the campground. Dad was quiet until we approached the bridge off the island.

"Tide going in or out?" he asked me.

I guessed without looking up from my letter. "Out."

"You're wrong."

There was an edge in his voice I rarely heard. His face was rigid and his mouth set. As we crossed the bridge water was rushing in from the sea. I put my pen on the dashboard, pulled my feet up onto the seat, and huddled my knees into my chest.

"This was my vacation too," he said.

"I know that, Dad."

"I might as well be camping by myself."

He banged his hands on the steering wheel. It was as if he had reached across the seat and slapped me. All the way to Bangor there was nothing between us but the wind whistling in my open window and blowing hair into my teary eyes. Dad broke the silence as we passed the life-sized statue of Paul Bunyan.

"I hardly saw you at all. We didn't go up Cadillac Mountain. We went to the beach once. What's gotten into you?"

I held my breath and waited.

"We used to have so much fun," he continued, "and now all I do is sit at the campfire, listening to ball games and waiting for you to come back smelling like cigarettes and beer."

"I wasn't smoking."

I finished the letter and mailed it to Katharine as soon as I got home, inviting her to come and visit me that fall. Her response came a few weeks later. It was short and had none of the warmth I had been expecting. I mailed two more letters after that one, but after a lot of silence and a long winter of heartache, I had to admit that what we shared meant more to me than to her.

*

This morning I hear meowing outside my tent. Lina and the cat are making breakfast. Her paws pound the path when she runs.

"Come on, Thunder!" Lina calls to her, and the cat has a name.

Our water situation is about to improve, though it will be expensive. This morning we're having a well drilled. The rig is part of a heavy truck that makes two ruts we'll have to fill. It takes out the corner of one of our carrot beds as it wends its way over the bumpy land to the place we've identified for drilling. Lina's water-witching friend, Jake, came yesterday and dowsed an underground stream seventy feet below the surface. I show them where Jake said to drill and they begin cutting into the volcanic rock.

After they have gone through fifteen segments of pipe at ten feet per, I start pacing. They charge ten dollars per foot. I have heard stories of these rigs never hitting water and you still have to pay. I tell the boss he had better call it off as I won't be able to pay for any more but he says he's going to keep going and not to worry about the cost. They hit water at two hundred and ten feet, I give them the money I had buried, and Lina and I are left with a capped well. We both wonder what we are going to do with water that far down.

She suggests we measure where the water is now, and for some reason it's only seventy feet down, just as Jake said it would be. We have no electricity, so I had hoped to be able to use a hand pump, which functions to a depth of thirty feet or so.

I buy a solar panel, a spool of eight-gauge wire, and a pump. We wrap the excess thirty feet of wire around the well casing. We connect the wire to the panel, aim it at the blazing sun, and wait. Nothing.

Lina goes to find Martin, figuring he may be able to troubleshoot. He takes a look at our setup, unhooks the wire from the panel leads, and unwinds it from the casing. He cuts the thirty feet of wire, telling us that we have inadvertently created a magnet that prevents the flow of electricity. When he reattaches the wires to the leads we can hear the pump, faint, and within a minute a steady flow of the best water I've ever tasted is pouring onto the ground. We whoop and dance. I even hug Martin, who is grinning. Lina grabs the pipe and sprays us.

On sunny days we flip a switch and have water, clear and beautiful, which we store in gallon pickle jars.

In early July our hard-necked rocambole garlic is more than two feet high. We snap off the curled tops so the bulbs will fatten up. We begin construction on my cabin. We work it out on graph paper first. It will be ten by sixteen feet. All my life I have been schooled from books. I have memorized, and forgotten, thousands of equations, names, dates. Little of that has prepared me to grow food, let alone build a cabin. When I came here I knew nothing about pumping water from a well, plumbing, mixing concrete, or how to frame a window. In the past year I have learned the extent of my ignorance.

We design the cabin with four windows and two doors. We buy the studs from the Reagh's family mill down in Margaretsville. Like the people in this part of the world, the lumber is honest. A two-by-four is two inches by four inches, not one-and-a-half by three-and-a-half like they sell at the building supply store in Middleton.

"Good, sturdy lumber from good, sturdy Christians," Lina says as we haul the lumber on our shoulders from the road, piece by piece. We build forms for the foundation posts and fill them with concrete we mix with a shovel in the wheelbarrow. We saw every board by hand, pound every nail with a hammer, and have the floor and four walls up by the end of July. It is magnificent to behold something we have built with our own hands.

I am satisfied staying at home, listening to Lina's voice or nothing other than the wind or the chatter of red squirrels in the woods. From the start, however, Lina has wanted to be involved in the community. She makes friends with people I haven't even met, folks who live down by the bay or a good bike ride away, along the dirt roads that traverse the top of the mountain. They are almost all Come From Aways like us: aging hippies, back-to-the-landers, young people escaping urban life for a summer of growing some of their own food, pot heads, and those escaping a world they can't comprehend. Sometimes I go with her to a music jam or a kitchen party, but I get bored and want to be home where it is quiet.

One night we go to a campfire at the land co-op where she met Jake. It is a fifteen-minute bike ride past Art's place, not far from the shore in East Margaretsville. I sit across the fire from her, pulling the label off the bottle of Keith's that has gone warm in my hand. I feel a tight coil in my gut as I watch her laugh with a boy I met for the first time an hour ago. Charles has a ponytail and a hairy face. I try not to stare as he repeatedly reaches over to touch her arm while he talks.

He puts his jacket across her shoulders when she mentions that she's chilly. Though I'm not inclined to jealousy, I don't trust this guy.

Our bicycle tires crunch the dirt as we head home in the dark along the ridge road. There are fields on both sides of us. She is singing ahead of me. We walk our bikes along the path to our garden then say goodnight as we go separate ways to our tents.

14

New York City

Benny's feet rested on the windowsill and she had her back to the lab bench. A warm cup of coffee in a paper cup in her right hand, a tedious journal article in her left. Snowflakes rushed past the window, yellow-bright as they caught the streetlights. She was glad to be inside where it was warm. She yawned. Success in research meant long hours at the bench. She dropped her feet and went through the doorway to see Leroy. She stood by the window, looking down on the street.

"I hate it when it gets dark this early. The only thing I like about this time of year is skating."

Leroy continued to mix reagents in Eppendorf tubes at his bench. The traffic crawled on the slushy street, taking people homeward or out for drinks and dinner.

"We should go out for dinner," she said.

"Can't," he said, not looking at her. His lab coat had coffee stains down the front and journal references and phone numbers written in black Sharpie on its left sleeve. He reached to vortex a tube. "Where do you skate?"

"In the park at Wollman."

He had tacked up a quotation from *Frankenstein* on the corkboard beside his desk:

> *What glory would attend the discovery, if I could banish disease from the human frame, and render man invulnerable to any but a violent death!*

Beside that, a Canadian Cancer Society sticker: *Cancer can be beaten.* The "can" was crossed out and covered with "WILL," also written with a black Sharpie. What he referred to as hopeful naïveté had brought him to the bench. He had told her that he had a mission to contribute to the fight to cure cancer because of his mother, who died when he was twenty-one. He had been embarrassed during his grad school interviews at the University of Toronto when he brought this up. He was told by the principal investigator interviewing him that such generalizations were innocent and emotional and had no place in the lab.

"Does it bother you to use animals in your research?" she asked.

He said it did a bit and that he never got used to killing them. Those mice that didn't succumb to the cancers they were encouraged to grow were eventually dispatched with a whack on the neck with a metal ruler. The ones that got cancer suffered, but it was work that needed to be done. With Leroy's mind and focus he was able to discover aspects of mouse genetics that nobody had known before. He told Benny that he relished these discoveries. They might be minor, some were cul-de-sacs, but they were his discoveries and his cul-de-sacs. His work involved observing the effects of DNA-damaging agents on DNA repair in normal and mutant mice. He bombarded them with X-rays, vinyl chloride, aflatoxin, UV light. These led to mutations, chromosomal breaks, and deletions of whole sequences of DNA. Most of the mice developed cancer, and he had to kill those. Some mice survived, and one, an agouti he named Chico, survived no matter what he threw at it. From Chico, he cloned a DNA repair gene, which he called AMF1. That gene, and the functional analysis of the protein that AMF1 produced, would be sufficient for his thesis. He looked forward to finishing his grad work, and not only because he disliked the city. It would mean he could go home and continue his research to find practical applications. Molecular biology gave him hope. His colleagues were developing the weapons to slay genetic demons. If they could prevent mutations from happening in the first place, or repair them after they occurred, cancer would be beaten. It was cellular eugenics, and a fight he took personally.

"But it's practical work. I don't want to just add to a pile of information."

"As we're doing?" she suggested, raising one of her eyebrows.

"No, from what I hear, Leach is going to solve the world's environmental woes."

She laughed. They had both sat in on departmental seminars in which Leach had waxed poetic about his microbes. He bragged that they would be able to clean up everything from oil spills to nuclear waste, from dioxin in rivers to CFCs in the air. The more soiled our nest, the sexier bioremediation became as a research topic. Yet, Benny and Leroy knew results were coming slower than her professor's promises.

Leroy bought a pair of Bauers and he and Benny went to Wollman Rink in Central Park that night and almost every Friday night that winter.

The next afternoon Benny stood in Leroy's doorway, shivering, water dripping from her hair onto her shoulders and down her back. Her hands were cold and pink.

"Come in."

Warm air blew in from the vent, a constant bronchial exhalation loud enough to cover the splattering rain and the hiss of traffic where she had been running. The crazy wind drove heavy rain first in one direction, then another.

"Annika said she'd be there when I got back, so I didn't take my keys. I've got to get warm." She peeled off the sweatshirt, her damp long-sleeved cotton shirt, and a T-shirt, leaving her white running bra covering pale skin, pruned as if she had been in a bath too long. Drops landed on the vinyl floor, where they made small puddles.

Leroy told her to take a bath. Once in the bathroom, she looked at herself in the mirror. Her heart had slowed since she arrived at his door, out of breath from running the stairs, but it continued to beat against her sternum. What did Leroy see when he looked at her? Her finger traced her clavicle to her throat. She was thin and knew that, though she was attractive enough, she was no Annika. She had seen Leroy staring at her roommate as though he had been hypnotized. The water in the tub was too hot for her chilled feet. She turned the cold faucet on and lowered herself into the tub. Once she was in, she turned off the cold and felt the heat on her legs. Benny closed her eyes and submerged her head. Her heartbeat under water had the rhythm of wings flapping. She moved her head from side to side, her long dark hair flowing between and around her fingers. The tendrils of hair, graceful and slow, moved like the tentacles of a squid.

She lost her virginity the spring of her freshman year of high school. It was painful to think too closely of that time. It reminded her that something was missing. Leroy had once told her that gin had become his drink of choice after his mother died because it reminded him of her. As Benny sat up, a wave sloshed over the edge of the tub. He said he liked its earthy tang and the way it made the sharp edges of some memories blur. Perhaps gin would blur the memories of inadequacy that were coming to her now.

He was two grades ahead of her. He was nice enough, and she thought for a while that she loved him. On one of the first warm nights of May they lay on the football field behind their school. Her arm was falling asleep under his head. As they kissed, his hand slid along her belly and moved under her sweatshirt. She didn't wear a bra. Her breasts had always been tender, but his calloused hand made her gasp. He pulled back. She told him it was all right and led his hand back to where it had been and kissed him. He told her that he loved her as he groped her, then pulled off her pants. When he entered her, it was sharp and abrupt. He seemed to mistake her moaning for pleasure. He came quickly, then flopped onto his back beside her and stared up into the murky sky. She stroked his face as she lay on her side, wondering at the distance between them, at the warmth between her legs where she had felt such pain. It wasn't long before he was hard again and wanted her. She asked him to go slower. It hurt, but not as much, and she wondered if sex was always like that. She shivered and pressed herself against him. The next day he passed her in the hall without even looking at her.

For a week after that night Benny was in bed with abdominal pains. She had had pains like this before but never this sharp. Was this her period, finally? She hoped so. She had friends who menstruated at eleven; she was seventeen. Benny faked cramps at school and kept a bottle of Midol in her locker for show. She occasionally gave one to a classmate in need.

She found the *Merck Manual* that had always been on her parents' bedroom shelf and looked for an explanation for her pain. Benny had been perusing it since she was in the seventh grade to diagnose every symptom she suffered. She had asked them at the dinner table once about the book. Her mother and father stopped eating and looked at each other, seeming to want the other to speak. After her dad started to say something, then bit his lip and stopped, she let it go. Now she found a section on chronic abdominal pain and wondered what was causing hers. Endometriosis? Not likely because she still wasn't menstruating. Hepatitis? She wasn't tired or losing weight. Ovarian cyst? Perhaps. She'd have to go see someone about it soon if it kept up. She put her hands on her breasts, wishing they were even slightly larger. Maybe they'd grow when she started to bleed.

She saw a doctor, who told her it was probably anxiety and wrote her a prescription, and her pains stopped for a while.

—

Benny submerged her head again, as if she could wash off the memory, then pulled the plug. When she came out of the bathroom Leroy offered her a pair of black track pants, a dry shirt, and his cableknit sweater. They sat in his room as her hair dried. She wrapped her legs in a blanket on his bed and curled them under her.

"That sweater looks good on you."

She was glowing from her run and the heat of the bath. He told her that the sweater had been a gift from his mother when his parents came back from a trip to Scotland. Its wool, now yellowed the colour of an old man's teeth and with a coffee stain shaped like the map of some imaginary country, had been white when he received it.

"It's from the Isle of Skye. Mom bought it from an old Macleod who spoke mostly Gaelic. She told her that each family had a unique pattern that acted as a signature to identify the fisherman who wore it. If he was drowned, and battered on the rocks, he would be recognized by his sweater."

That sounded to her like the kind of thing that sold sweaters to tourists. He wore it raking leaves, playing Frisbee and football, and tobogganing. He had worn it until there were holes in the elbows, and he patched those holes with green, orange, and brown yarn he'd woven into a tight knit. Though he might not recognize the pattern if the sweater was lost, the patches he added had made it unique and recognizable as his.

A few days later Benny returned the track pants and T-shirt but kept the sweater. He never asked for it back.

15

Forest Garden

On the hottest day of the summer Lina and I decide to make raspberry jam. Across the road is a clear-cut that slopes toward the valley. Out of the thin, gravely soil and mounds of too-small logs left behind grows a tangle of raspberries, alders, and skinny birch. The wild raspberry canes push through the piled logs, now soft with rot, and knot them in place. We pick berries into baskets hanging from our necks with sisal we cut off the straw bales in our garden.

Once we have eight quarts we walk back and pour the mushy berries into a pot and add sugar. The sugar feels like sand against the wooden spoon as I stir it on the stove outside. Sugar-filled steam rises from the pot and lands on us as we stir the bubbling jam. We both have our shirts off and I try—I really do—to keep my eyes averted from the drops of sweat beading between Lina's breasts.

"It's kind of hard for me to focus on making jam," I say.

"Focus on what you need to," she says as she bumps my hip and smiles. "I'll look after the jam."

Why can't I simply tell her how I feel?

"I love what we're doing here," she says.

It's dark by the time we pull the final batch of jars out of the canner. We spread the last, half-filled jar on flaxseed bread from the bakery in Middleton, with Jersey butter we bought from the Reaghs.

A big moon beckons us to stay outside. Lina suggests going for a swim, so we put our shirts on and go down the hill to the pond. We stop talking as we pass the cemetery. On the shore she slithers out of her shorts and T-shirt as if shedding skin. I pull off my shirt but leave my shorts on. She looks at me and smiles.

"Coming?"

My heart is rowdy as I stand as naked as I dare in front of her. She turns and wades in. She stops when her bum, taut muscles curving up to her sacrum, is half submerged. Then she dives, arching like a porpoise, her calves and pointed toes disappearing with hardly a wave. When she emerges she calls in a whisper.

"Take off your gotch and get in here!"

I walk in with my shorts on. We swim in the moonlight as silently as we can, keeping our hands underwater so they won't splash. I get her to float on her back while I grind the soles of my feet in the coarse sand and cradle her, my hands under her neck and knees, her breasts and belly on the surface. With my eyes I trace the tattoo snake spiralling around her belly as it shines in the moonlight. It lies coiled like a blue vein under her skin. The quicksilver washes over the flesh of her stomach, over her nipples, and brushes her long hair looking like fronds of kelp swaying.

Onshore I wrap her in a towel as she shivers.

"Don't you like skinny-dipping?" she whispers.

"No." My shorts are clammy.

We go back up the hill. I have to tell her sometime. When we get close to our place I count to three and dive in.

"There's something—. It scares me shitless."

She stops walking and puts her hand on my forearm. Her eyes are glistening in the moonlight.

"I'm afraid once I say it, everything will change. I love this summer."

She doesn't say, "Trust me," she doesn't say, "Tell me." There's a glitter in her eyes that makes me believe it's going to be O.K., that she'll go on liking me even if she might never love me.

"I, I was—" But I start to cry before I can finish.

She takes a half-step and puts her arms around me. I let her hold me.

"Lina, I'm in love with you."

Her jaw drops and she swears. We continue past our place to our neighbour's field of mown hay and sit under the moon. Finally, she turns to me.

"This has happened to me before. I make a good friend. Then he falls in love with me and the friendship is ruined."

I want to argue, but the illusion of our simple life has been broken. My hope that she can love me has proven as fragile as a soap bubble.

Things fall apart, 1993

The last spring I lived at home, the final semester of my last year of high school, my father let his flower beds go. The tulips at the end of the driveway bloomed in April like an echo from the time when he was happy. For a week when I walked home from school I passed the fading tulips, watching their petals droop and fall to the ground, hoping he'd do something with them. I cut lilacs, purple and white, from the path to my old school and put them in a vase on top of the bureau in my room. I'd have to tend his flower gardens by myself.

I dug up the bulbs and stored them in a box in the garage, as we always had, then replanted the triangular bed with petunias. The lilacs took on a funky smell by the third day, a pungent note of decay, and I threw them out before the water grew stagnant.

I tended his peonies, roses, and dahlias all summer. I didn't ask for help and Dad didn't seem to notice. The purple-flowering clematis climbed the light pole of its own volition. The ants crawled on the pregnant peony buds, preparing them to open once again, and the roses bloomed provocatively whether or not he chose to smell them.

I was without a job that summer, choosing instead to stay home to be near Dad before I went to college. Perhaps I should have moved out, but it felt as if someone had clipped my wings and I could not fly in a straight line.

He was disinterested in me and in what I was doing. I stayed out of the house as much as I could. When I was home we circled each other like tired prizefighters in the twelfth round, morose and taciturn. Or I went to my room to read or smoke a joint and listen to Dad's old records. Dylan, The Band, The Allman Brothers, Clapton, Bowie, The Who.

Since our last camping trip to Maine, he rarely asked me to go for walks with him, complaining of being tired all the time. When he did have the energy to go, he either overcompensated by being garrulous or he made no effort to talk and there were long silences I wanted to fill but couldn't.

In the evenings, when my bedroom was stuffy with the day's leftover heat, I sat on the back porch. Sometimes my friend Steve joined me and we listened to a ball game and talked. But I was usually content to be by myself, and on those nights I'd smoke some pot and brood. I liked sitting in the dark after washing the dirt and sweat off my skin from my day in the garden. The sun stayed stored inside me, radiating its heat outward as my skin cooled in the dark.

One night in early August I couldn't sleep. I got a can of ginger ale from the fridge on my way out to the patio. I sparked up a joint and had been there less than ten minutes when the breezeway door opened behind me. I threw the joint on the flagstones and ground it out under my flip-flop. I stood too fast, tipping my chair backward with a slap on the stones. I bent to pick it up, then bumped the table with my hip.

"Smooth," he said, then laughed.

It was the first time he'd sought me out in weeks. He held a bottle and placed it, along with two highball glasses he held with two fingers and his thumb, on the round table. Gin. How could he drink that straight?

"It's too damn hot to be inside. I can't sleep."

He unscrewed the bottle and began to pour. He asked if I wanted some. I shook my head.

"Not your drug of choice?" He winked.

His breath was heavy as if he'd just come back from a jog. Something about the still night and him joking about catching me smoking dope made me feel closer to him than I had in a while. It made me take a chance.

"Do you think Mom left because of me?"

He looked at his glass and then at me.

"I got the feeling sometimes that she didn't think I was all right," I said.

"There's nothing wrong with you, Bean."

He hadn't called me that for such a long time that my eyes filled with tears he couldn't see.

"Something is wrong, though," he said.

"With me?"

He shook his head. He poured himself a bit more and drained the glass.

"Tomorrow I'll show you what to do with those raspberry canes. I've let them go and they need pruning."

He picked up the glasses, wrapped his fist around the neck of the bottle, and disappeared into the house.

The next day I waited in the garden, but he never showed up.

Steve and I were wrestling on the lawn the day after my birthday. Dad came home as I pinned Steve. Dad got out of the car and stood staring at us as though he were trying to remember where he'd met us before. It was weird. I jumped off Steve and waved at him.

"Hey, Pop!"

He stared a moment longer, then yelled at me. "Stop your childish nonsense."

He looked miserable as he turned and went inside. I felt like he had kicked me in the gut. I sprinted down the driveway and along the road. I kept running until I was exhausted.

My father was quiet at supper, solicitous, and he avoided my eyes. With my head cradled in one hand I pushed food around my plate with the fork. I could feel his eyes on the top of my head but I couldn't look up. I went to my room and wept.

The noxious cloud that crossed between us that afternoon lingered like a bad smell. His anger came and went without obvious provocation. It was inexplicable to me. I had passed through some door of my childhood and was being pushed into a dark space as the door locked behind me. He moved into the spare room in the basement with its pull-out couch in front of the TV.

I left home for college that September. My father pulled himself together long enough to help me pack my boxes in the car and drive me there. He was reminding me of the man who had always been my best friend. We talked the whole way, he joked with me, but I couldn't relax into the belief that he had come back.

We stopped outside my dorm. He turned off the ignition and faced me.

"You know I'm proud of you, right?"

I assumed that, but it was hardly enough. I imagined him alone in our house.

"Are you going to move back upstairs?" I said.

"Probably."

My new roommate was not only unpacked but seemed to have been living in that room for months. There were pizza boxes stacked on the floor by the door, a wet towel on the unmade bed, a lacrosse stick on the windowsill, an empty

Pepsi can on the desk. Dad rolled his eyes and smiled. Once all my stuff was in neither of us could think of a good reason for him to stay. I followed him into the hall and down the stairs to the entrance.

"Is everything going to be all right?" I said.

He squeezed me hard, then left. I ran up the stairs two at a time and to the window of my new room. He got into the car and sat there. He gripped the steering wheel with both hands, then rested his head on it. *Come on, Dad, pull it together.* I looked away and prayed for the car to start.

I was home for the weekend the night of the first snow that year. Snowflakes settled onto the pavement, where they melted. I was in bed studying. Other than the occasional car splashing along our street, the only noise was of my father downstairs in the kitchen. Sounds that had become familiar but that I was trying to ignore: his footsteps, the cupboard door opening, the unscrewing of the metal cap of the Gordon's bottle. *Glug, glug, glug* into a glass. The cap again, bottles clinking as he returned it to the cupboard, and the *click* of the magnet on the closing door. Then later that night unexpected sounds. The deadbolt on the side door and the car backing out of the garage. I read for a bit more, then went to bed. An hour later, maybe two or three, the garage door opened and the car returned. I peeked through the curtain. The snow had stopped. The early morning light seeped through the clouds on the horizon beyond the pines. Dad sat hunched over on the edge of the driveway, his feet on the lawn, his head in his hands. A crow tilted its head back and bellowed a predawn cry. My father shook his head, muttered profanities at the crow, and hobbled into the house.

Then it was Christmas. Aunt Irene and Uncle Bob were staying with us for three days. I think they were worried about me and wanted to see for themselves what was happening. Dad hadn't moved upstairs, so they slept in my parents' old room. For the first couple of days Dad was fine, joking with his sister and brother-in-law. He and I even went for an after-dinner walk, our first in months. On Christmas Eve, the four of us walked in the rain to an Italian restaurant. Dad had too much red wine at dinner and became first loquacious, then, when the bill arrived, surly. He wanted to pay and argued with Bob about it, threatening to lay into him if he didn't shut up. The temperature had plummeted while we were eating and we had to watch for patches of ice on the sidewalk the whole way home.

I went outside the next morning before anyone else was up. When the sun rose it looked as if the entire neighbourhood had been covered in glass. I went back in to get my skates. I left the breezeway, and though it was bumpy, the freedom of skating wherever I wanted — on the street and sidewalk, over the schoolyard, all the way to Crystal Lake and back — was glorious. For that hour I thought of nothing. There was the ice in front of me, the vibrations in my feet, and the glittering branches sheeted in glass. There was a happiness that wouldn't quit.

The rest of Christmas Day was quiet, and I didn't see much of Dad. He insisted on carving the turkey. When he cut his hand, he threw the knife on the table and slumped in his chair. We ate in silence.

I laced up my skates again after supper and went out to the backyard hoping to retrieve something from that morning. I left the floodlights off because there was enough light coming from inside the house. I had been skating alone for ten minutes when the breezeway door shut and Uncle Bob was standing at the edge of the ice in my father's old brown-and-tan leather skates. His hands were stuffed into the pockets of an old ski jacket of mine. He stepped gingerly onto the ice.

"I haven't done this in years," he said. He shuffled like a penguin across the ice. "Ah, there we go," he said once he got the hang of it. "Like riding a bike."

We skated side by side in circles.

"Not such a merry Christmas, huh?" he said.

The next time I faced the house my father was standing behind the picture window watching us. He was motionless. I stopped and stared at him, wanting to wave but unable to will my hand from my side. Then he turned and left and the curtain covered the spot where he had been.

16

Forest Garden

It's been three days since my confession, and Lina hasn't brought it up. The tomatoes are ripening nicely for early August, and soon we'll be overwhelmed by them. I can't wait and snap off a beefsteak with green shoulders. I cut it with my Swiss Army knife and offer half to Lina. The zucchinis are loving the heat, and we find one we missed that has grown as big as a baseball bat. We slice off all the smaller ones down to the size of a hot dog. Then we pull up spinach and arugula that's shot to flower, weed the bed, and sow kale and chard for the fall. I keep my distance from her and try not to stare. We swim in the afternoon, this time with our shorts on. Lina is wearing a T-shirt.

After we eat and say goodnight at the fire I lie in my dank sleeping bag waiting for it to warm up so it will feel dry. I hear Lina's footsteps.

"If we do this," she whispers through the canvas, "I need you to promise to keep treating me like a friend. You can't own me."

I unzip the flap. She's carrying her sleeping bag all bunched up under her arm, and I take it from her. She climbs in. We kneel facing each other, holding hands. She lets go of my hand and reaches up to my face. I close my eyes as one of her tapered fingers brushes my face. I haven't slept with anyone since I left the city and I'm trembling like poplar leaves on a stormy day.

"Hey," she says, looking me in the eye. "It's O.K."

Then she kisses me and I wonder if it will be anything like O.K. An insistent voice cries within me, tells me I am getting in over my head. I press her lip between mine, her tongue tickles inside my mouth, and my hands come up to touch and explore the body I have worked next to and desired all summer. She pulls my shirt over my head, then her own. Though we have both worked shirtless in the sun I am startled by the contrast of my body, with its edges and angles, against her softness. She shuffles closer and I hug the muscular frame of her shoulders, her stiff nipples and full breasts pressed into my chest, and the warmth emanating from her skin. My desire propels me beyond the anxiety that continues to wash over me and allows me to let her reach between my legs, take me in her hands, and love me.

I stay awake watching her peaceful face while she sleeps. She is lying on her side facing away from me. She fell asleep soon after we both came. I envy how uncomplicated falling in love seems to be for her. For me it feels like I'm swimming in the ocean when a big wave curls and breaks on me, grinding me into the sand along the bottom. I come up spluttering, disoriented and anxious, but wanting to do it all over again.

I reach down and draw my finger over her cheekbone, along her chin, and down her neck to her clavicle. Then I lie behind her and drift away.

—

We haven't left the land for three days. We have been rising late and going to bed early. This morning I'm balancing on two ceiling joists and holding a rafter board while Martin hammers it into the wall plate. He is the first person we've seen since Lina came to my tent. I asked him to help us because he knows how to measure and cut the rafters properly. I look over him to where Lina is sawing another two-by-eight on the sawhorses. I grin at her like an idiot. Once the rafters are up we nail strapping along them, then screw on the sheets of green metal roofing. It takes all day to finish but we have a waterproof space by late afternoon.

Martin takes his cordless drill and his saw home, whistling along the path. I sell him short at times. He really has been generous to me. When his hat disappears among the foliage I run to Lina and throw my arms around her. She sneaks her hands under the back of my shirt. Sawdust clings to the hair on her forearms and rubs against my skin. The sun is on us, hot and intense, and her breath is warm as we kiss. I press her tight against my dirty, sweaty, and tired body.

We decide to take a break from work since it's my birthday. We plant the oak seedling, a foot tall, that I grew from an acorn I found in Middleton last year. I pull it from the pot and put it in the hole we dug, tamping earth around the ball of roots. We surround it with chicken wire to protect it from foraging deer. Then Lina walks a little way off and returns holding her menstrual cup full of blood. Without a word, she empties it on the soil around the seedling. The blood soaks into the ground. My mouth is agape.

"What?" she says. "It's good for the plants."

We need to wash off so we decide to swim in the bay. We get

our bikes and walk them along the path to the road. On the way we pass the waist-high garlic. The lower leaves are brown and dry.

"Is it ready to eat?" She rubs her thumb and forefinger along a hard stalk.

I lay my bike in the grass and grab the stalk below her hand and pull it up. The soil is loose and the bulb remains attached to the stalk. Up it comes, this gorgeous treasure, erupting through the dirt and the straw above that into the sunlight. Lina's beautiful face breaks into a wide grin. I hand her the whole plant. She massages the bulb and the dry dirt falls off the skin. She finds where two of the cloves meet and presses her thumbnail into the depression between them, breaking through the wrappers. Then she wedges her thumb between the top point of one of the cloves and the hard stalk that runs down the centre of the bulb and pulls the clove away from the stalk. It is as large as a good-sized cherry. She hands the rest of the plant back to me. She peels the moist skin away from the flesh of the clove with her nail and pops the whole clove between her lips.

"Can I taste it?" I say.

She bites it and beckons me to her lips. I kiss her and her lips open and a chunk of garlic comes to me, spicy and astringent.

We bike to the Bay of Fundy past Port George, where there's a beach with a waterfall that Jenifer told me about. Lina and I walk along the sand to a spot where water drops over the edge of the cliff. We strip and stand under it, shrieking as the water washes over our bodies and continues along the beach into the waves. We put our shoes on and hike to the top of the cliff where there is a pool on the ledge. It is deep enough that we can lie in the water. It looks like liquid silver as it flows over and around us on its way to the edge of the cliff. We hike back to the beach, lie in the sun to warm up, then bike to Margaretsville. We buy fish 'n' chips, then sit on the stony beach to eat. There is a fat gull pecking at ketchup and some greasy-looking fries in a plastic basket someone left behind on the rocks. Twisted within the dry bladderwrack above the high tide mark is nylon rope, faded orange and green, an ice cream bucket, and a shattered stackable chair. I can almost see the beauty of this detritus, catching the slanting rays of the sun. I am in love with this land and its relationship to the sea, with the warmth of summer and the breeze blowing away any insects, and with the slanting light. Most of all I am in love with Lina. I remember then, lightning across a lake, rain on water, my orange towel wrapped tight against my skin, and I know it's true, that everything is relative and depends on its opposite for definition. I had a long, lonely winter, cold and wet, but sitting on the rocks this early evening with Lina makes it all worthwhile.

"Do you want to go to Art's?" I ask.

"Let's go home."

I'm not ready to go home, wanting the evening to last, and I convince her to bike along the bay road to Art's place. He hugs Lina, Lucy nuzzles me, and the four of us sit in the kitchen. Art goes to the freezer and brings us each a chocolate-chip cookie. They are frozen. He sucks on the third. Once we finish eating them he tells us they have pot in them. I look at Lina. She shrugs. It's homegrown, local, and not like the potent skunk that comes from BC. I haven't smoked pot in years, not since it was bred to disorient you completely, but this is mild enough. We go outside and sit by the cliff to watch the sun set. The water is still, and other than Art chattering and the two of them laughing, it's quiet. The sky seems gentle, pink and blue, beneficent. Venus shines over the dark mass of New Brunswick. Weaker points of light follow.

Back in the house Art makes us coffee, which we drink in the kitchen. His eyes are closed and he seems to have retreated to some inner dimension, whether brought on by the dope or his memories I can't tell. Lina sits beside me in a rocking chair, the warmth radiating off her sun-soaked skin as we hold hands. I am confused. The intensity of falling in love again after so many years of being alone is like the heat I feel on my skin when the sun comes out after a thunderstorm. I look into Lina's eyes, black and big and crinkled at the edges, with dumbstruck affection, and I laugh. That affection is all for me and I am amazed.

Tonight while we are at Art's and I tell Benny's story in his kitchen I look over at Lina. She is staring at me in disbelief, as if to ask, How did this good thing we have come to be? Weed makes me reticent, then voluble. Once I start talking it's tricky to get me to stop. I might not be telling this with Lina here if I wasn't stoned.

17

New York City

"Damn," Benny muttered at the jars and bags polluting her fridge.

She stood with the fridge door open on a Sunday afternoon in August. Annika sat at the table behind her. The one-room kitchen and dining room was utilitarian in its blandness: walls painted primer white, grey carpet, pressboard cabinets tacky with years of vaporized grease. It had been muggy and hot for days in New York, the kind of conditions that fermented and moulded the food in the fridge.

"Fucking plastic."

Annika was a patient roommate and put up with most of Benny's idiosyncrasies. In the year they had lived together she had watched as every piece of plastic that could be removed from the apartment disappeared. Benny had taken the table and chairs that came with their apartment to the storage room in the basement late one afternoon while Annika was on clinical rounds. Benny replaced them with wooden ones she bought second-hand from a graduating med student. The Venetian blinds disappeared, as did the clock on the wall in the kitchen. Despite these efforts, Benny felt like Sisyphus;

everywhere she looked there was more plastic, as if containers were reproducing in the night.

There were the compromises she had to make in the lab. Polyethylene tubes and vials. Polystyrene petri dishes. All this equipment in turn came wrapped in polyethylene bags. Every day in the lab she had to open disposable packaging and throw it out, even the stuff that could have been recycled. But there was no recycling in the city. Everything was thrown out. They discarded the syringes they used in a plastic box and threw that in turn into a garbage bag. On and on it went. Interminable.

She pulled out the peanut butter. Glass jar, metal lid. The heat wave had culminated in a spectacular thunderstorm the previous night. She had woken to bright sunshine and a breeze from the west that had ushered the stench of garbage and fermenting urine out to sea.

"Why do you do this to yourself?" Annika said from the table. "Who told you that getting rid of the world's plastic was your responsibility?"

Benny spread peanut butter on the two slices of bread, pressed them together, and took a bite. They'd been through this before. Benny had joined the Sierra Club, lobbied her local government to recycle, wrote letters to her congressmen, and formed a group at her high school to encourage the use of alternatives to plastic. There was little recycling, Congress was ineffective, and her classmates laughed at her. When it became obvious to her that this kind of action was futile, she wrote a letter to the Sierra Club, stating her reasons for renouncing her membership. They weren't active enough to alter the environmental landscape. Altering human behaviour was glacial and required a Gandhi or Malcolm X to make it budge. There was no longer time to wait for the cultural evolution that might bring sanity to our way of living. What was needed was a real solution, "perhaps like pouring botulism toxin in Boston's water supply." She read *The Monkey Wrench Gang*, joined Greenpeace, and considered bombs, spiking trees, and chaining herself to backhoes and skidders. What was needed was rapid planetary triage. Throwing a spanner in the gears was the obvious means of disabling the machine that continued to spew all over the planet.

"Someone's got to do it."

"You think too much," Annika said.

There was a knock at the door. Annika shut her textbook and stood. She opened the door wide enough that Benny could see Leroy. He stood with his hands in the pockets of his shorts, gawking at Annika, his jaw open, "catching flies," as Benny's grandmother used to say. Benny found it funny to watch how confused he seemed every time he was around Annika. It was obvious to Benny what flustered him: the Norwegian accent, her straw-coloured braids and fair skin, her ample curves. Guys hovered around her like fruit flies over a ripe melon.

Benny waved at Leroy from the counter she was leaning against as she chewed her sandwich. He stepped into the apartment as Annika let go of the door, scooped up her textbook and notes, and headed for her bedroom.

"Leroy," she said, right before she closed her bedroom door, "can you convince Benny not to take things so seriously?"

"You heard her," Leroy said. "Let's go for a walk."

"I'm headed to the lab."

"But it's your birthday."

Benny relented. She went to her bedroom and came out

wearing a Red Sox cap and carrying a football. She put on running shoes that were well past their prime. She and Leroy crossed Lexington with a dozen busy people. A yellow cab nudged forward to find a hole in the pedestrian line.

"When I first got here I waved them on like a polite Canadian," he said. "Then I lost my patience one day and kicked a cab. Big mistake. He opened his door and I thought he was going to get me with a baseball bat or a gun or some other weird American shit."

The cab cut them off, its bumper coming a few inches from Leroy's leg. He gave the cabbie the finger. Once they were across, Leroy asked Benny about her research.

"Can we not talk about that? My *Pseudomonas* transformants aren't surviving for some reason. They're so slow growing even without being transformed."

"Is this not talking about it?"

She shook her head. "*Pseudomonas* is supposed to grow on anything moist. Shit, it grows on soap, in sinks, in distilled water that's been sterilized. But it won't grow on my plates. They found it in the hospital last week on IV catheters."

"And they let you work on that in the hospital?"

"It's safe. Leach had hoped to be marketing one of these organisms months ago."

The last time she was in his office he had the patent office on one line and a vice-president from DuPont on the other.

They walked through the park to the Sheep Meadow. Sunbathers, in various stages of undress, sat and lay on towels and blankets in clumps. The spaces between were sufficient for the occasional game of Frisbee. A man with dirty high-tops and T-shirt weaved from group to group selling cans of Budweiser out of a dripping grocery bag filled with ice.

Benny shook the football at Leroy. He ran straight out and cut left in front of a couple making out on a blanket. Benny reached back and let go of the ball. She watched the ball arc up and toward him gracefully, the laces spiralling against the cloudless sky and tracing a parabola. He tossed it back. The ball wobbled in flight and landed in front of Benny. She ran to pick it up and yelled at him.

"What was that? You throw like a fucking girl."

She hurled the ball back with a vengeance. It came to him horizontally. No parabola this time. It hit him in the gut.

"All right, all right."

He wound up but again his throw was tentative. It tumbled through the air, off course and far wide of the mark. It rolled end over end toward the towel of a man who was reading by himself.

"Heads up!" Benny shouted as she ran after it.

The man didn't even look up but reached to grasp the can beside him and kept on reading. She came jogging back to Leroy with the ball in her hands.

"I'm not made of glass, man."

Leroy laughed. They threw the ball a few more times, then found a spot to sit and read. Late in the afternoon they passed the roller skaters on their way out of the park. One skater, fortyish and bald, danced around the elliptical surface with a static smile and an open can of Coke balanced on his head. As they stood on the boulevard of Park Avenue waiting for the light, Leroy said, "There's something I need to tell you."

Benny interrupted him as a cab honked, switching lanes in the intersection.

"What?" he said.

"Don't."

"Don't what?"

They walked to Madison before she spoke again.

"I don't want to spoil a nice afternoon. It's rare for me to enjoy a guy's company the way I enjoy yours."

"If you like being with me, why can't we—"

"I need a friend like you. I value that too much."

"We could still be friends."

"It would be different and you know it."

He stopped and put his hands on her shoulders. When he leaned toward her, Benny pushed him away.

"No," she said.

He pouted all the way to Third Avenue.

"Can I at least take you out for your birthday tonight?"

*

Late each Friday afternoon Dr. Nawthorn's lab had an informal get-together. Gabe bought beer and they sat in the lab to gossip and laugh. Doug, the most recent addition to his lab, had decided to brew beer in the equipment room. He used flasks, beakers, and thermometers from the lab as though it were another experiment, and shared the results. His first attempts were strong. Leroy said it tasted like cheap champagne with an aftertaste of cough medicine, but he drank it anyway and found that a litre of the stuff, drunk from a beaker, was enough to obliterate his ambition for the night. He had to be certain that his work was done before he began drinking.

Students from neighbouring labs were invited to join. Melvin Leach saw it as counterproductive, however, and discouraged his students from joining. Benny and Jon ignored the dictate.

One Friday, Benny was sitting beside Cheng, a grad student from mainland China doing a rotation in Nawthorn's lab. Benny sipped Doug's latest experiment out of a 250-ml beaker and half listened to the usual round of crap that flew around the room on these afternoons. Doug was describing, in a booming voice, some live music he'd heard the weekend before. He was a drummer whose weekends were about jazz and beer. Cheng was nodding, but Benny had little interest in a recitation of percussion lore. Over by the incubator Jon was drinking coffee and regaling Lynn, also in Leroy's lab, about the success of the book he had published.

"The royalties don't amount to much more than beer money," he said, "but I have a name for myself now. My next book will be about getting in on the ground floor of the biotech IPO boom. You could get some useful hints from it."

"When do you find time to do this?" Lynn said. She had earned the nickname the Nun, not only because she buttoned her blouses up to the neck and wore calf-length skirts, but also because she cloistered herself in the lab no less than sixty hours each week.

Jon tossed his Styrofoam cup into the wastebasket.

"Recycling is so 1970," he said, looking at Benny.

Leroy and Gabe came into the room from Gabe's office. Gabe walked over to Benny, pulled a bottle of beer from a paper bag he was carrying, and raised his eyebrows at her. She smiled and nodded and he passed it to her. She trusted Nawthorn, and he was one of the few people she ever had a drink with.

"Hey, Timmins, did you see Leach's latest squeeze?" Jon said.

"What about her?" Leroy asked.

"She's got these buck teeth. She looks like Bugs Bunny."

"Jon," Lynn said, laughing, "you're mean."

Leroy sat down beside Benny. The next time Doug got loud, Benny put her beer down and touched Leroy's sleeve.

"Let's go for a walk," she said.

He nodded. While the talk continued, they left the lab.

Once outside, as they crossed York Avenue heading west, Benny said, "I owe you an explanation."

They went two blocks before she spoke again.

"My father drowned four years ago," Benny said. "In a lake near our house."

Leroy exhaled and shook his head.

"After his funeral, I went back to school and studied. People told me to cheer up, find a boyfriend, to get out and do things. But it's not like turning a tap on and off." She looked at him. "You know that."

He nodded.

"I was on the track team at college," Benny said. "I trained for long distances. Anything over 10K. I thought of running a marathon."

She told him how the summer after her father died she lost interest in training. She went from running seventy miles a week to ten. Her body missed it, her mood grew darker, and she didn't know if it was because she stopped running or because of her father's death.

"Your body must have been addicted to the endorphins," Leroy said.

"It could have been that. So I started to train hard again."

"Did the depression go away?"

She shook her head.

They ended up in front of the Met, and Leroy suggested

going in. The lobby was quieter than the time she had been before, when it had been full of boisterous schoolkids. Leroy asked if she had seen the European sculpture room, and because she hadn't, he took her hand and led her there. The white marble pieces were inviting her to touch them. How could Rodin's lovers, made of stone, look so warm, so animated? The lifelike bare limbs, lips, and breasts demanded to be caressed.

"Get back from the sculpture," a voice boomed behind them. Benny flinched, then turned to see the guard who had spoken to Leroy.

"I was only looking," Leroy said.

"Look with your eyes, pal, not your fingers."

After a few uncomfortable seconds, Benny smiled at Leroy, then went to join him.

"It's hard to keep your hands off them, isn't it?" she whispered.

"I've spent whole afternoons here, just sitting."

They wandered through the maze of rooms, then walked back out into the twilight of the hot evening. The light, dim and glowing on one horizon, turned navy blue on the other. They went out for dinner at a Thai place on Third. When her meal came, Benny picked up her chopsticks, but they merely hovered over her plate.

"How did he drown?" Leroy said.

She twirled one of the sticks between her fingers.

"Nobody saw it happen. He probably slipped and banged his head on the way into the water. Maybe he had a seizure."

"At least I got to say goodbye," Leroy said.

"Was she sick long?"

Leroy shrugged. "It seemed like forever."

She told him how, after her father died, she was left wondering where he had gone and how she would carry on without him in her life. These were questions unanswered and unanswerable. She chose to be an engineer, then a scientist, not to solve these mysteries but to skirt around them. Heartache taught her to appreciate the hard facts of life, the mathematical equation and the classification system of organisms. That which never changes. She revered Newton with his calculus and billiard-ball universe that allows humans to control the physical world. She envied his certainty that cause and effect could be measured with precision, and that light could be taken apart and measured, without ceasing to believe in the Creator of that light. She honoured Linnaeus for binomial nomenclature, for his assurance that the nuthatch was a discreet species and different from the blue jay, and that everything had a name. She clung to the certainty of fact like a bird on a branch in a storm.

Leroy stared at her as she ate.

"I'm not ready for a boyfriend. Come back in five years."

"I'm in love with you now. I might be dead in five years."

She took his hand. How could it be that she could like him, really enjoy his company, but not want more than what she already had?

They walked back to his lab. The lights were off. The place smelled yeasty and a couple of drained cans decorated Doug's bench. Leroy went into the hall where the fridges stood against the wall between Gabe's and Melvin's office doors. He opened the fridge that belonged to his lab and found the cans of beer he was looking for. The stand-up freezer next to it held a clear bottle of pure ethanol they used to isolate DNA and he carried that, and the beer, back to his desk.

"What are you doing?" Benny said.

"Refuelling for the night." He poured the ethanol into a beaker the size of a cappuccino cup and held the cold shot of pure alcohol. "Leach calls this stuff rocket fuel." He lifted it to his lips and downed it, then winced and shook his head. He chased the alcohol with a sip of Budweiser. "I refuse to be morose."

"Well, I'm going to leave you to it," she said. She turned her back to him and walked out.

"Hey," he called after her, but she flipped him a wave over her shoulder without looking back.

Eight months passed from the time Benny explained to Leroy why she wanted to remain single. For a while Leroy visited her lab less frequently. She watched as he developed crushes on other students, even a virology professor down the hall. None of this went anywhere, and, try as he did to find an alternative, he was drawn back to sit by Benny's desk while she worked. On a Friday afternoon in April, Leroy brought a beaker of beer and sat down.

"You still drinking that shit," she said. She was replenishing her stock of growth media and solutions for DNA purification.

"Potent stuff," was all he said.

The squeak of heavy-soled leather shoes signalled the approach of Dr. Leach. He wore his lab uniform, a white polyester lab coat that fell to below his knees. It was buttoned up, leaving a V-shaped frame for his navy tie.

"Timmins, do you *live* here?"

It was Leach's greatest anxiety that one of his discoveries

would be stolen by another scientist. There was money to be made and fame to be won.

"You know us grad students, Melvin. We basically do live here."

"Melvin, can I order some glass petri dishes?" Benny said.

"What do you need them for?"

"We could reuse them instead of throwing them out."

"The weekend's here, Ben. Time to relax, let your hair down, have a bit of fun. Would you like to come into my office for a soda?"

"Please don't call me that."

"If she won't, I'd like to, Melvin," Leroy said, grinning.

"I was asking Benita."

"Benita? Who's that?"

"I need to talk to you about something," Leach said to Benny, ignoring Leroy.

"I was going to go for a run."

"On a Friday night? I bet you've got a date. A good-looking girl like you must have plenty of dates."

"You never know, Melvin."

He looked at Leroy, shook his head, then strode back to his office. He called over his shoulder. "Glass dishes are too expensive."

Benny left the lab. She had been looking forward to this run all day. She was going to meet her new friend Rachel at the south end of the park. Benny jogged west, into the park, and headed south. She passed the zoo and ran around a lone horse, which looked weary and defeated as the hack urged it on with the clucking of his tongue. Its shod hooves clip-clopped on the pavement. She waited for Rachel on the sidewalk across from The Plaza. Even though Benny was living in a polluted city, with plastic everywhere, the barnyard smell from the row of horses and their manure piled against the curb, the fresh breeze coming out of the park, and the trees that towered over the street made her feel like she belonged there.

Then she spotted Rachel running along Central Park South toward her. She was happy to see that ragged hair bobbing up and down over the backs of the tired horses. There was a fluttery feeling in her belly, and she started to run again to meet her new friend.

18

Forest Garden

The days are getting shorter but continue to be hot and sunny. Today we will harvest potatoes from Lina's no-till experiment. The dying tops of the potato plants lie on the brown straw. My fingers move the crumbles of straw and plunge into the friable ground, cool and moist. The grass is gone. An earthworm glistens in the soil. I push more straw aside and my fingers bump against a potato. Then another one beside it. There are teeth marks in many of them where mice have nibbled. Despite this we have a crop of gorgeous baking potatoes that will last all winter. No digging, no weeding.

It is time to plant garlic. After lunch we take the largest bulbs from what we harvested in August and separate the cloves, putting the largest of them aside in a pot to be pressed into the ground. We rake the decaying straw off the potato bed and leave it in the walking rows. I step on a fork to loosen the soil. We pull out grass, dandelions, and hawkweed, and then rake the bed level. It's a rectangle of dark earth with sharp corners and neat sides, weed-free and ready to plant. We shovel composted cow manure into the bed.

We push the cloves into the soft ground, one every six inches, until we run out of garlic. I cut the sisal from a bale of oat straw, grab a flake, and shake it so it loosens, then spread the straw thickly on top of the bed. Finished, the blanket of golden straw contrasts with the green around it and the blue of the sky.

The straw is dry and dusty, and the mixture of shit and straw aggravates my asthma, long dormant. I wheeze and cough. Lina goes to her tent and when she returns she hands me a pipe.

"Smoke this."

"You want me to inhale smoke into my already messed-up lungs?"

She tells me it's medicine from her grandmother and I take it from her, find a match by the stove, and light it. I haven't smoked anything since I left home. As soon as the smoke hits the back of my throat I cough it all out. She laughs at me.

"Not so fast. Take a smaller drag."

It's hot and rich. I hack up a wad of viscous, near-solid mucus, take a few steps into the trees, and spit it onto the ground. She's laughing at me when I come back.

"That was fast. You O.K.?"

"What is it?"

"It's a mixture. It's old, though. I'll have to collect new leaves."

She takes my hand and we walk across the road to the clear-cut where we picked raspberries. She shows me the tall stalks of mullein with their spears of musky-smelling yellow flowers and, below these, the hairy leaves the colour of sage.

She pulls a few of these off. We find elecampane growing in Martin and Jenifer's garden and coltsfoot in the ditch along the road. We tie them up and hang them from branches above the stove in our outdoor kitchen beside the gummy leaves of tobacco she grew in our garden and harvested recently.

I continue to smoke her grandmother's mixture while the leaves we gathered dry. Once they dry, she crumbles them and puts them in her leather pouch. I smoke a bit each afternoon and my bouts of hacking and wheezing abate. My asthma all but disappears. Go figure.

We wake to frost one morning the night of the full moon in September and Lina moves into my tent full-time. She says it will be warmer that way. Not that she needs an excuse. We hustle to finish the cabin, shingling the walls with cedar, framing the windows, and installing a wood stove and chimney. All this we do using only hand tools. I know that's not saying a lot—it's not the Chrysler Building—but it makes me proud every time I see the cabin in the clearing when I come home. And now it's finished.

We take our tents down and move into the cabin. What a difference. I sleep better because it's always dry, especially once we have the wood stove lit.

We finish splitting and piling our winter's wood supply against the cabin. On a warm afternoon in early October we walk through the woods to the pine grove. We make love on that spongy mattress, with bits of sun reaching the ground to keep us warm. I lie on my back. The pine branches have made room for one another over the past century, filling the sky but not criss-crossing, not getting in one another's way.

These trees have spent a century and a half learning how to live together. My arm is around Lina and her head is on my chest.

"Could you see living here a long time?"

There is something unattainable about her. It's going to cause me pain.

"My father wanted me to have his name when I was born, but my mother wouldn't let him. She's a proud Wendat. Traditional. She wants me to come home and have a family."

"Will you?"

"Maybe one day. I'm not through roaming."

The sun moves behind the trees and I shiver in the shade.

Drowning, October 1994

The last night I saw my father he was dazed in the basement. It was Sunday night and I was headed back to college after coming home for the weekend. He had been drinking since suppertime. My ride was waiting out front as I went down to say goodbye. The car honked. Dad called me back from the hallway.

"How'd your exam go?"

"It's not till tomorrow."

He shook his head. "I'm sorry, I forgot."

On the way back to Lowell I sat in the back seat of my roommate's Civic, her friend in the passenger seat and some old Bowie playing too loud for me to hear what they were talking about. I didn't care, stuck in my own thoughts as I was, except that they kept turning around to include me in the conversation and I had to make an effort to hear them above the music. We pulled up to the house and I went straight to bed.

October 25

When the phone rang the next morning, I was lying on my back with my eyes open. I went to the kitchen, past the cat, and took the phone from my roommate, Justine. Who is it? I mouthed at her.

She shrugged and said, "Ask them not to call so early next time."

The radio was on, broadcasting the day's news from the city. I took the phone.

It was the police. He was saying something about my father that I couldn't hear. There was a ringing in my ears that hadn't been there before he spoke. He said it again.

"There's been an accident. Your father was found un-conscious."

Then the ringing stopped. I had to pull it out of him by asking if Dad was all right before he told me he was dead. It was as if I had been expecting it for a long time and it was only at that instant that the realization surfaced. He said I needed to identify the body, and I didn't hear much after that because the word *body* floated through my head. *Body, body, body.*

"Do you want an officer to drive you home?"

I told him no and hung up. Justine was brushing her teeth. *That is such an ordinary thing to be doing at this moment, this moment that is stretching so long.* I didn't want to have to tell her or anyone. As long as I didn't say a word everything would be all right. But she could see something was wrong and I had to say the words, as awkward as they felt fluttering out of my mouth.

That's not how it was meant to work, was it? To tell someone I barely knew that my world had capsized while she stood in front of a mirror getting ready for class. Where were the explosions and the blackouts and high winds knocking down trees? Justine hugged me but I was rigid; I was already calculating how to get the twenty-six miles home. There was a bus that didn't leave until late that evening, but I had to get home sooner than that. If I had been in better shape I could have run it. A marathon.

Justine offered to drive me. She talked most of the way, lightening the atmosphere and keeping my mind partially diverted. It was a beautiful fall day and I felt crummy for liking it. We pulled into the driveway and I got out, then watched the car back onto the street for the hour-long drive back. I needed to be in the house first, before I went to the morgue, so I would have something familiar to hold on to before I saw him. The place was tidy and smelled like it had been recently cleaned. I had been associating death with disorder. The police officer had implied that Dad had killed himself, which I didn't believe. I looked for a note on the counter, by the phone, on his desk. Nothing. But then I went upstairs to my room. The cover on my bed was neat and lying by the pillow were his skates, laced up and tied together.

Friends of his I didn't remember came to the house the night after the funeral. There were cousins I had never spent much time with, Dad's two siblings, a few of the teachers he had worked with, and a couple of students who had liked him. I assumed my mother would have to turn up, that she would walk through that door as suddenly as she had walked out of it. How could she not? As I stood in the kitchen that afternoon, after leaving Dad in a pine box at the church, I looked beyond each person I was talking to at the door. Her absence that afternoon stung more than the pine box had. My father's death hadn't solidified; I had spoken to him too recently to believe he was gone. But my mother? Wind whistling across an empty parking lot.

The darkness was gathering as the last guests left. I stood on the driveway looking at the garage door. I grabbed my hockey stick and a ball from the garage and started shooting it at the door, one-timing it again and again as it bounced back to me. Never again would I clean off the ball marks I was making. I ate some tuna casserole one of the neighbours had brought and went upstairs to bed. It was three nights before Halloween, the end of the year when the Celts say that the veil between this world and others is flimsiest. Things were dying, receding into the earth — that was obvious — and the air was crisp and clean. The living and the dead, what is spirit and what is flesh, more easily communicate when the veil is thin. I felt myself being tucked in. There was a pressure first at the sheets by my feet, then working its way up my back until finally my neck and shoulders were covered against the draft from the open window. I turned to the door, yellow with light from the hallway, but saw nothing.

A card from my mother arrived two days after the funeral, again in an envelope with no return address. She had heard about my father's death from a friend and said she was sorry that I had to deal with it alone. She said she wasn't well, that she had had a malignancy removed from her colon the previous summer, and that she would try to see me when she was feeling better.

Two weeks after the funeral I went home to bury my father. I picked up his ashes at the crematorium on the way. The clerk shook my hand and stared into my eyes without blinking. He handed me a heavy metal box over the counter as if I were buying a pizza. There was no way Dad was in that box.

It was late afternoon when I got to the house, and the sunlight was slanting through the kitchen window onto the counter where I had eaten all those breakfasts and carved pumpkins. The house was inhabited by a silence that was corporeal. I held the metal box filled with his ashes and bits of bone and struggled to remember what my dad's voice sounded like. The harder I concentrated, the farther away it receded. I put side three of his copy of *Quadrophenia* on the turntable and turned it way up to drown out the quiet.

Later I got the shovel from the garage and headed out to the backyard. At one end of where the rink had been, behind one of the goals, was the apple tree I had given my father when I was nine. A dozen shrivelled apples that I hadn't picked in October clung to its bare branches. I pushed the shovel into the ground beside the tree. Was this even legal? I folded the watercolour of Sam Peabody I had painted for him as well as a note the tooth fairy had left under my pillow, in his handwriting. *You have lost your last baby tooth. Here's 25¢. You are no longer a child.*

I knelt beside the hole. I would have to sell the house; I'd never live there again and I could use the money. I pounded the ground and swore out loud. It wasn't money I wanted. If you have kids, you owe it to them to stick around, not disappear like a wisp of smoke. I lowered the box and the two pieces of folded paper into the hole. It wasn't until I received that lame card from my mother that I felt really angry. Did she give him the idea—the permission—to do his own disappearing act? I wanted her to leave me alone. I threw dirt into the hole until it was full, then hammered the mound down with my fists. When I stopped, the indentations of my knuckles were on the surface.

I went back to school, got my degree, and two years later moved to New York. By the time I got there, my wish to be left alone had come true. My mother was dead of cancer.

19

New York City

Benny ran up the stairs again, gut-punched by nausea at the eleventh floor but carrying on. On the landing of the fifteenth she stopped, bent over gasping, and checked her pulse. Thirty beats in ten seconds. Her heart was ready to burst through her ribcage. Rachel was there already, doubled over with her hands on her knees, having finished a few seconds ahead of Benny. When Benny's heart slowed down, she was able to revel in the blood coursing through her limbs and the breath heaving into and out of her lungs. They walked back down the stairs to start again.

"I love this feeling," Benny said. "It's the reason I run."

"It's for *this* that I run." Rachel grabbed her own butt and laughed.

"There's nothing wrong with your ass."

"Nothing that running seventy miles a week won't cure."

Benny had met Rachel while running in the park late one afternoon. She caught up with a pack of women jogging together and spoke to the one nearest her.

"What running group is this?"

"Lesbian environmentalists."

The woman was fast despite being short. She wasn't straining herself as the others in the group huffed along, red in the face. Benny sped past them and carried on around the loop before heading home. She saw the woman again a few days later, running alone one morning. This time Benny had a difficult time catching up with her.

"Where are your tree-hugging girlfriends?" Benny asked once she had.

"They only run once a day. Wimps."

"I usually run by myself," Benny said.

"I noticed. When you passed us the other day I wondered if you'd be into running with me. I prefer company, but only if she keeps up with me."

With that Rachel picked up her pace, moving ahead of Benny before she could figure out what was happening. When Benny caught up with her again, Rachel smiled as if Benny had passed a test. They ran together, saying little, the rhythmic pounding of their feet on the pavement and their exhalations serving as conversation. As they approached the path leading out to Fifth Avenue, Benny slowed her pace.

"This is where I leave," she said.

They stopped and faced each other. The skin of Rachel's cheeks and forehead was pocked from an adolescent bout with acne and her dark hair had the beginnings of dreadlocks, cut like a mop above her shoulders. It looked like she was her own barber. She wore a hoop ring through the right nostril of her pudgy nose. She held out her hand straight in front of her and Benny gripped it. After they told each other their names, Benny searched in vain for something else to say to prevent her hand from being let go. Time stopped. There was no sound, the trees had ceased to sway in the spring breeze, the birds were caught in mid-air. There was a runner frozen mid-stride on the road. Then, just as quickly, her hand was let go and she was returned to time's irreversible march forward.

"I'm here every morning at quarter of seven," Rachel said. "Rain, sleet, ice."

Benny jogged crosstown, dodging cabs. She altered her training schedule to maximize her morning runs. She and Rachel were a boon to each other. Rachel was fast and pushed Benny further in her training than she would have gone by herself. Rachel ran 10K races in the park every second Sunday and was training for the marathon as well. Rachel liked Benny's company since she didn't like to run alone. Rachel studied herbalism at the New School, and once a week, after her classes, she ran uptown from the apartment she shared with her ailing grandmother on the Lower East Side to run stairs in Benny's building.

Once they got to the first floor they started up again. Rachel pulled ahead. There was nothing wrong with her body. She was muscular and healthy.

Benny had won a spot on her college's cross-country team after her father died. She trained hard and became as fit as she would ever be. Her abdominal pains recurred. Still no period. She started to see herself as separate from her body. She gorged on bagels and cream cheese, strawberry Pop Tarts, and Oreos before going to class. Sitting through class, she loathed herself for giving in. She stuck her finger down her throat if she could find a private bathroom. She tried Correctol, up to thirty in a day, but this got in the way of her training. She would go a day or two without eating, subsisting on nothing but pots of strong coffee. She went from feeling bloated and so full her stomach ached to an emptiness that could only be filled with more food. Or else she'd run and run and run.

It was her college classmate and friend, Alicia, who knocked her out of this cycle. Being the only women in most of their engineering classes, they sat beside each other. Near the end of term, during a physics lecture in which Benny kept dozing off, Alicia passed her a piece of lined paper torn from her binder, on which she had written, *Purger or non-purger?* Benny folded the note into a tiny ball without looking at Alicia and poked it into the back pocket of her jeans. She was awake now but couldn't focus on the rest of the lecture. Alicia looked at her when the class ended, waiting for a response.

"What?" Benny said.

"Don't fuck with me." Alicia sounded fatigued.

Benny left the class and didn't go back for the next week. She was lying on her bed when there was an insistent knocking at her door. She continued to count the marks on the ceiling and trace the cracks in its stark white paint. Alicia came in and sat on the edge of the bed. She stayed there a long time before speaking. She had been a purger, she said. Alicia made her an appointment at the university health service and soon Benny was admitted to a psychiatric clinic. Young women were bingeing and purging and starving themselves all around her, hiding from one another. She had group and individual therapy, but no matter how much she talked and was listened to, the void inside did not shrink. She wanted it filled.

She ran, adding more miles to her training. She wasn't running as a means to punish herself, nor as a means to stay slim. She didn't need running to do that. Her body, with its narrow hips and muscular limbs, was programmed not to gain weight. She ran because she felt disconnected from her body. Running hard connected her to it. It made her body real. She ran to inhabit a body in which she had never felt at home.

Now, she and Rachel ran the fifteen flights twice more, slowing each time, then agreed to call it quits for the night. They went back to Benny's apartment.

"Do you want to have a shower?" Benny said.

"You forward little skank." She punched Benny on the arm. "You wanna soap me up?" Benny blushed. "I'm teasing you. I'm going to run home. I'll shower there."

"At least stay for supper."

"Can't. Brian's gonna meet me at my place. Gotta run home, and I don't want to puke."

Benny walked Rachel to the elevator.

"Brian?"

"A boy I like to shag from time to time."

Rachel was smiling as the elevator doors closed.

20

Forest Garden

It's January and we spend the morning trudging through the snow in the forest, cutting birch and maple, working together on either end of a crosscut saw. The low-lying area froze before the dump of snow we got last night. I slide on it in my boots.

"It's like glass. We should come back with our skates."

"I don't know how to skate," she says.

I tell her I will teach her. We carry some of the logs back to the cabin and will get the rest tomorrow. Then we'll buck the logs and split them into firewood for next year. I make a lunch of rice and beans and garlic on top of the wood stove while she reads poems to me. This winter we have been visiting Art at least twice each week. The only other place we go is Middleton, and then only when the roads are clear. Otherwise we stay at Forest Garden. I am enraptured, finding joy each morning when I wake. I have Lina all to myself.

She borrows a pair of figure skates from Jen and we walk back into the forest. I'm carrying a shovel. I lace her skates as well as mine, then lead her onto the ice. She stands for a few seconds before her feet slip out from under her. I help her up and she falls again, this time on her tailbone.

"Ow!" She sits on the ice, waving off my offer of assistance. "Just go and skate around and let me figure it out."

I shovel a path curving around the little islands and outcroppings that shape the pond. My blades make a slicing sound on the smooth ice. Crystal Lake often looked as smooth as the ice under my blades, a mirror on which the lights from the houses surrounding it were reflected. As Lina gets up to try again I lean into the curves, turn backwards, revel in lush movement. Soaring on ice, especially on a pond, is the closest to flight I come. Skating allows me birdlike grace. I glance over at her but she isn't getting it. Soon, she's sitting on the bank and watching me.

She gives it a try again at the end of the month. The full moon shines off the snow. Lina is hesitant to go out in the cold again.

"You will remember this night forever if we go skating," I say, "but not if you go to bed."

She bites and our shadows follow us through the trees to the pond. She has Jen's skates laced together hanging over her shoulder, one white skate bouncing against her back. I lace up on the bank and go onto the ice. There has been a slight thaw since we were last here, then high winds and sleet, then the cold of last night. The slushy snow that fell froze and made the surface bumpy. The bumps reverberate through my shins, up to my chest and arms. I call from ahead, skating backwards over the rough surface. Lina's picks keep catching on the roughness, nearly sending her tumbling. She surprises me by running instead of skating after me. She grabs my scarf. As the rest of her body catches up with her lunging arms she stumbles and falls into me, knocking us both down. Her nose is cold and her cheeks are cold but the warmth of her lips is enough for me, enough to keep me warm and moving. Once we're up she stands without falling. I hold her hand and pull her up whenever she starts to slip. After tonight I think she'll be hooked.

Back in the cabin, with the wood stove crackling and orange firelight shimmering on the wall, we lie under the blankets on the bunk. The skin on her neck is smooth under my lips. She is so healthy. It's the joy of having skated outdoors under the moon, surrounded by trees, that has put me in this mood. It's her body next to mine, her skin smelling of wood smoke or olives or something else I can never quite discern, that is feeding my sense of domestic bliss. She nestles her mouth against my throat and hums. The vibration ripples down my side, through my chest, and into my belly. She looks up at me.

"Will you marry me?" she asks.

I laugh. "I'm not the marrying type."

She stares at me with those eyes.

"Why don't we go to Lorette next fall? See your grandmother?"

She doesn't answer. I nuzzle against her flawless skin.

Lina is sitting cross-legged on the bed with her back against the wall. She has my sweater on, and her hair flowing over her shoulders looks like a black waterfall. I am sitting on the floor with Thunder and half a scarf in my lap. Lina is teaching me to knit. My bowl of porridge and a cup of nettle tea are on the floor beside me. The cabin is warm; the wood stove is large enough for a house, but without insulation in our walls or roof, it's the right size for here. We are waiting for the sun to be higher so it will hit the solar panel and we can get water to wash. Then we're going to visit Art.

The road is clear and dry, the shoulder crusted with frozen slush where we walk. We share two pairs of mittens Lina has knitted, so we each have an unmatched pair. We are hand in mittened hand, the red ones clasped while the green ones swing at our sides. We find Art in his chair by the stove, the *Chronicle Herald* waterfalling from his lap onto the floor. He waves us in and tries to make sense of the paper all around him as he stands up. I shake his hand. He hugs Lina, then kisses her on the lips. It makes her blush, something I have not seen before.

"Says there," he tells us, waving one of his hands at the newspaper, "that Nova Scotia used to be attached to Africa. Then it broke away and floated off by itself. It used to be an island."

"It could happen again, with the ice cap melting," I say. "Your place will be underwater."

"I won't be around to find out, will I?"

"It's happening fast."

He shakes his head. "I'm not long for this world."

"Don't say it if you don't mean it."

He shrugs. "There's also a piece about all the plastic that's disappearing." He glares at me from under those two bushy brows. I reach for the paper.

CREDIT/DEBIT CARDS SAFE
FROM PLASTIC-EATING BUGS

There is a small bit of good news amid the crisis surrounding the degradation of many plastics. Credit and debit card manufacturers report having

some success with cards coated with a type of
plastic they claim is impervious to biological attack.
Unfortunately, the technology is taking time to
perfect and few people have access to it.

"Why's Benny so hot and bothered about plastic anyways?
What'd it ever do to her?"

"The same thing it's doing to all of us. She was sick of
seeing garbage everywhere, of seeing loons washed up on
the beach strangled by six-pack rings. Getting rid of plastic
seemed as good a place to start as any."

"I think she's a kook. I lived without plastic. It's easy to say
you could do without it if you haven't had to. But you couldn't
and neither could she. She wouldn't last a day. We've got
things I never dreamed of as a kid."

"And you don't think our quality of life has been degraded
by all the plastic crap we deal with?"

"That's sentimental rubbish. I use plastic bags every day. At
least I used to when I could get them. I drink out of a plastic
cup that won't break if I drop it. The telephone I use to call
Louise every day is made of plastic. We'd be lost without it,
son. You've seen how hard it is to get sewer pipe."

"Benny told me once, 'I chose one thing to do that would
make the world better.'"

"Well, she chose the wrong thing," Art says.

I wonder sometimes myself.

21

New York City

Benny tried on a pair of Annika's earrings in the reflection from the wall-to-wall windows of her bedroom looking south over Manhattan. She moved so that her face was superimposed on the Chrysler Building. Open copies of *Applied Microbiology* and *Molecular and Cellular Biology* lay on her desk by her neatly made bed. Her bedside table held a glass, half full of water, earplugs, and a beeswax candle on a saucer. It was Friday night and she was getting ready for dinner out with Rachel at an Italian restaurant in Rachel's Lower East Side neighbourhood. Benny leaned closer to the window and pressed Annika's red lipstick across her mouth. She puckered her lips together, feeling the sticky grease.

On 4th Street, off Second Avenue, the door to Cucina di Pesce opened onto the bar. Warm, thick air smelled of mussels steaming in garlic and butter. There was Rachel, with a glass of red wine in front of her, talking to a man in a dark suit and short hair. As soon as Rachel saw Benny, she put her hand on his forearm and excused herself. The green of her blouse shimmered in the darkness of the restaurant. Her mouth was stained with wine.

Benny ordered linguine with gorgonzola, sun-dried tomatoes, and capers. They shared a bottle of wine. Rachel drank more of it and was tipsy.

"I came here once on a blind date," she said.

"How'd that go?"

"Crappy. I was set up by a guy friend of mine. Men don't know what a girl's looking for in a date. He kept staring at my tits all night. I ordered some pasta dish with a mushroom cream sauce. I was so distracted I forgot that mushrooms make me nauseous. By the time the bill came I had to excuse myself and go outside. I thought I was gonna puke."

"I'll watch for that ruse when the bill comes."

"So long as you don't stare at my tits."

Benny blushed. "I'll do my best."

She took another sip of wine.

"These engineered bugs of yours, will they eat the vinyl siding on my parents' house?"

Benny nodded.

"Good. I hate that ugly shit."

"Where was this house you grew up in, with the vinyl siding?"

"I moved here from England when I was twelve. My mother married an American and moved us to California. San Francisco area mostly. But my stepfather was in the army so we moved around a lot."

"Where's your home now?"

"Here, I guess. Though nowhere really feels like home to me."

"No place feels like home till you stop," Benny said. "It's

something my father used to say. He said our generation is rootless, that we take up migratory lifestyles that are going to be painful when we decide it is time to settle down. He figured we wouldn't know how."

"Your father *used* to say that? Has he changed his mind?"

"He drowned a few years ago. He slipped off a dock. I wasn't there, but I think he had a seizure and fell in." Rachel seemed on the verge of asking more but Benny didn't want to talk about it. "Tell me about Brian."

"He's nothing serious. He's intense but he has his moments. I wouldn't want him to father my children or anything." Rachel laughed.

"You're going to have kids?"

"Lots. Everything I'm doing is a prelude to that."

"It doesn't sound like Brian is a prelude to that."

"How about you?" Rachel said.

"I wouldn't bring kids into this mess."

She had used this argument so many times that she had almost begun to convince herself. For, truly, how could anyone bring children into a world where there was more plastic than plankton in the ocean for whales to eat?

"The only choices we have," Rachel said, as if reading her mind, "are to participate in the destruction or do something about it."

"Yes, and I see my work as my child. I'm building a frigging monster and then I'm going to unleash it on the world." Benny laughed.

"Wouldn't it make more sense if we stopped using plastic? You guys are always looking for a technical fix. We need social change."

Benny told her that the social solution would never come.

Even if they stopped using plastic, the seas would be awash in the detritus of their desire for convenience for centuries to come.

They left the restaurant. Benny felt the warmth of Rachel's hand sliding into hers.

"You'll have to help me here. I'm a bit wobbly."

Benny's heart thumped and her arm stiffened. Her friend was smiling up at her. They walked up Second Avenue and to Rachel's building on 6th Street. It was a red brick tenement, five storeys tall and four windows wide. She turned to face away from her place and pointed down the short street that ran one block to the tavern at the end. Loud laughter and arguments echoed down the street.

"That's the reason I prefer to sleep at Brian's most weekend nights. That's my window there." She turned and pointed up to the second floor.

Up in the room Benny sat on the floor with her back to the window and Rachel sat against the door jamb facing her as they talked. Around midnight, the number of noisy beer-guzzlers milling about outside the entrance to McSorley's increased. Two college-aged men wove their way down the street and were standing in front of Rachel's building, saying goodnight to each other as though they were never going to meet again.

"Every weekend it's like this."

Rachel got off the floor, closed the window, and sat back down. She put her arm around Benny. Her head inched forward toward Benny's until their foreheads touched. Rachel smiled and sighed. She rubbed her nose against Benny's from side to side. Benny smelled her breath, sweet and boozy.

Rachel parted her lips and was about to kiss Benny. Benny pulled her head away.

"What're you doing?" Benny said.

"What do you think, silly?"

"You're drunk."

Benny leaned away from Rachel and stood up. "I think I should go." She grabbed her coat from the bed. Rachel followed her down the stairs to the front door.

"Are you sure?"

Benny bit her lip and nodded. She headed toward the tavern on her way to St. Mark's Place and the subway home. She was halfway up the short street when she heard Rachel calling from her second-floor window.

"Keep running!"

22

Forest Garden

Our days are numbered. We choose to ignore this for blissful stretches of time. All winter I have lived in one of those stretches with Lina, imagining this time going on forever, the two of us living together and nothing changing but the seasons.

But things are changing. Something is wrong with the sun, with the air, with the food we eat from the store. Most of us ignore the toll this takes on our minds and our souls. What is impossible to ignore is what's happening to our bodies. Almost everyone has flaking skin, rashes, unexplained sores. All winter the backs of both my knees are unbearably itchy. I wake in the night scratching them raw. I also have cold sore after cold sore, a new one every few weeks, always on the same part of my upper lip, where they've left a scar. Winter illnesses used to be predictable and familiar. You'd get a cold or the flu and you knew what you were in for. It might be nasty, but you knew what it was called, what it felt like, how long you'd be vomiting or blowing your nose. The new diseases seem to come on faster, be more intense, and they are more intractable to treatment. The symptoms, like everything else these days, have become exaggerated. Their names—Norwalk, H5N1, West Nile, SARS—are on everyone's tongues but these sicknesses were rare not that long ago.

The snow has melted, the ground thawed, and the muffled atmosphere of the forest in winter has given way to spring. The rain and mud make it impossible to keep our small space clean. The sheets on our narrow bed are gritty and, along with our pillowcases and the floor, are covered with Thunder's muddy prints. We need to get outside. Lina and I bicker about silly things, like the dishes, which are never easy to do, or her habit of leaving her washable menstrual pads to dry on a line over the wood stove. The cabin is too small for that.

"Pileated woodpeckers have it worked out," I tell her. She's sweeping the floor for the third time today. "The male and female have holes in separate trees."

"They also mate for life," she says.

Lina sweeps. She tells me it's time for her to pitch her tent again. I disagree, but she's adamant. Later that day she sets it up, far enough away that it can't be seen from the cabin. Then we cross the road to explore the abandoned homestead. Huge, gnarly apple trees from what must have been a well-tended orchard are covered with pink blossoms. Spruce and alder are growing throughout the once-cleared land. This home must have been a lovely spot, southward sloping and sunny. There's a dug well lined with stones, formerly used to water cattle, and a stone foundation for a small house, the masonry chimney broken off five feet above the ground. It's nothing more than a tombstone for the lives that were lived here. Bumblebees and flies are going from flower to flower and the air is alive with the buzzing of insect wings against the petals. We lie under one of the trees, the sunshine warming my face, my whole body.

"I'm beginning to feel like I belong on this land," I say.

I imagine continuing to build something like this homestead, with apple trees, maybe one day even cattle.

"I wish I did," she says. "Most places feel like foreign geography to me."

I tell her it was that way for me too when I first arrived.

"The difference is, you people have a few hundred years of victorious armies and land-grant agencies behind you to make you feel at home wherever you choose to live."

It's too nice a day to argue. Besides, I can see that she is surrounded by an alien culture. She is a turtle, carrying her home on her back wherever she wanders. Notwithstanding her marriage proposal, I doubt she can settle down here with me. For her, no place will ever feel like home.

After I left the city I wanted to keep moving for no other reason than that there was always the next spot a bit farther that was hiding its treasure from me. I used to think I would have been a failure as a pioneer. I kept moving without even the kind of purpose someone as rootless as Johnny Appleseed had. Some search for a home they never had. I was searching for the one I couldn't get back to.

Then I ended up at Martin and Jenifer's, saw this land, and stopped, perhaps forever. It's a good feeling, like I have become successful at least at this one thing. I can grow food, build a home, husband the land. I can plant a tree and stay to see it bear fruit.

No place feels like home till you stop.

23

New York City

Most days Benny arrived at the lab before Melvin or any of the other graduate students. Today, a Saturday, she wasn't so lucky. She had gone for a longer run than usual and Jonathan was already at the centrifuge spinning down some cells from a culture.

She had been too embarrassed and confused all week to phone Rachel. Her run that morning had cleared her head. If Rachel wanted to kiss her, despite her relationship with Brian, why should Benny care? Rachel knew what she wanted and wasn't afraid to ask for it. It was clear to Benny what she wanted as well, but in her case she was anxious to ask for it. She waited until Jon had left the room, then phoned Rachel. She asked her to meet her in the Sheep Meadow after lunch.

Tacked on the corkboard on the wall to the left of Benny's desk were a photo of her sunburnt and freckled sixteen-year-old self on top of Mt. Washington surrounded by clouds, a list of reagents she needed to make for her experiments, and a *New Yorker* cartoon—a rat in a lab coat was watching a naked man scurry through a maze of streets that looked like New

York. She pulled a notebook from the shelf and opened it. She couldn't concentrate.

She hoped to create a strain of *Pseudomonas* capable of digesting soda bottles as its source of carbon. This required manipulation and splicing of DNA fragments into a plasmid that could replicate in *Pseudomonas*, transformation of the bacteria with the recombinant plasmid, and antibiotic selection of successful clones. Luckily, what she needed to do today didn't require much focus. She had to put Rachel out of her mind and get to work.

She filled a black bucket with ice and went to the hall to retrieve the plasmid DNA and restriction enzymes she needed. A researcher at Berkeley had sent her the estA gene on a plasmid. This gene encoded an esterase capable of digesting PETE, albeit weakly. Benny would splice this gene into a plasmid that would over-express the enzyme in bacteria, then select for strains that could live off PETE as their sole source of carbon. She used SmaI and EcoRI to liberate a 1.2 kilobase fragment that contained the estA gene. She poured an agarose gel, then loaded the digested plasmid into the gel. Electrophoresis would separate the gene fragments according to size. The separation would take four hours at least. She left it to meet Rachel in the park.

They spent the afternoon lying in the sun. Benny saw a red-tailed hawk fly over the field looking for rats and mice. His mate followed after, screeching. Rachel lay on her stomach in her shorts and bikini top. She was well on her way to sunburning her back, as she said she had done at least once each summer since she was a girl. Benny traced the raised tissue of a scar on her back as they talked.

"What's this from?"

"Mole. They cut it out."

The white scar was an island surrounded by tanned skin, evidence that Rachel's living had consequences.

"You should be more careful about the sun."

Rachel rolled over and reached for Benny's hand. She led her finger to another scar, this one on her sternum above her left breast.

"This one's even more interesting."

Benny used Rachel's cell to phone the lab and ask Jon to turn off the electrophoresis. She and Rachel went for dinner at the Great Jones Street Café. Rachel had to sit with her tingling back away from the chair. She drank a couple of shots of cayenne-infused vodka, hoping it might relieve the prickly heat of her sunburn. They went back to Rachel's apartment. The sunburn had progressed to the point where Rachel couldn't lie on it at all. She pulled her shirt over her head, took her bra off, and lay on the bed on her stomach, moaning. Benny rubbed a mixture of aloe and oil that Rachel had made onto her back as gently as she could, feeling the trapped heat coming off.

For the rest of the summer and into the fall Benny and Rachel trained together for the NYC Marathon. Five mornings a week they met in the park and ran as many as ten miles before Benny went to the lab and Rachel jogged another three miles back to her apartment, then went to school. They entered a 10K race in Central Park in October. Rachel was out of sight soon after the race started and Benny was left pushing as hard as she could. It was quiet out there after the rush of the starting gun and the jostle of legs and arms. There was the grunting and puffing and occasional spitting of the runners near her. She always went faster in a race, pushing herself to the point of puking, the pain in the centre of her chest unfamiliar from her training. She paced herself well and passed two men in the last five hundred metres.

Rachel had finished almost two minutes ahead of Benny and was waiting for her, cheering her as she crossed the finish line. They walked together out of the park and went looking for something to eat.

When the first week of November arrived, Benny felt prepared to run the marathon. It helped that she had run twenty-five miles at a decent pace with Rachel two Sundays before. Rachel and Benny started the marathon side by side, running across the Verrazano-Narrows Bridge to the rhythm of twenty-five thousand pairs of pounding feet. They stayed together for the first eight miles. Benny's breathing was fluid, her legs grabbing the pavement effortlessly as if she were levitating. She went ahead of Rachel despite her friend's warning to slow down. It was in the Bronx with six miles to go that her early speed caught up with her.

The fatigue she experienced and assumed she could run through increased until her body quit on her. There was no sensation in her hands or feet and she had to stop running. She continued to breathe easily, but her legs were on the verge of not working. She took a few awkward steps. There was an ambulance nearby, its rear doors open to the sunshine, an attendant leaning against the panel watching runners pass. Benny staggered toward him. He helped her into the ambulance and drove the short distance to the next pit stop, where two women were sitting in lawn chairs behind a table. They sat her down in a chair, wrapped her in a Mylar blanket to keep her warm, and offered her something to eat. They left her to her thoughts and returned to watching the racers pass by, runners unhindered by the embarrassment of polyethylene capes and bologna sandwiches on white bread.

Benny asked for directions to the nearest subway station when sensation returned to her feet and hands. One of the women pointed over her shoulder. Benny had to convince the man in the token booth that marathoners were entitled to ride the subway free that day. He shrugged at the crazy wrapped in a silver blanket. Commuters glanced over at her, bemused. She shivered on the subway and on the walk the few blocks home. She looked straight ahead. When she got to her apartment she took off her running clothes, drew a bath, climbed in, and beat her fists against the sides of the tub. When she pulled the plug, her tears and seven months of training went down the drain.

24

Forest Garden

Nothing stays the same for long, especially joy. Lina is scything long grass along the edges of our garden. Constant vigilance is required to keep the wild spaces from encroaching into our beds. She swings the scythe back and forth, bare-breasted in the June heat like a bronzed fertility goddess. The hawkweed and birch saplings are laid low with each swing. I lean on my rake, admiring the muscles on her shoulders and upper back, and then she yelps. I drop the rake and run to her. She is bent over, looking into the grass. At her feet is the writhing gloss of an Eastern Green snake, nearly cut in half.

"Aw, shit," I say.

It leaks a little blood. She picks it up and it wraps the tip of its emerald tail around her finger. She places it beside a stump out of the way. I try to hug her, but she pushes me away and stomps off. I don't know what's bugging her. A few minutes pass and she comes over to where I work.

"It's all right for you to live up here by yourself and never see anyone but me. I feel like I'm in a cage."

She walks away again. She launches herself into her tent,

where I hear furious shuffling, then she emerges with her backpack and water bottle.

"Where're you going?"

"Away. I don't know when I'll be back."

Late that night I listen to AM radio. The news of epidemics and environmental collapse would make it hard to get to sleep even if I weren't anxious about Lina's whereabouts. There's an upsurge of TB, cholera, and typhus, and not only in the Third World. Something resembling Marburg virus has hit Toronto, hundreds of cases of flesh-eating disease in Buffalo. The gangrenous limbs, the deliquescence of internal organs, the cases of bloody tears. There are rumours that terrorists have got hold of Russian stockpiles of smallpox virus.

Being animals, we are hardwired to anticipate disaster. Our ancestors were like the sparrow in a bush, stressed by the crow flying in to steal its fledglings. Those of us who, until recently, have lived our lives in peace and abundance translate our fears of starvation, predation, and war into an imminent retributive holocaust. As much as I hate religious fanatics, especially Christian ones, their vision of the Apocalypse as punishment for our sins makes sense. It's just that ours are collective misdemeanours, not personal ones. And where many see retribution coming from a patriarchal god created in their own image, I see a planet that we have left no choice but to fight us — as if we are a contagious disease. She uses plagues of insects, droughts, and mudslides, hurricanes in Nova Scotia at the wrong time of year. She wants to drown us, swallow us up, or blow us off her.

I sleep fitfully, wondering where Lina is.

25

New York City

Benny was in a funk and hadn't run all week. It was Friday night and she had come home from the lab to lie down. Dropping out of the marathon had discouraged her. Lab work was not going well. Something else was bothering her that she couldn't quite grasp. She felt panicky, as if she had forgotten to do something important and time was running out. The phone rang and Benny picked it up to stop it from ringing, not caring whose voice was on the other end of the line.

"I won more tickets for us."

When she heard Rachel's voice, Benny realized what had been eluding her. Her friend was going to Peru to study with an ethnobotanist for six months. Benny was going to miss her. She had seen Rachel at least five times every week all summer and had grown reliant on having her around. Her flight to Lima was on Sunday.

"Congratulations."

Rachel had a habit of winning tickets to concerts and ballet and theatre from NPR when she called them during her lunch break at school. She had won two tickets to see the Tokyo

String Quartet at the 92nd Street Y the following night. They agreed to go together so they could say goodbye.

Benny walked to the park in the sun to meet Rachel under the elms near 69th Street. She arrived early and found a bench to sit on. People passed by on the paths and on the grass, pushing strollers and rollerblading. A woman was chasing her young son as he headed for the road. A short man with a silver crewcut and a black leather jacket was bent over talking sternly to a puggle with an intent look on its face.

"You little devil. You know daddy only brings one bag with him on our walks."

Benny heard footsteps behind her and turned to see Rachel, who wore a blue hoodie under her jacket, a black ball cap, and black Converse sneakers. Her ragged hair hung into the hood of her sweatshirt. They walked uptown to the Y.

They held hands as they listened to three Mozart string quartets. The music pressed under Benny's wings, offering her the lift she needed to move through the close air of the hall, above where they sat. She hovered near the ceiling, like the couple flying in the Chagall painting she loved to look at through the windows of the Metropolitan Opera. There she was with Rachel, sitting side by side below her, their arms entwined and Rachel's breath audible when the music was gentle and quiet. The music brought a simultaneous sense of happiness and loneliness.

The magic ended with the music and they were outside, walking through the park to the West Side. They headed to Café Lalo for dessert, where they talked of the music and Rachel's trip. Rachel invited her to her apartment for a drink.

She offered her brandy once they were inside.

"Could I have a cup of tea?"

Rachel put the kettle on and while it was heating poured herself a drink. Benny stood at her bookshelf looking at the spines. *Still Life with Woodpecker, Their Eyes Were Watching God.* There was a photo of her skiing at Stowe on the windowsill. Rachel put a tablespoon of sencha tea in the pot and poured the boiling water over it. Benny opened a cupboard and found a mug with Chagall's "Promenade" on it. The artist holding his wife's hand as she floated above him.

Rachel stood beside her and Benny leaned in for a kiss. She smelled the lemon soap that Rachel used, an exhalation of brandy between the lips, and then felt tacky lipstick. Rachel's lips were ripe fruit, a persimmon, with their rosy red flesh. Benny lingered for a moment, then pulled her head away. Rachel was biting her lower lip, wide-eyed and sighing.

"I thought you'd never get around to this," she said.

Rachel raked her fingers through Benny's hair. When their lips touched again Benny was reawakened into the dreamy anticipation that had enveloped her earlier in the evening. Rachel turned out the light, took her hand, and led her to bed. The faster they moved, the less Benny could worry about what was to come. She had no idea what to do other than kiss Rachel and run her hands over her back.

Benny grabbed Rachel's hoodie at the waist, wanting to get inside. She pulled it over Rachel's head and threw it on the floor. Benny traced a line on her skin from her throat, across one shoulder, and down her upper arm. She continued down the downy hair on Rachel's forearm until she found her fingers. Benny wrapped her palm around each one and gently pulled, then let go. Rachel's eyes were fixed on hers.

Benny let her fingers return up the underside of Rachel's arm and felt the fur in her armpit. She ran along the fullness of the edge of her breast and down her waist, as if she were sculpting a lover from her warm flesh. Benny buried her nose in the scent and softness of Rachel's hair and neck. Rachel was strong, her hands kneading the muscles of Benny's back. Benny reached down and unzipped her, pushed her pants off her hips. Rachel did the same for her.

They didn't get much sleep. They dozed off, but desire would wake one or the other of them, and they began once again to kiss and love each other. Rachel fell asleep in Benny's arms. Benny wondered how she had let her fear and the pain she had experienced in high school prevent her from enjoying sex for the past six years. She regretted that. Once in the night she woke with Rachel staring at her, resting on her side on one elbow. She smiled at her.

"What time is it?"

"You do this thing in your sleep where your lips keep pressing together as if you're about to say something."

How could she know such a thing? She had always slept alone.

"What are these from?" Rachel had an index finger on one of the scars below her belly button.

"I used to get pains when I was a younger. They did exploratory surgery to see what it was."

"And?"

"And the pain went away."

Rachel lay down and put her arm around Benny. Benny nuzzled into the crook of her neck and felt her head rise and fall with each of Rachel's breaths. She could hear Rachel's heart.

"Does Brian know about this?"

"*I* didn't know about this until last night." She laughed.

"Will he care?"

"He knows what I'm like."

Benny took a deep breath and exhaled.

"These scars? They mean I'm sterile."

Rachel raised herself up on her elbow. "What? How do you know?"

"It's probably genetic." She paused. "It *is* genetic. Definitely genetic. There were telltale signs when I was younger. I never had a period. I had to go to specialists who poked and prodded and did everything but bleed me with leeches. That was their diagnosis. 'Genetic abnormality.' That's when I got these."

She pulled the sheet down again and touched her scars. She closed her eyes. She told Rachel the whole story, just kept talking so she couldn't think long enough to stop. When she finished she wanted neither of them to leave that bed or to speak ever again. She wanted to dissolve into Rachel's arm, sleep deeply again and wake in some other time. She had never told anyone the whole story. They made love again before falling asleep.

Early the next morning Benny sat up in Rachel's bed, a blanket covering her outstretched legs. A thin band of light under a bank of clouds showed the sun was threatening to rise. Rachel was packing for her trip to Peru.

"I have a bad feeling about this."

Rachel straightened from stuffing T-shirts into her backpack. She yawned.

"About us?"

Benny shook her head. "You going away."

"We'll be running again before you know it. You'll be so busy you won't have time to miss me. It'll be a blip of absence."

A blip of absence. There was no such thing. Benny had learned that absence was half of a binary switch. On or off. There was nothing in between. Of 0 and 1, this felt a lot like 0.

"Promise you'll come back."

"I promise I'll come back." Rachel got off the bed. "I'm going to be late if I don't get ready."

Downstairs Rachel kissed her goodbye and retrieved her coat from the hall closet. The two friends left the apartment onto 6th Street and waited for the cab. They hugged when it pulled up and Rachel whispered in Benny's ear, "Keep running."

She would as soon as she got home, but first she decided to walk all the way uptown. The roads in Central Park were icy, bare branches silhouetted against a bright sky. She thought of how it felt to have Rachel's hands on her back and wished she could have shared with her the light coming through the trees, the metallic breeze against her face.

26

Forest Garden

I am sitting on the little stone wall smoking Lina's herbal mixture. Down the gentle slope in front of me grows a young chokecherry tree that hasn't borne fruit yet. I really should cut that tree down before it gets too big and shades the vegetables, but I like the look of it and its speckled bark in the midst of the garden.

That Mylar blanket of Benny's is probably long gone by now. It was made of PETE.

Lina walks her bike up the path, past the tree, and sits down beside me. She looks sheepish and contrite.

"Where'd you spend the night?"

"In a tree house."

Puff, exhale.

"Who has a tree house?"

"Charles."

Chucko. The guy from the land co-op. The tree house is intriguing, but I don't want to hear her say anything else out loud so I don't ask. I know what happened, and she knows I know, but as long as we don't acknowledge it I can pretend that nothing has changed.

I may not say anything, but I can't stop thinking about it. I don't know what she sees in Chucko. I know she admires his politics. His self-righteous, activist, holier-than-thou politics. Lina is quirky for heavy beards and long, lanky hair. Chucko has this disgusting furry thing on his cheeks and jowls that makes me shiver. His facial hair is thick enough to store objects in, and he does: chopsticks, pens, bits of his last meal.

"I don't trust him."

"Don't be jealous," she says.

Jealous? I've never been jealous in my life. That's a stick people use to measure love.

Lina bikes over to Margaretsville, leaving me alone in the woods for the night. Chucko has invited her to harvest kelp from the sea in his canoe early the next morning. I am in my cabin trying to think of anything but them, but what they get up to before they begin paddling is a source of vile speculation on the part of my disobedient mind. I imagine her kissing his beard, trying to find his lips. Lina has always encouraged me to stop shaving. Perhaps I should have, but I've never liked having facial hair.

Chucko takes to visiting our homestead. He drives an old beater. He seems proud of the fact that he found a '73 Satellite Sebring Plus, in excellent condition, and is driving it into the ground. He covered it with yellow house paint, then painted over that with green slogans. "Say no to GMOs!" "Would you eat YOU'RE dog for dinner?"

His bedroom is in a forty-foot white ash. She tells me it's fun to sleep up there. The tree sways with the slightest breeze at night. Each morning the resident red squirrel—she says they call it Pete—visits them, dashing in one window, eating table scraps, then darting out another. No doubt Pete pees on Chucko's pile of unwashed clothes on the way out.

When I ask, she won't tell me whether they are having sex. She says I'm being possessive.

"If you want to know for a good reason," she says calmly, "then I'll tell you."

"Are you doing this because I didn't say yes to you?"

"I'm doing it because I need more than to live here alone with you."

When she is at Forest Garden I can pretend that nothing has changed. We cut firewood and garden together. We sit by the fire at night together. We continue to sleep together and sometimes have sex. When she isn't here, though, and even sometimes when she is, I miss her.

One late summer day she comes to the pine grove with me. I'm frisky and hope we will have sex. It's warm enough in the sun that I can take off my shirt and place it on the pine needles as a blanket. She lies on it and I kiss her and scratch her scalp. I can tell she's distracted. I put my hand under her T-shirt and stroke her belly, then move up to her breast. She nudges my hand away and makes an irritated sound.

"They're sore," she says. "I think I must be getting my period."

I pull my hand out and lie on the needles beside her, looking up at the branches of the pines mingling in the sky. She snuggles up to me, putting her head on my shoulder.

"I can see having my home base here. With you. I can go

off and travel and do the things I need to do and come back to you each fall to overwinter."

She makes it sound like she's a Canada goose, waiting to fly south to Georgia. She's with me now, however, and it seems we might work something out.

Less than a month later and she's changed her mind again. We are sitting in the dark by the fire. It is late September and we woke this morning to the first frost. We should get a few weeks of warm days and crisp, clear nights. She sits in front of me on the dry ground, my arms wrapped around her.

"Let's drift apart slowly like Morocco did from Nova Scotia," I whisper in her ear as she leans against my chest.

The firelight reflects orange off her face. Something in the look she gives me offers little warmth. I know I am alone now, that the best I can hope for is pity, and pity is worse than nothing at all.

"Charles is going to take me to see my gran and to visit Georgian Bay," she says. "He wants to go on a road trip to the West Coast and spend the winter out there. Then, next summer, we'll drive up to the Yukon for the Solstice."

All the places we have talked of going together. I ask her when she's leaving.

"Sometime in October."

So much for Forest Garden and me as her home base. I could have said yes when she asked me to marry her and she might have stayed, but that would be like clipping a hen's wings. Thousands of tiny lights ray down above the horizon of treetops that encircles us. In the years to come I intend to thin these woods with a handsaw and a felling axe, buck my firewood by hand, split it with a sharp maul and axe. And then, five hundred years from now, a mature forest will stand here, oblivious to the pain of loving and losing that came so long before. Sooner than all that, sooner than the sawing and felling, and a lot sooner than the white pines growing to their full height, I'll be alone again. She is Morocco, drifting with her half of our shared geology. One day soon, once she's gone, if you look down from where those stars are shining you'll be able to see, despite the expanse of sea between us, that we once fit together. That our edges would still mesh like two pieces of a puzzle.

27

Benny's run, after walking three miles home from Rachel's, made her tired. She was still recovering from the marathon. She slept in the next morning and was late getting to the lab. She hung her jacket on one of the hooks on the wall by her desk and sat down in the chair. It was 10:45. Underneath the clock Leach had hung a quote from Einstein:

> *Perfection of means and confusion of goals seem to characterize our age.*

She pulled a notebook down and opened it to the previous day's entry. This one was written in cursive, from right to left and in a private shorthand only she could decipher. She was left-handed and her handwriting was elegant only when she wrote backwards. It wasn't often that she associated that adjective with herself. Pushing her hand across the page the way she was told to since grade school felt like shovelling gravel. Her everyday handwriting looked like it had been scratched by an eight-year-old. It did not bring her joy to look at her experimental results because her research had not been going well. The past two weeks had been full of setbacks. First her bacterial cultures had been contaminated. Then, once she'd solved that problem, the bacteria wouldn't take up the recombinant plasmid DNA she had engineered containing the estA gene. She was at a standstill.

She pushed the book away. Somnolence tussled with the exhilaration of being in love. But she was exhausted from getting little sleep the night before. The fluorescent lights settled the match and she laid her head on her folded arms and dozed. She chose an awkward position, knowing that her body wouldn't let her sleep for long in discomfort. It was delicious to give in and float away from the lab.

"Good morning."

The voice came to her as if through fog. She raised her head and rubbed her hand across her mouth, afraid she had drooled on her chin. Her hair was damp with sweat and both her shoulders and upper arms tingled, half asleep.

"I hope I'm not interrupting anything," Leach said, looking like a cat with the flutter of wings in its mouth. "If you're not too busy, I'd like to speak to you in my office."

The open notebook glared accusingly at her from the desk. She closed it and returned it to the shelf above her desk.

Leach was moving a stack of copies of *Molecular and Cellular Biology* and *Applied Microbiology* journals from the couch when she entered. A beige filing cabinet stood against the wall behind the door. She walked over to the lone window. Grime-encrusted, it faced into a shaft that was bordered on four sides by offices like this one. That space, no more than six feet square, was designed by an architect—either a hopeless optimist or a fool—to allow light into the rooms from the roof three floors above. It was dark, even in daytime, and it was a trap for any bird that made the mistake of dropping into the space. Leach told her to sit on the couch. Three storeys below lay the carcasses of half a dozen birds. She turned away from the window and sat down. Above his desk were two framed magazine covers. One was a framed cover of *Time*, showing Leach with lips pursed and his eyebrows drawn down, both fists on the bench in front of him, staring out at America in his impeccable white lab coat. At the bottom, in bold orange letters: *Is this the scientist who will save us from Superbugs—and ourselves?* Underneath it was the cover of the latest *SI* swimsuit issue, with a woman with lush blond hair, plenty of flesh hanging out of her yellow bikini, and a sultry pout.

Leach leaned back in his chair to reach a bowl of mints he kept on a shelf behind his desk. He threw her a mint and unwrapped one for himself.

"I heard about our little marathon disappointment." He smiled and appeared to be offering sympathy. "Shot your wad too quickly, huh?"

Benny gaped. The smile drained from his lips, leaving traces only around the eyes.

"Ahem." He made a throat-clearing attempt that rattled convincingly. "Anyways. Be that as it may, I'm concerned about the status of your research. You've been here almost three years. By this time you should be thinking about how to wrap up your story. Your experiments should be directed toward the apex, reaching a point that will culminate in a body of work that is unique." She knew this. PhD candidates ate, drank, and slept with these things on their minds. "Beginning, middle, end. That sort of thing. Your beginning here was full of promise. You found those mutants that had adapted to metabolize polystyrene and nylon. Good work. You isolated the plasmid-borne genes that were responsible. Good work. And then *pfft*. You stalled. Nothing has happened since when, last year?"

"I've been having trouble getting the plasmid to be stable in *Pseudomonas*."

"I know, I know," he continued in a paternalistic tone. "But we've got to move quicker on this project."

"Why can't we publish my results about the enzyme?"

"Are you nuts? We're not publishing anything until we have a strain that eats plastic, and eats it like a fat man at an all-you-can-chow Chinese buffet." Leach laughed. "A really fat guy who whimpers at the sight of moo shu pork."

"It's going to take more time. It'd be faster to publish what we have and team up with other labs."

"You don't get it, do you? There's something I need to explain to you. Again. BioGreen Enterprises will buy anything we have that is capable of digesting plastic. Every municipal and state government will want it for their waste disposal programs. BioGreen knows this. They will pay us money for it. Lots of money. Well, not us, me. But it will benefit you, trust me. You will be the lead author. I have the patent application here, in this pile, completely filled out except for one thing. It's waiting for the details of the strain that you are going to create. Not data on an enzyme. Not preliminary findings about how, with a few more modifications, you might come up with a strain that eats plastic. I need the strain."

He told her that if she couldn't get results soon he'd have to bring someone else on board to lend a hand. He was thinking of what was best for her. If she'd reached a dead end it was important to realize that as quickly as possible. They could find a simpler project for her to complete. He wondered if she'd be interested in pursuing a more theoretical angle, to look into the evolutionary aspects of the mutants she'd found.

"Are you trying to force me out of your lab?" Her voice squeaked.

"Don't get all hysterical on me. This isn't about your abilities as a graduate student. It's about getting these products onto the market as quickly as possible. I'll need some real progress by the end of the year."

Less than two months. He was giving her an impossible task so he could justify taking her work from her.

"When I first met you," she said, "you led me to believe it was the environment you were doing this for."

"You misunderstand me. I know you think I'm in this just to make a buck. It's not true. But, hey, what if it was? If what I'm doing helps the environment, why shouldn't I be rewarded for it? But you've got to remember that the competition is stiff out there, Ben. Stiffer than a sixteen-year-old in a harem."

"I have no idea how to respond to that." She got up to leave. At the door she turned to him. "I'll have results by Christmas."

"Good girl."

Benny left Leach's office and went up to the roof to think. It didn't help. Back at the lab, she paced the floor with her head down. Leroy came to her lab to weigh out some acrylamide.

"You O.K.?"

She shook her head. Then she nodded. He laughed, put down the spatula, and screwed the lid back on the jar. "What's up?"

"Two things. One you know. Leach is up in my face for results that I don't have."

"And?"

"And I've fallen for Rachel."

"Oh."

"I didn't mean to. I mean, I didn't see it coming."

"At least not for another five years." He picked up the jar of acrylamide and the paper on which he'd weighed out what he needed, and left.

"Shit," she said.

She went home at lunch. She needed a nap.

28

Forest Garden

I lie awake in the night with Lina breathing lightly beside me. There's no moon and no light and it's quiet. When I couldn't sleep in the city I could turn on a light and read or watch a movie. There is no light switch here, no humming fridge to derail my thoughts from their anxious track. Lina's sleeping face is relaxed. She was my touchstone, allowing me to be deceived into believing I wasn't alone. I try to rouse her by nibbling her ear and rubbing her belly, but she murmurs something that sounds nothing like encouragement and turns away. I get up and go outside.

The night air coming up the mountain from the bay is thick and damp. I feel the fog settling on my hands and hair. I find the path to the road and walk in the dark. It reminds me of being with Dad and playing the World Without game. Given the news these days I have an easier time imagining the world without plastic. He and I had worked on that one for a week-full of walks. Plastic utensils and tools would disappear. Cutlery, shopping bags, garbage bags. Cars, computers. Prostheses, pacemakers, condoms, contact lenses. The machines that make all these things. Parts of rifles, Kevlar, and cruise missiles.

Septic tanks, water cisterns. Food packaging, refrigerators, and freezers. The polystyrene components of phones, computers, radios, and TVs. The logical end to all this would be industrial collapse.

I am out until the sky begins lightening in the east and I am sleepy. As I get near home there is movement in the ditch. It's a fawn with a speckled coat, trembling by itself on splayed front legs. It looks at me directly with its immense brown eyes. I glance behind it for its mother but she may be hiding in the woods. It must have been born late to have those spots visible in October. It will be hard-pressed to survive the winter. I want to pick it up and save it, but I have to let it fend for itself against coyotes, hunters, and the probability of starvation. A crow somewhere nearby calls.

Lina is still asleep when I return to the cabin. I take off all my clothes and climb in behind her. She mutters about my cold skin and pulls my arm around to her chest. Soon enough her warmth against my front lulls me down wispier mental pathways and I fly along them from branch to branch until I escape.

She is at the foot of the bed stretching when I wake. Thunder weaves between her legs as Lina rises in downward dog. I call the cat and she looks quickly at me and jumps onto the bed. She purrs as I scratch her ear. Lina smiles at me.

"Were you up last night?"

I nod. I want her to care where I've been. Otherwise how will I know she cares for me?

She continues her yoga. I nudge the cat aside, climb down from the bunk, and step outside. Yet another blue sky. A few leaves falling in the breeze. The colours have peaked. I am torn by the last gasp of warm sunshine, by the Michaelmas daisies that have struggled past the two frosts of the past week, and by a junco eating garden seeds on a stalk not a body's length from me. A turkey vulture soars low over the treetops. One after another, members of its flock come into view until there are seven of them, looking for something dead to pull apart. Their wing tips curl up as they brush the spruce tops.

Lina comes outside and stands beside me.

"Eagle?"

I could never confuse the two when they're in the air. As soon as I see their outline I know what it is. I am proud of my hawkish eyesight and my ability to discern shapes and sounds that birds make. It's not an innate characteristic, though one could be fooled to believe so. It's like learning to ride a bike; once you know how, you can't forget.

"Turkey vultures."

But she doesn't really care. Her mind is elsewhere.

"Hey," she says softly. "There's something . . ."

"What?"

"I'm pregnant."

Silence.

"Since when?"

"I think about eight weeks."

I am dizzy. I sit on the ground.

"I'm sorry."

"About what exactly?"

"That things didn't work out for us."

That was fast.

29

New York City

Patience was not one of Benny's virtues. She found it trying to work with *Pseudomonas* because it was a slow-growing bacterium. Cells plated on a petri dish took seven or eight days to form minute colonies. She stood at the incubator outside Leach's office and for the umpteenth time she looked inside at the petri plates. The 30°C air was moist and smelled sweet, like the soil of a flower garden.

She picked up the stack of petri dishes and held the uppermost one to the fluorescent light above her. No colonies. She'd have to wait another day. Leach called to her from his office.

"Ben, is that you?"

"Yeah," she said absentmindedly.

"Can you come here?"

She moved to the doorway.

"Come in, come in," he said from his desk, ushering her with his hand to sit as he continued to write a note. "Shut the door behind you." He looked up. "I told you in November that your pace wasn't quick enough to get this job done. It's March. I've given you all this extra time."

"I'm getting close."

"I asked Jon to fiddle with one of your plasmid constructs to see if he could get it to work more efficiently."

"Jon works with staph. Antibiotic resistance. What does he know about *Pseudomonas* and plastics?"

"It's his versatility I appreciate," he said. "Jonathan's capable of moving in more than one direction at a time."

"So are slime moulds."

"Ben, Ben, Ben," he said, shaking his head.

"I've asked you a hundred times not to call me Ben."

"All right, calm down. We'll get these products out more quickly and you'll still be the lead author on whatever we publish. Here, have a mint."

She waved her hand and shook her head. He popped a mint in his mouth before continuing.

"He's had some success getting the plasmid to be expressed. You should welcome—"

"Interference?"

Leach lost his smile. "The other thing I appreciate is team-work. We're all part of Team Leach, pulling together for the good of the lab. We're like a braided rope, stronger together than as separate strings. It takes a village, Ben, a whole stinking village to raise one kid. I've applied that principle here to my work. To *our* work. These recombinant bacteria are my children and you're all my village. Now is the time for you to be part of the village. Part of Team Leach. We have potential products that are worth a lot of cash. Dilly-dallying won't get them to market."

Team Leach? Leroy would love that. If he were talking to her she could tell him.

"Besides, now you can focus your attention on your other

project. You can really get a handle on the molecular evolution of the nylon-digesting bacterium. That's a good, interesting project for your little thesis."

She was leaving the office with her head down as Nawthorn walked through the door. She didn't see him until it was too late. She threw her arms up and her elbow hit him in the solar plexus and knocked him onto one knee. Benny reeled sideways and landed on her bum, stunned. Leach began to laugh.

Once Nawthorn caught his breath, he stood and helped Benny up. She moved past him, through the door, and went to her bench. She paced the aisle by her bench, turning circles in the confined space. A few minutes later Nawthorn found her and motioned with his head toward the door.

"Come and have a beer."

She followed him into the hallway, where he reached into one of the fridges and pulled out two cans of Bud. He closed his office door behind her. She sat on the couch. He opened a can and passed it to her. She admired Nawthorn and tried to imagine a life of pure research, with no application, pursued solely for the sake of satisfying curiosity. That was Gabe. He was a scientist for all the right reasons. He loved discovering stuff. He was not venal and he was not sussing out how he could make a killing by connecting his work with some biotech start-up. Although she was trying to create something practical, if anyone could appreciate what she was trying to do, it would be him.

"I've seen women rushing out of Melvin's office plenty of times, but never that fast," he said. He sipped his beer. "Why not finish your thesis on molecular evolution and get out of his lab as quickly as you can? Then find a post-doc working on plastic degradation and write your own ticket in that lab."

"There's nobody else. Besides, my research career is almost over."

"Why don't you come to my lab?"

"Thanks, Gabe, but that project is the sole reason I'm here."

"Get the plasmid to work, and I'll deal with her."

It was Leach, talking to Jonathan at his bench. Benny had come back from her beer and was about to enter through Leroy's lab when she heard her name. She stopped at the door.

"I want my name first on the paper," Jon said.

"Absolutely. You won't regret it, my friend."

"Sure."

"You know what I don't get? I don't get how she can run so fast and work so slow. I saw her during the marathon running up First. She was really moving. She looked good too, in her tight leggings and T-shirt."

"Instead of those ridiculous army pants she wears here," Jon said.

They laughed.

"She's got no tits, though," Leach said.

"Whatever. Let me get back to work."

Benny left the lab and wandered around the neighbourhood. The sky in the west was darkening as heavy clouds rolled in. She found them comforting, as if the world was mirroring her feelings. Her mind was an ouroborus, swallowing its own tail, passing all the familiar landmarks of pain: the doubts she had that her work would be successful; the way her body continued to confuse her; her father's demise. She had to exhaust herself or go crazy with these thoughts.

She walked with her head down so nobody could see her

crying. The sidewalks were a map of crevices, splits, and cracks leading nowhere. At the intersection of 79th and Lexington, a crew was working on the road. A jackhammer pounded the pavement rhythmically, like a woodpecker drilling holes in a spruce. It probed under the city's skin for a purchase for the sidewalks and subway tunnels, the concrete footings of skyscrapers. All it would find was more concrete and asphalt, layer upon layer, laid down by the city's builders from Stuyvesant to Trump. Scar tissue. Year after year, decade after decade, the island's flesh was reopened, then sutured with beams, rebar, concrete, and wire. At the base were the bones of the Lenape people and under them middens of discarded oyster shells. The jackhammer seemed intent on getting there, as if only then would it have a chance to put down roots.

She went home and took the stairs to her apartment two at a time. There, she stripped to her underwear and stood in front of the mirror that hung on the back of her bedroom door. Her face was puffy. Her clavicles protruded, casting shadows on her chest. She cupped the soft flesh of her breasts and looked at the sharpness of the bones below them. When she sucked her belly in, she could count her ribs. Below her belly button were her scars, running vertically for two inches. She turned around and looked at her ass over her shoulder in the mirror. It was taut from running and as flat as always.

She pulled on her black track pants, her sports bra, and her white sleeveless top. She tied her hair back in a ponytail and laced up her shoes. It was drizzling by the time she got to the street. She had run through heavier rain than that. She headed west, dodging cabbies driven insane by the ever-changing red and green. At the corner of 70th and Lexington a mother pushed her infant in a stroller ahead of her at the crosswalk. A lull in the traffic allowed Benny to pick up speed between Madison and Fifth and she sailed into the park fully warmed up. The contrary wind of the coming storm was churning the leaves, offering their lighter underbellies up to the sky. The heavy clouds were moving to cover up the last bits of blue remaining behind her to the east. As she reached the road and headed north it began to pour. This urged her to pick up her pace. As she passed the Met she thought how Leroy was able to sit among the sculptures and stare at them until he wasn't seeing them anymore. It was his form of meditation. For her, the park was the only place she could be herself and think clearly. It was the city's masterpiece, the one work of art essential to her sanity.

Today was different though. She hadn't come to think. She was there to run thinking into the ground, to push herself until there was no thought left except the desire to stop. She wanted the beating of her feet on the pavement to jackhammer all thought from her mind. For this to happen she had to run fast and hard until her heart knocked against her ribs. The rain cooled her off and her tears mixed with the rain and fell to the ground, where they were washed in rivulets along the road, down the storm sewer, and into the river. Her tears were inconsequential to this rain. By the time she was running south her shoes sloshed uncomfortably with each step. Her shirt clung to her skin. As she passed Strawberry Fields two men passed her jogging the other way. They were as soaked as she was but they were obviously having fun in the rain, laughing with each other.

"Looking good, girl," one of them shouted at her as she zipped past them.

"Fuck you," she yelled without breaking stride. Still she cried. Even the rhythmic pounding of her feet on the pavement couldn't stop the ceaseless chatter in her head. She returned to the street where she had entered the park and jogged home around the few souls who braved the sidewalks in the storm.

When they ran together, Rachel insisted that they not retrace their steps. "I hate gerbilling," she said. Benny had laughed at the image of them running in circles on a wheel, but she didn't see any way around winding up exactly where she'd started. You run and run, but you always end up back at the beginning.

She stopped at The Food Emporium, knowing what she was about to do and powerless to stop herself. She bought two bags of Oreos, a loaf of the fluffiest white bread she could find, a package of cheese slices, and mayo. Her tears were gone, replaced by a resolve that felt ominous. The pimple-faced cashier checked her out.

"Wet out there?"

"Yes, it's wet out there," Benny said. "And you can stop staring at my nipples."

She shocked him more than she had anticipated. A whimper escaped his lips and she saw that his eyes were watering. The tiniest flicker of compassion fluttered in her chest.

"Oh, shit." She looked at his nametag. "Jason. Forget I said anything, will you? Forget I was even here. I'm not having a good day."

She pulled the groceries out of the bag he had packed them in and left the store under a full head of steam. The tiny flicker of compassion notwithstanding, she was a one-hundred-car freight train and had just thrown on her screeching brakes, seeing something on the tracks ahead. She wouldn't be able to stop for a mile or more. Momentum carried her forward, the product of the mass of pain her body had caused her over the years multiplied by the velocity of her mind trying to ignore, avoid, or resolve that pain. She had hated her body for too long, hated what it had been doing to her, what it lacked when she came into the world and what it lacked now.

Annika was out when she arrived home. Good. She opened one of the bags of Oreos and began eating them the way she had when she was a kid watching *The Cosby Show*. She unscrewed the cookie, lifted off the icing, and ate both the wafers. She collected the icing as she went and rolled it into a ball. After eating six cookies, she bit into the ball of icing. She was empty, a hollow tube wanting to be filled. There was no turning back, no temporary solution this time. No laxatives, no finger down the throat.

She had eaten a bag of cookies and was into the second one as she stood at the stove making a grilled cheese sandwich. Doing two things at once was never a good idea for her. She would get warnings to slow down and she got one now. One of her canines came down on the inside of her cheek, hard enough to draw blood. She threw the spatula down on the stove.

"You fucking piece of shit!"

Her tongue bathed in the salt of blood pooling under her tongue, then probed the puncture in her cheek. It tasted like the metal on the chain-link fence she once licked.

Benny turned off the stove and slid the grilled cheese sandwich onto a plate. The plate was the second indication that the freight train was slowing down. She wasn't going to stuff the bread, mayo, and cheese in her mouth. She cut the sandwich in two, dropped the plate on the table, and went to her bedroom to lie down. The bag of Oreos sat like a log in her gut and she cried again. The salty tears ran down her face and into her ears. The blood had stopped flowing, yet her tongue continued to probe the wound in her cheek.

There was DNA in the cells lining her cheek. Easy to scrape off and analyze. There was DNA in the blood spilled from her cheek. All she needed was a few cells and she could sequence the DNA to learn what she needed to know.

What is wrong with me?

The combination of running and crying and eating all that sugar worked to draw the mantle of sleep around her. When she opened her eyes later, outside the bank of windows at her feet was a cloudless sky. She lay and loved that sky. Her mouth was full of the detritus of the bag of cookies, sickly sweet. She had a desperate need to brush her teeth and have a glass of water, but she loved that sky and didn't want to move.

She wanted to corral her unhappiness of the previous evening, then put it in a stable where she could prevent it from roaming free. Her body was flawed, her father was dead, and she was failing in the lab. But she still believed in her dream. All she had to do was get her creations to work.

She didn't want to move, or get up, or figure out what day it was. She merely wanted to lie there and relish the joy of the golden glow coming through the window onto her legs and pelvis. Her mind had cleared, the clouds of confusion had dissipated, and she felt a clarity of purpose that was calming. She would stay in Leach's lab and work on molecular evolution. Clandestinely, she would continue to create strains of bacteria to degrade and destroy plastics. She figured she had worked out all the angles by this point, knew everything that could go wrong. From here on in she would be alone. If she was going to realize her dream it would alienate her from the lab, the city, and from everyone she knew and loved. It had to be secret now, and she would have nobody to share her ideas with. Not Leroy. Not—and this caused her heart to contract—Rachel.

Before she could finish her work, however, she needed to know what was at the root of her body's woes. What was the genetic cause of her abnormality? She would need to sequence her own DNA to find out.

30

Forest Garden

"When's Lina leaving?" Art asks.

"A week or so."

We are among the stunted trees on the way to the bluff. The barrel of his .30-30 Winchester is pointing down. He's got me wearing an orange vest and cap like his. Lina is spending less time at home. I have got back in the habit of seeking out Art for company. Ostensibly, he is teaching me to hunt deer. I asked him to, but my heart's not in it. I go out of my way to step on any dry branch that is near my hiking boots. If that doesn't work, I hope that we're talking loudly enough to scare any deer away.

"That's a bugger. I'll miss her."

At the edge of the forest we come to a cliff that overlooks the bay. Art sits on a stump and I lower myself to the ground next to him. His gnarled hand reaches into his jacket pocket and pulls out a pouch of tobacco. He rolls a smoke, then offers me the pouch. I have run out of Lina's herbal mixture and now smoke tobacco. In addition to alleviating my asthma, it grounds me, especially when I'm upset, anxious, or lonely.

31

New York City

"You should see the farming they have there," Rachel said.

She had been home for three days and finally Benny had returned her calls, asking that they meet in the park at their usual spot. Benny wore her cotton shorts and running shoes and jogged in at 69th Street to wait under the elms. It felt like she had a basket of bees in her belly and might throw up.

Rachel arrived wearing red shorts, a T-shirt, and flip-flops. She ran up to Benny, threw her arms around her, and kissed her.

"You should have told me we were going to go for a run."

She wouldn't stop talking, her arm around Benny's waist.

"They have these terraced gardens on the mountain slopes. The hills are so steep that farmers have actually fallen off their gardens." She told of campesinos cultivating varieties of crops that had originated in Peru thousands of years ago. "There are tomatoes, peppers, potatoes, and eggplants like I've never seen before. Every variety different. And tobacco. Do you want to jog?"

Rachel kicked off her flip-flops, picked them up, and began running. Benny, not knowing what else to do, followed her. Rachel set their pace and it was fast. She had run in Peru, at high elevation, and her body was thriving on the higher oxygen concentration at sea level. They ran past the Met, the only sounds being the slap of Benny's sneakers on pavement and her heavy breathing. They were running up a hill, Benny struggling to keep up.

"Hey," Benny said, reaching for Rachel's arm and stopping. "I can't run and talk."

Rachel stopped too.

"I'm sorry," Benny said. It sounded so pitiful to her ears.

"What?"

"I can't do this. It's not fair to you."

Rachel shook her head. "You chicken."

"You should never have left."

Benny knew that wouldn't have mattered. She hated having to let go. She loved Rachel, but she was leaving and was not coming back. She thought about the possibility of Rachel coming with her but knew it was impossible.

"I have to go," Rachel said. She took off in a sprint. By the time Benny knew what was happening, Rachel was far from her, and though Benny had been training, she never was as fast as her friend. She tried to catch her but despaired as those red shorts receded farther. She stopped.

Benny began to run in the late afternoon to avoid bumping into Rachel. The following week she saw Rachel running toward her, either oblivious of Benny or determined to ignore her. Benny didn't want to find out which so she turned abruptly down a path she had never run on before. From then on she ran either right before her lunch or at three o'clock.

Now, on Saturday, she stood before Leroy's door. They had barely spoken since she told him she had fallen in love with Rachel, though their benches were only thirty feet apart. Benny needed his help. She thought she had a defective chromosome and she had a good idea which gene was mutated. Although it looked like human mutations would be correctable *in vivo* in the near future, there was nothing she would ever be able to do about her defect. But at least she could have the knowledge of what had gone wrong during her development. She had no right to ask Leroy to do the sequencing of the mutation for her. What did he owe her? She wasn't even going to tell him the truth about which gene she was looking at.

Leroy opened the door. He seemed surprised to see her but smiled. His roommate Mike waved at her from the kitchen. He was wearing a short-sleeved dress shirt in the heat.

"Leach was hounding me all day to find out where you were," Leroy said.

It was heading toward evening and they hadn't yet turned on the lights. Benny pulled up a chair to the round table, which was covered with a few beer cans, a tin of smoked oysters, and the crumbs of crackers. The room smelled like a beach with a smoky fire. Leroy pulled a can of Coors from the six-pack ring and handed it to Benny.

"These Canadians really know how to live the high life, huh?" she said to Mike.

"There's not much choice at The Food Emporium," Leroy said. "I still can't get over being able to buy beer at the grocery store."

"Can't you do that up in Canada?" Mike said.

"Nope. Our liquor laws are tighter than the flapper on a goose's ass."

Leroy put an oyster on a cracker and handed it to Benny. She poked it with her index finger. She joked that she was checking to see if it was male or female. Oysters could change their sex, she told them. One year an oyster produces billions of sperm, the next it will release eggs. It all depends on the water temperature. In the winter, when the water's cold, they hibernate and their gonads are flat and neither male nor female. They never know what sex they'll be the next summer. Mike said he thought that would make planning difficult.

Once Mike left the room, Leroy asked her if she wanted another drink. She put her hand on his arm and shook her head.

"Can we go to your room?"

He grabbed his can of beer and followed Benny into his bedroom. She went to his desk, littered with journal papers, CD cases, and gum wrappers. He turned on his lamp, threw the quilt over his unmade bed, and sat down. Benny picked up *Blue* from the desk and put it in the player. She sat beside him and told him that she had stopped seeing Rachel.

"I wanted it to work out. I love her, I do. But . . ."

He reached out and put his palm between her shoulder blades. Her breathing changed and she began to cry.

"Lie down," he said and sat beside her. She turned onto her side, facing away from him, and he rubbed her back. She relaxed and stopped crying. She shouldn't talk to him about Rachel anymore, it wasn't fair. She turned her head to face him.

"Can you sequence some DNA for me?"

"What sequence?"

"A stretch on the fourth chromosome." She paused. "Mine."

"What are you looking for?"

She picked at his quilt.

"I told you that my father drowned. There was more to it." With an index finger she traced the outlines of the squares on the quilt. "I'm convinced he had Huntington's disease."

"Does it run in your family?"

"He was depressed. It began all of a sudden. He forgot things and snapped at me for no reason. I want to know if he had it. He might have had a seizure on the dock that day."

"And if he had it…"

She nodded. Any father with Huntington's has a 50 percent chance of passing it on to his daughter. The normal gene has a short sequence in its DNA repeated about twenty-five times. The mutant form results when that short sequence was stuttered over during DNA replication so that the sequence was repeated forty to a hundred times.

The apartment was quiet. The traffic had all stopped. No honking horns. She breathed, in-out, in-out.

"What do you need from me?" Leroy said. "They've cloned the gene, right?"

"In 1993."

She wanted him to do the test. It would take one polymerase chain reaction and sequencing fewer than two hundred nucleotides. He routinely sequenced DNA fragments from Chico and his other mouse mutants. It would take one evening to do most of the work and she'd know the result in less than a week.

"Why don't you go to a clinic and get tested?"

"I need it to be anonymous."

"Where are we going to get the probes?"

"A Huntington's researcher in Madison sent them to me."

"O.K., but this goes no further than you and me. If you test positive you go to a doctor and get a proper test and don't mention this one. If they find out I was using the lab for genetic testing they'd drum me out of school quicker than you could say Jack Robinson."

"Leroy?" She was smiling.

"Yeah."

"Does everyone up there talk the way you do?"

"What?"

"Does everyone in Canada use archaic expressions like 'Jack Robertson' and that thing you say about the flapper on a duck's ass?"

"It's Jack *Robinson* and it's a goose's ass and, no, not everyone up there talks like that."

Leroy grabbed the pillow from behind Benny's head and bopped her with it. She laughed and he lay down beside her. Leroy put his arm around her and Benny snuggled into his chest.

"No funny business, O.K.?" she said.

He squeezed her. "You can sleep here if you want."

They listened to the music for a while and then she realized he had drifted off. She got up to turn off the light, then lay down again. There were voices in the neighbouring apartment coming from a TV and the white noise from the street. She wanted to stay.

Partway through the night Benny woke up and went to the kitchen for a drink of water. When she returned, Leroy had undressed and climbed beneath the covers. She lay down beside him. In the morning Leroy lay with the covers pulled up under his chin. They talked for a long time while Benny sat on the windowsill.

"I like sleeping with you," she said.

"Me too."

"But I don't want to have sex."

"I wasn't asking you to." He grinned and shook his head. "You're a strange girl, Benny, but I do like you."

He made her oatmeal for breakfast and they went to the lab. At the end of the day she invited him to spend the night at her apartment. They ate supper and then went to bed. She opened the blinds so they could see the city lights and climbed in beside Leroy. She leaned over and kissed him, and her hands began touching him before she caught herself and pulled back. She lay awake long after Leroy had fallen asleep, wondering if she was being foolish to insist that they not consummate their unusual friendship. They liked each other and she found him attractive, but soon enough she would be saying goodbye to him too.

32

Forest Garden

We are sitting on the bluff. No buildings in sight. No crowds of people. We are alone and farther from New York than I have ever felt. Across the bay lies Cape Chignecto, a band of green against the water's grey. Isle Haute, the solitary island, rises out of the water like a disc to our east. Art calls it the clitoris of the Bay of Fundy.

"Benny was a fool to get him to sequence her DNA," Art says.

I ask why.

"If your biography was written down, including what hasn't happened yet, would you read it?"

I say I would.

"You didn't take time to consider the question." Wisps of smoke from his cigarette carry out to sea, then dissipate in the gentle breeze. "Because that's what she wanted. She might have got some really bad news that she'd be able to do nothing about. And what if·there was a cure for that disease? What if they could have changed her father's DNA and cured him? Would she have chosen that?"

"Anyone would want that."

"I don't think so. We all have to die. He died young, before his joints and bones began to rot."

"At least she would've had him around longer."

He isn't listening.

"That's what's always bugged me about Lazarus. Christ wasn't doing Martha and Mary any favours bringing him back from the dead. He forced them to mourn their brother's death twice." He laughs. "As if we need any more suffering than life already brings us."

One minute we're talking about DNA and the next he's getting all Biblical on me. I ask why Jesus did it.

"I doubt he did. I haven't believed in that hocus-pocus since I came back from Italy. But if it's true, he was showing off. Trying to convince them he could do magic."

"I thought we were talking about science."

"Science is our magic. We expect scientists to raise our dead. Benny's father died and she wanted an explanation. You can explain that he had a mutation in his genes and it killed him. But she'd never know why he had to die anymore than you and I know why we're alive. Magic. We're marvellous machines, that's all."

I get up, wiping the dirt off my pants. "I'm going home to see Lina."

"I don't blame you." He grunts as he stands, rubbing his hip. "You had a good run with her."

We go back into the woods, heading toward his house. We pass a maple, its upper and outer leaves crimson, the lower leaves still green with red outlines. Beneath the tree is a blanket of red on the forest floor in a perfect circle, as if the tree had been dripping paint. The only sound is the crunching of our boots on the leaves and twigs. Then Art stops in front of me,

reaches back with his right arm to still me, and raises his gun
to his shoulder. I follow the direction of the barrel to where I
see the tail of a deer twitching against a white rump a hundred
feet away. Then a blast and the deer bolts.

"Damn. I ain't used to missing."

He seems embarrassed to have me watching. We start for
home.

"You know she's pregnant?"

Ahead of me, he nods. "She told me."

33

New York City

Another night, Benny and Leroy were reading together in her bedroom, lying on her bed, their legs touching under the comforter, like a decades-married couple.

"What's that?" Benny said.

He closed the book on his finger to mark his place and showed her the cover. *The Good Life*.

"It's about a couple who move to the country and grow all their own food," he said. "Doug's girlfriend told me about it. It reminds me of this daydream I had as a kid of living in a cabin in the woods. Growing my own food. Skating on a pond."

"Do you think you'll go home after you graduate?"

He nodded. "When I was a boy, my father would come home from work with construction paper. Before he took off his tie he'd sit beside me on the floor and we'd cut up the paper and draw on it. I was always making elaborate skylines of hills and trees, with one house on the edge of the forest that had smoke coming out its chimney and with a garden in front. I really don't belong here."

"That's so far away from here."

"Do you remember," he said, "when I told you that first night that we'd be living together in Canada with our children?"

"You don't still believe that, do you?"

"We make things happen by believing they will. We dream where we're headed and one day we arrive there."

"You're such a fatalist," she said. "Your belief in destiny is always going to disappoint you."

"I saw Rachel in the park yesterday."

"What?"

"I took the afternoon off and went for a walk. She was running and stopped to say hi. We talked for over an hour."

"How is she? What's she doing?"

"She's great. She said she misses you."

"I doubt that."

She wanted to know more, to know what she looked like, what she was wearing, but she couldn't ask. When Leroy's breathing told her that he was asleep, Benny got out of bed and sat on the windowsill to look at the skyline. The horizon, visible between buildings, was nothing more than a grey line separating heaven and earth. Benny knew that Leroy found Rachel attractive and she had a hunch that the two of them would like each other. It was bittersweet to see him become so animated when he mentioned bumping into Rachel. She pictured Rachel and the scar above her breast. Leaving her and Leroy felt like a deep cut. She wondered if all she was doing by imagining them together was trying to dress a wound she was making by running away.

Benny and Leroy stayed at their benches late that Friday. Lynn was the last of the others to leave and then they were alone. Leroy decided it was best to collect DNA from her blood even though sequencing could be done on a few cells scraped from the inside of Benny's cheek. He was used to drawing blood from his mice and he wanted a larger amount of DNA in case he needed to do the procedure twice.

He unwrapped a 21-gauge needle and pressed it onto the syringe. He unscrewed the cap from the glacial bottle of Leach's rocket fuel and brought it to his nose for a sniff. He held the cotton ball against the bottle's neck and inverted it. The ethanol he brushed along the crook of Benny's arm was cold. His teeth gripped his lower lip, his squinting eyes were held in anticipation. He slid the bevelled point of steel into a bulging vein, tattoo blue, slithering beneath her skin like a snake. Blood darted from the vein, deep red, eager for somewhere to go.

"You never mention your father," she said.

"That's because I don't want to talk about him." He paused. "I remember laughing with him a lot when I was a kid. I wonder where that went."

The vial filled with her warm blood. He detached the vial and jammed it into the bucket of ice on his bench. He pressed the cotton ball onto her skin to staunch the flow and pulled the needle out from under it. She rested her index and middle fingers on the cotton as he leaned into her. The bristles on his upper lip outlined the shape his moustache would take, although he had shaved that morning. His incisors were both chipped and uneven along the bottom surface. She felt his whiskers first, tickling her lips, then the warm lips themselves. Benny held her breath, then pulled her head away gently. Leroy straightened his back and put both hands on the bench to steady himself.

"What happened the day your dad drowned?" Leroy said.

"I don't know for sure. A neighbour saw him leave the house. He must have walked to the lake and wound up at the public dock. He slipped and drowned."

"Can I kiss you again?"

She shook her head. He leaned toward her but she pushed him gently. "I can't."

"I don't get you."

She nodded.

"I'll isolate this DNA while it's fresh."

"Here's my key if you want to stop by on your way home."

He poured ethanol into a small beaker and downed it. She tried to kiss him on the cheek but he pulled his head away. She dropped the key on the bench beside the bucket holding her blood. "Annika will let me in."

It was after two. There was a tapping on Benny's door, then it opened. Leroy climbed in beside her. She put her arm over his hip and he huddled in closer.

"Do you remember showing me that falcon's nest on the roof?" he said.

"Uh huh."

"I remember looking over at you and you were smiling and looking down at the nest and I said to myself, 'This is her. This is the one I've been waiting for.'"

She murmured into his shoulder blade.

"Huh?"

"Hopes are different than prognostications," she repeated.

"You keep telling me that."

"Rachel's your girl."

"You think?"

Soon, she could tell from his heavy breathing that he had dropped off. She wished she could fall asleep as quickly as he always did. Instead, once again, she lay and thought. She loved him and she loved Rachel but she knew she wasn't being fair to either.

Two days later Benny ran into Leroy on his way from the freezer to the dark room, carrying a sequencing cassette the size of a thin coffee table book. Inside was a piece of film waiting to be developed.

"This is your sequence," Leroy said, tapping the cassette. "I'm going to develop it now to see if there's too many repeats."

"I'll look at it when I get back."

She went down the hall to another lab in search of glass petri plates. She had constructed plasmid DNA that might allow her bacterial strains to digest polystyrene. Now it was time to transform the bacterium with the DNA and see. Polystyrene. Rigid, with the potential to be transparent, it was ideal for storing fresh food. All those to-go boxes holding hamburgers and sushi and roast chicken would one day be gone. An alternative to the Styrofoam insulation in the walls of plastic houses would have to be found. Ditto ballpoint pen barrels. In the meantime, the petri dishes they used in the lab were made of polystyrene; she needed to find glass ones.

Benny went to the lab of a classmate of hers who studied

signal transduction in human cells. Kim used glass dishes for tissue culture of human cell lines. She lied that she was trying to get *Pseudomonas* to grow more quickly. She had altered their medium, fiddled with the incubation temperature, tried different wavelengths of light. Nothing had made much difference. It was a long shot, she knew, but they might grow better on glass.

"Not likely to make a difference," Kim said.

"Maybe not. I wonder if the bisphenol A the plates leach out is affecting their growth."

"I doubt it. They're over there. Take as many as you need."

Leroy was waiting for her at her bench when Benny returned.

"You got the wrong primers from Madison," Leroy said.

He handed her the film. She held it up to the window and studied it.

"There are no repeats in this sequence at all," he said. "There should be at least twenty-five."

"Leave it with me."

She rose from her stool and left the lab to retrieve a flask from the autoclave down the corridor. Leroy was gone when she returned. She poured the hot liquid medium in twenty glass petri dishes, covering each one as she went. Once she was done, she sat at her desk and looked at the film he had given her. She knew there would be no repeats. She wrote down each nucleotide—A, C, T, G—as a band appeared. She worked her way down the film. When she came to the end, she found her copy of the 1993 paper from the *American Journal of Human Genetics* reporting the sequence of the SRY gene. She compared her sequence to the wild-type sequence. There it was. One nucleotide different. A transversion mutation at position 1846, putting a C where an A was supposed to be.

In the beginning was a mutation. That small change—one typo in her three-billion-letter autobiography—changed the way the whole book had been read.

That night the blinds were open and light poured onto the single sheet that covered her and Leroy. It might keep her up. She put one arm underneath her head to look at the lights blazing from the Citibank building. She thought of the songbirds that were being lured to their deaths, confused by the lights, dying for the city's fabulous skyline. Leroy was pressing her about the sequence of her DNA.

"Did he send you the wrong primers?"

"I need to sleep."

"I could have kept the sequence, you know."

"But you didn't."

"Was it even on chromosome four?"

"I got what I needed."

Leroy sat upright. "Why would you lie to me?"

"I don't want you to know."

He rested his back against the wall.

"Can't you relax about anything?" He bit the words off. "All this secrecy and your obsession with plastic. You're like Joan of Arc, burning with this passion to save the world. It's bullshit. No one asked you to save us."

She whispered, "Please leave."

He jumped from the bed and, as he was pulling his pants on, said, "I have more fun in my bathroom than in your bed."

He was tucking his shirt into his pants as he left her room. She only saw him once more after that.

34

Forest Garden

Martin and Jenifer are out for the evening. I'm taking advantage of their absence to bathe in their clawfoot tub. The emptiness of the house gives me time to think, and time to think makes me sad, and that sadness has no bottom. Many months after my father died, I became determined to will the sadness away, thinking that only by effort could I return to some semblance of normal. I saw no rational reason to be depressed anymore. Sometimes in life you flew into a window. Best to shake your head and fly on.

If only it were easy for me to obliterate grief with drink. Instead, what I've got is a cup of tea, a hot bath, and *Sophie's Choice*. The tub is too short for me and my feet rest on the taps out of the water. I turn the hot water on with my left foot from time to time. William Styron also wrote a book about his depression. He said that some people who had a parent die when they were young resolve their grief by creating a lasting legacy to their own life. Long after his mother died of breast cancer when he was a boy, Styron did that by writing *Sophie's Choice*. I hold the hardcover with damp hands but I keep reading the same page over. I can't focus on it and am thinking about Sophie's alcoholism and depression. It is too familiar for me to let go. I close my finger in the book and hang my hand over the tub's edge.

Smells from my past overwhelm me when I reach for the lukewarm cup of tea on the other side. Cigar smoke and juniper berries. I turn, sure that I'll see my father in the room. There is nothing there but the door with a towel hanging on a hook. I close my eyes. There are the stalks of corn, eight feet tall, yellow scallopini squash, and row after row of green beans in our garden. Then I do see him, his sunken cheeks, a day's stubble on his chin.

"So, it is you. I was remembering."

I feel no embarrassment at my nakedness. I put the tea down and he reaches for my hand. I enjoy that firm grasp once again. I motion for him to sit on the lid of the toilet. He asks what it is I don't understand.

"What do you mean?"

"You were remembering. We remember what we don't understand. That's why you can't let it go."

"Shit, Dad, I'm just trying to get it right."

"Listen to me. It passes quickly. One minute all that matters is you're playing goal for your college team, keeping the puck out of the net and hoping that pretty girl is in the stands again watching you. Then the next thing you know all the good stuff is behind you and you're staring down a dark road leading nowhere you want to go."

I felt like throwing the book at him.

"I don't understand you leaving without a word. I don't understand Mom disappearing. I don't understand how a child who was so happy ends up in the woods alone. That's what I don't understand."

"You're not still trying to figure out whether I killed myself, are you? That's like trying to figure out what caused someone's cancer. You may never understand what you're remembering. Learn from my mistake. Be content with what you have. Let it go."

The smell of cigar smoke is getting fainter. Panicking, I sit up in the tub. Water rises in a wave to the end and sloshes over the side. I'm desperate to grasp his hand again but he's gone.

"Fuck you!" I shriek. "Why are you always leaving?"

It was only eight years that he and I went camping. When I was young and each of my years passed slowly, those few weeks we spent together camping were a large fraction of my temporal and imaginative life. Yet as I grow older, time shrinks those weeks and that time falls away like dead skin, like dust.

The tides continue to ebb and flow through that sheltered bay off Somes Sound on Mount Desert Island twice each day, raising and lowering the wooden wharves I played on. It's just that I'm not there to see them.

It's one of those autumn days, warm, bug-free, without a cloud. There's a heavy joy that comes at the end of the growing season, when the air is still as time holds its breath, waiting for us to catch up with all changing things.

I'm eager to have Lina's help to plant the garlic before she leaves at the end of the month. We weed this summer's potato beds, loosen the soil with the fork, and rake the surface smooth. Then we mark off seven rows in each bed, running the handle of the rake along the soil to make a line we can follow. We push the large cloves into the ground with thumb and index finger along this line. After each row I run my hands over the crumbly earth and cover the cloves until the bed is completely planted. We cover all five beds with straw and when Lina and I are finished it has the same satisfying effect as seeing dry cordwood, split and stacked against the cabin.

She and I lie on the grass in the sun, no longer concerned about ticks or mosquitoes or blackflies. There's brilliant sunshine to soak up, as if we are storing warmth for winter as red squirrels store fat. Her black hair is shiny in the sun and warm on my palm that cups her head. I lean toward her and whisper in her ear.

"I knew at the beginning it was going to be hard to love you. I just didn't know how hard."

She squeezes my hand. "Do you keep all your letters?"

I keep most of them.

"I'm thinking of burning mine and burying the ashes under a tree."

I face her and look into the black eyes of a stranger. It's awkward, as if I haven't hugged her, slept with her, and loved her intensely.

"You're going to have a hard winter," Lina says.

There are pieces of me that I have left in her care with an uncertain future. Envelopes tucked in her backpack, slips of paper I've written notes on folded into her journal.

"I saw a black wasp nest over there at shoulder height. They want to be sure to be above the snow."

"How about I get through the fall first?"

A crow glides down, wings folded in, to land on the straw of one of the garlic beds. It expresses a curve from crown through rump and down its tail. Its feathers glisten in the light and are luscious, black and sleek like the head on my arm. I stroke Lina's hair as if my hand is running along its smooth and glossy back as it hops on the straw we have spread out. It caws as more crows fly overhead.

"Hey," she says softly. I look at her again. "You should know I think you're a good lover."

My consolation prize. "When are you leaving?"

"He's coming to pick me up the day after tomorrow. Early."

The weight of her head on my arm annoys me. I wish she would pull it away, but fear she will. I could float away myself, to grow wings and fly over the garlic beds with their straw blankets, but my feet are leaden and my heart is leaden and I have no wings.

The crow pecks at the straw, looking for bugs without much effort, then flies up into the trees. It cries again, arcing its back and tilting its beak to the sky. Then it takes off to the west into the spruce woods to join others.

I am looking past the time that Lina is gone. I learned years ago that if I had a long distance to walk I only needed to keep my feet moving and, in time, I'd get there. If I was sick in bed, I ignored the milestones of recovery—the cessation of puking, the headache going away—and focused on two or three days in the future. I knew that time kept moving and that things would get better. I learned to use sleep as a way to pass time. When Dad and I were driving a long distance I would fall asleep imagining supper as the sun was setting and the car was parked. After he died I used sleep as a diversion from stress and a place where sadness didn't follow me. I was like that breed of goat—bred to protect more expensive livestock by acting as a decoy to predators — that falls unconscious at any sudden sound. Clap your hands and the stress makes them fall down and go to sleep. But I can't do it anymore; I keep waking up.

While I'm lying there in the quiet, with a heavy head on my arm and crows flying away, a rifle shot explodes from the woods close behind the cabin. I'm on my feet fast but frozen in place. Someone shouts in distress. I run toward the sound, crashing over fallen debris, ducking the low branches of spruce.

"Where are you?" I yell.

I follow the voice, aware of Lina's footsteps behind me, deeper into the forest. I find Art propped against the trunk of a maple. Blood soaks through his pant leg. Drops of red are sprinkled on the brown and gold leaves carpeting the ground around him as if they have been flicked from the end of a paint brush. The .30-30 rests a few feet from him.

"Seems I shot myself," he says with a lopsided grin.

He's been hit somewhere below the knee. I lift his pant leg and feel faint. The bullet has entered the boniest part of his ankle, shattering it. The white of bone contrasts with all the blood and flayed flesh. I pull off my shirt and tie it around his ankle. Lina applies pressure to staunch the bleeding.

"You're damn lucky you didn't aim above your knee," I say, "or we'd be leaving you here for the coyotes."

I pretend it isn't serious, as much to calm my nerves as to reassure him and keep him from going into shock.

"I saw the flash of a buck's white ass over there." He points lamely. "I lifted the gun and it went off."

"Too bad you didn't forget your shells this time, huh?"

"How bad is it?"

I'm sure he's seen far worse during the war. "Do you think you can stand on your good leg and we'll get you out of here?"

I haul him up, his arm around my shoulder. We hobble and skip out of the woods like two drunks in a three-legged race. Lina follows us with his rifle. We get him into the cabin and I run next door to Jen and Martin's place. It feels good to be moving over so much ground so quickly. It's as if I haven't run in years. I find Jen in the house and she drives me and Art to Soldier's Memorial Hospital in Middleton.

Lina is gone by the time I get home. Maybe she's at Chucko's. I roll a smoke and sit on my stone wall facing the garden. Dead brown things and dirt. The wind blows the hair away from my face. A pileated woodpecker makes its monkey screech from a treetop nearby. The big bird swoops out of the tree, making an arc down, then back up to a dying fir tree at the edge of the garden. It cocks its head, turning its eye to the trunk to see any tiny movement. I don't know where the woodpeckers spend spring and summer, but it's in the fall that I see them. They fly away at the sight of me but their shyness belies their true nature; they are feisty birds and I see in them the grit and resourcefulness of the Nova Scotians I've come to know.

Nova Scotia ain't for sissies.

35

Benny picked up the stack of glass petri dishes and held the uppermost one to the fluorescent light above her. She smiled. Scattered on the plate were hundreds of tiny colonies of *Pseudomonas*, transformed and surviving the lethal dose of vancomycin in the agar medium on which they grew. The cells could only be growing if they had taken up her recombinant plasmid and were expressing the antibiotic-resistance gene. The transformation had worked. The gene conferring the ability to digest PETE was piggybacking the vancomycin-resistance gene. These transformed, genetically altered bacteria should be capable of eating plastic. The glass plates had colonies too, cells containing the polystyrene-digesting gene.

She put the plates back in the incubator, closed the door, and walked back to her bench. She wanted to test her creation right away but would have to wait for liquid cultures of cells to grow. She made liquid media to grow the cells in and sterilized the flasks in the autoclave. She checked the petri plates again on her way home, though she knew they couldn't have grown any larger in that short time.

Three days later she analyzed a crude extract of the transformed cells for enzyme activity. She crushed some cells to release their contents and mixed that with a piece of a soda bottle she'd cut up. She left that for an hour, then performed chromatography on the reaction mix. There was a peak characteristic of ethylene glycol, one of the products she expected of esterase digestion. The transgenic esterase enzyme could digest PETE; the ethylene glycol would be, in turn, a source of carbon for the bacteria.

Benny left the lab early and took a vial of cells home. She found one of Annika's water bottles in the garbage under the sink. She poured the cell slurry onto the bottle and left it in the sink. She couldn't sleep. What had been theoretical to her, an imagined vista beyond the next hill, was now spread out before her. Her creations would divide ceaselessly, driven by the blind need of their DNA to reproduce. Once released there would be no stopping them. No antibiotic could kill all *Pseudomonas*. It was capable of reproducing every hour and was found on every human body, on countless other animals, and in the soil of every continent.

After waiting for sleep she turned on the light and read. That took her mind off her work and she dozed. A car backfiring — or possibly a gunshot — woke her at 4:30 and she couldn't get back to sleep. She rose and dressed for a run. She went to the kitchen to get a glass of water and saw the bottle in the sink. It had melted. The little plastic that remained around the cap was slimy to her touch. She put the glass on the counter. She had stopped breathing. This was going to work and a lot of people were going to be angry. She must not be caught. She needed a smokescreen so that once she released the bacteria they could not be traced to her.

She threw what remained of the bottle in the trash, tied a knot in the bag, and took it with her when she left the apartment to throw down the garbage chute.

Her run began in the dark and the cool of the night brushed against her skin as she moved. By the time she headed home from the park the sun had risen. It was going to be a hot day. She showered and rushed to the lab. It was too early for Leach to be there. For the few days she had left in the city, Benny had decided to work when the lab was most likely to be empty.

She needed a lot of bacteria to release and she wanted them in powder form. In the absence of water the cells would be able to survive but could not metabolize or divide. For the past week she had grown liquid cultures of them, spun and washed the cells with distilled water, centrifuged the solutions to concentrate them, and desiccated the cells to remove all moisture. She poured the powdered cells into glass vials, capped them, and put them in a pocket of her backpack hanging on a hook on the wall.

Once water was added to this biologically inert powder, metabolism in the cells would resume, digestion of the plastic was possible, carbon would be released from the enzymatic degradation of the plastic, and the cells would begin dividing. The daughter cells would digest more of the plastic, providing more carbon for other cells. A chain reaction would begin, one she hoped might never stop.

There was a bit of powder left in the tube she had used to desiccate the cells. She was about to throw it in the garbage when she stopped. An impulse to mess with Leach gripped her even though she knew it was unwise. She added a few drops of water to the tube and pulled a swab from her shelf. She opened the incubator in the hall that held Leach's experimental plates and swiped the bottom of two of his plates with the mixture of cells before leaving the lab.

Benny was back in the lab early the next morning when she heard the outer hall door open. Then the magnetic fastener on the door of one of the incubators in the hall clicked shut. She heard Leach's voice over the hum of the fan in the fume hood.

"Who's been fucking with my plates?" He addressed the corridor with the arrogance of the omnipotent, knowing he would be heard, assuming whoever heard would care. Leach's footsteps approaching Benny's bench signalled the definite end of peace. She considered hiding under her desk, but that would make her look guilty.

"Look at these plates. It looks like someone's put them on something hot."

"That's weird," she said.

He threw one of his petri dishes onto her bench. The plastic was thin enough in places that the agar seeped through and left a trail of slime where it skidded across the surface.

"Look at this."

Benny didn't move.

"They're all like that. Every damn plate in the incubator."

"Looks like they've been melted on something."

"I can see that. Shit."

Benny put a latex glove on and picked up the plate. As she squeezed gently to hold it, the plastic gave way and her fingers went through the plate. Leach threw the plate in the garbage can by her side, turned, and strode out of the lab to his office. She followed him. He wore a short-sleeved shirt tucked into his pleated pants. He took his fedora off his balding head and hung it on a hook on the back of the door.

"I'm going home for a couple of weeks," Benny announced.

Leach picked up a reprint of a journal paper from his desk and, without lifting his eyes from it, said, "It's hardly an appropriate time for you to leave, Ben, right after you've decided to switch thesis projects."

"I have family business to attend to."

He dropped down in his chair. "Someone who wanted to succeed would buckle down after a setback and get right back at it. A certain maxim about getting back on the horse springs to mind." He began sorting his piles of notes and journals.

She forced a smile. "And that's what I'll do when I get back. I've been going through a lot lately and I need a break. This trip will give me time to clear my head, analyze my project, and come back refreshed."

"Suit yourself. I have to admit you're a hard worker and you haven't taken any time off for a while. Let me tell you, though, that success in research comes not only from hard work. You've got to have inspiration and mental agility as well." He tapped his temple with an index finger. "I suggest you use this little holiday as an opportunity to be creative. Come up with some novel ideas for experiments you want to do when you get back."

"I'll see you in two weeks." She turned to leave.

"Oh, before you go, see Jon and go over the maps of the plasmid construct you gave him. He's having trouble getting the esterase cassette out of it."

The trouble was that *she* didn't give it to Jon and, ergo, she wasn't able to explain that he was probably using the wrong restriction enzymes to remove the fragment he wanted.

Back at her desk she leaned over her binders and found the pages with the schematics of the circular DNA constructs she had made. The images were concise and spare. She pulled the map out of her binder and put it on Jon's desk with a note explaining how to extract the esterase cassette.

She returned to her desk and went through her notebooks, flipping through sheets and sheets of raw data. She would not miss the lab once she was gone. Not the experiments, nor many of the people she had worked beside for the past three years. She wouldn't miss the smell of the caged mice down the hall, a smell of fear, not hope. She wouldn't miss seminars, like the one in which that benighted scientist from Cambridge had described her work infecting cats with herpes simplex virus by scarifying their eyes. No cure was worth torturing cats and mice. It was like arguing that inventing, then using, the atom bomb was justified because it ended the war and diminished suffering. Any evil that entered the world contaminated the world. That sort of thing—the mice, unethical experimentation—was of no use to her. She only ever had one purpose; the rest was a distraction. The lab had outlived its use to her and now she was ready to be far from it.

She pulled out all the pages related to her plastics digestion work and stuffed them into her backpack. She went to the freezers in the hall, removed the DNA samples and bacteria that were hers, and put them in her backpack too. Once she had disposed of all this, she would have her smokescreen; all signs pointed to Jonathan as the one working on this project. He was the only one with data, the only one in possession of DNA samples. Benny took the capped vials of desiccated cells from the pack and put them in the pocket of her pants.

Leach and Jon knew it was her, but if things got bad they wouldn't be able to convince the authorities of it. And by then she would be long gone.

When she left for the last time, Leach's office door was closed. Gabe's door was open, as always, and he was sitting on the couch, his feet on a chair, reading. She smiled at him and he waved. Benny walked partway up the street before turning to take one last look at the building. It was as beautiful as the first time she'd seen it, solid and immovable. She heard a high-pitched cry and, looking toward the top of the building, saw a falcon circling.

She took the stairs in her building to the fifteenth floor and went to the garbage room. It smelled of rotting food. The handle of the chute was greasy. She turned her pack upside down and shook its contents into the shaft where they clattered to the ground, echoing against its metal sides as they fell. She opened the door, looking left and right, and went to her apartment.

She poured a glass of water and drained it. She reached into her pants pocket to remove the vials of desiccated bacteria. One each of bacteria capable of digesting polystyrene, nylon, and PETE. She turned the faucet on again so that it dripped, then she added a few drops of water to each vial, sealed them, and shook the contents. She put them back in her pocket.

She left her apartment and walked up 70th Street. She passed the Lebanese lunch place where she got her falafels, the deli beside it, and the newsstand where she bought her Sunday *Times*. An ambulance stuttered down the clogged street, its siren wailing impotently. She saw the people on the street anew, really noticed each face, as if she were moving in slow motion. She turned right onto First Avenue and went into

The Food Emporium. She pulled the vials of recombinant bacteria from her pocket. She selected the right one, putting the other two back, and opened it. Her index finger felt the mud of cells, brought out a clump, and touched plastic soda bottles of every brand and size she could find. Two-litre bottles of cola, ginger ale, seltzer, root beer, cream soda, and tonic water. Smaller bottles of cherry-this and grape-that, and all the brands of water she could reach. All of them manufactured from PETE. Tomorrow she would know if she had been successful.

The next morning, Benny ate some toast, then filled her backpack with underwear, socks, two T-shirts, her toothbrush, and the sweater she had borrowed from Leroy. She spent the morning going through her belongings. She would leave it all behind except the letters—from her father, among others—that she'd carried with her from Newton to Lowell to New York. They fit in a shoebox. She taped the box shut, addressed it to herself where she was going, and put it in her backpack. She threw out her papers, her journals, and clothes she no longer needed.

She slung her pack over one shoulder. Leroy was stepping out of his apartment as her door closed. He seemed ready to ignore her. She said hello and he looked up. She asked him to go to the roof with her.

They walked to the end of the hallway, up the stairs, and out onto the gravel of the roof of their building. The city hummed with a combination of air conditioners, traffic, and elevator fans. A fat bumblebee flew around them twice and continued east toward the hospital.

"Where'd he come from?" Leroy said. He was smiling. "I miss being among trees and stars. I don't belong here."

He told her about watching a moose cross the road in Fundy National Park, the Northern Lights above a stony beach off the coast of BC, the thrill of sheet lightning across a lake at night. He talked as if he needed to get out all the things he hadn't told her since they fought.

"My three years here have almost fooled me into believing that I can find whatever I need within a few blocks."

The city had done its best to trick him into believing that any other place he chose to live would be second-rate. He had lost perspective by being immersed in it, the way fish don't know they live in water. He had been swimming in its cavernous streets. He had been drowning in the lights, the food, and the smells, as well as the endless flow of people on the street.

"I've spent too much time indoors, in a toxic, chemically infested, airless room, with people who are stressed and overworked. Most of what we do only adds to a heap of useful facts. I belong where there are trees and Northern Lights and no Irish pub for a hundred miles."

"Where will you go when you're done?" she asked.

"Home."

She felt his arm reach around her and rest on her shoulder. Though they were looking at the same view, she thought the light, the cabs going up First, and the man hosing down the sidewalk below them were the kinds of things she would miss about living there if she never saw it again.

She kissed him on the cheek and they left the roof.

*

What Benny found at The Food Emporium when she left the roof was beyond her expectations. She stood at the end of the aisle listening to a conversation the store manager was having with one of his employees. The two men stood in the aisle looking at the brown liquid dripping off the shelves onto the floor where it joined an ever-expanding puddle.

"I stacked them the way I always do, sir."

"Well, how the hell do you figure they exploded then?"

"I read on a website that Coke cleans rust off cars," the clerk said. "You can use it as radiator fluid. It cleans toilets. Maybe they sent us a defective batch and it's melting the bottles."

"It's not just Coke, pal. It's everything on the shelf." The manager walked away, calling over his shoulder, "Get a mop and clean it up."

Benny saw that the clerk was Jason. Their eyes locked as they passed each other. She shouldn't have come back. A mother with her child sitting in the cart approached him and he looked away from Benny. The mother lifted her feet, marching in place, watching them come unstuck from the floor.

"Everything's sticky. All I want is some root beer."

"There's cans at the end of this aisle," Jason said.

Benny rushed out of the store. She put her hand in her pocket and rolled the vials of nylon-digesting and polystyrene-digesting *Pseudomonas* between her fingers. Once she felt them click together, like a talisman, she began to run. She knew where she could hide. She was afraid to take the subway, afraid to be below ground with no escape. She ran south, dodging cabs and the traffic of the late-afternoon rush hour. Her pack jostled against her back and she cinched the waist strap tighter.

The intersections and their red lights kept hemming her in. She passed a post office on the way, ducked in to mail her shoebox of letters, and continued her run downtown.

By the time she got to the Lower East Side it was getting dark. She was jogging now, almost where she wanted to be. She walked down Second Avenue, past a grocer with signs in Russian and Ukrainian, a fish 'n' chips place, Thai, Mexican, and Italian restaurants. There were signs in Spanish too. She was passing the world on the street. There were punks, street people talking to themselves, an Asian guy delivering groceries on his one-speed bike, and a cabbie yelling in French at the driver of an another cab blocking his way. Across the avenue, two monks in robes were helping a man lying on the street as an ambulance pulled up. She turned west on 6th, went past the church, and rang Rachel's doorbell.

The two women stood facing each other. Benny caught her breath.

"I made a mistake."

Rachel made a come-here motion with both of her hands and Benny fell into her arms. They stood in the hall, hugging, not saying anything. Then Rachel led her up to her room.

36

Forest Garden

A week later the morning is bleak, grey and cold, as I bike down the hill to visit Art in the hospital. He is lying with his foot bandaged and raised. He's dopey from the morphine they've given him.

"I'm glad you came back. I'm going crazy in here. There's too much time to think."

The man in the next bed is in great pain, lying on his back and groaning.

"What's his story?" I whisper.

"The big C. His stomach."

The man's wife sits in a chair by the bed complaining about a sandwich she ate on her way to visit him.

"Just some old dark brown chicken and mayonnaise. I hate that. I left your suitcase in the car. I saw no need of dragging that thing in here until I see where they're going to put you."

Art shakes his head. "If she doesn't shut up about that chicken sandwich I may throw up."

I pull up a chair by his bed.

"My ankle's killing me. I'm going to go mad in this place. I may tie a helium balloon to my prick and sail over the mountain, waving, 'Here I am!' Take my mind of it, will you?"

37

New York City

The wall at the foot of Rachel's bed was bathed with golden light in the morning. Rachel's pyjama bottoms and T-shirt lay on the pillow beside Benny's head. They smelled lemony like Rachel's skin and were warm against her cheek. The tinny voice on the clock radio butted up against the softness of that pile of clothes.

What started with soda bottles at The Food Emporium on First Avenue had spread, first to other neighbourhood stores, then to far-flung ones all over the city and beyond. Unlike Frankenstein's solo creation, lonely and hopelessly searching for a mate, Benny's were capable of creating themselves in their own image. They ceaselessly divided into identical daughter cells. They replicated without tiring, like machines on an assembly line, while humans fed them. People had extracted what was imagined to be an endless supply of oil, converted it to plastic, and distributed it throughout the world. To the bacteria this was food in clothing, cars, and computers. Food on the scrubbed-clean cruise ship, food under the grime of the city, and food in landfills, under sinks, on our backs. A neighbour's pacemaker, the telephone line, lunch bags, paraffin wax on store-bought tomatoes. There was food for Benny's creations wherever they roamed.

She burrowed into the sheets, bringing them up against her face, inhaling Rachel in her absence. She figured she would be all right if she didn't move from that bed. The reporter told of windshield wipers smearing slime trails of decomposing PETE on the glass and eyeglass lenses melting like crayons left out in the sun.

When she finally got out of bed, she went to the bank that held the inheritance from her father and directed them to transfer all funds to Rachel's Citibank account in four weeks.

38

Forest Garden

On my bike ride up the mountain after visiting Art at the hospital, I stop to fill my backpack with large, scabby apples from a wild tree by the side of the road. They will make fine applesauce once I cook them and squeeze the pulp through the food mill.

I see what Lina and I have accomplished when I pass between the ash trees into the clearing. The path leads to my cabin, and from my cabin to her tent, and it shows that we are married to this land. The two of us created something from nothing more than dreams and effort. We have eaten simple meals of rice and olive oil, peas, cut chives, onions, and garlic. We worked hard every day until light failed, night fell, and then we dreamed some more.

Yet it is all so fragile. August, laughing with the land's gift of tomatoes, onions, carrots, and blueberries, has passed. November is over there scolding me for thinking that such bounty could continue.

Lina is singing in the cabin. She's stayed a week longer than she had planned to spend some time with Art. But now she is packing her stuff and intends to leave early tomorrow morning.

"How is he?" she asks.

"He would've liked to have seen you one last time. Where were you last night?"

"Don't go there now." She lays a hand on my arm.

I leave the cabin and go to the garden wall for a smoke to let her finish. The chokecherry standing sentinel over the garlic beds has lost all its leaves.

We eat supper in the last of the afternoon light, enjoying the heat radiating from the stove. She rises after we eat and it's as if I am seeing her for the first time.

"I have something for you in my tent," she says.

She has always been slow and graceful, but now there is something careful about her movement. Can this be the same woman I once lay with above that waterfall, naked on the ledge, the two of us slippery as perch, watching water pour over us, sheets of liquid ice?

I don't know if what I feel is love or fear.

When she returns she is carrying a canvas, two feet wide and four feet tall. She hands it to me and I turn it around.

It is the finished painting of me she started the first day I met her at Art's. It's like the others I saw in her studio last summer. My face is blurry but recognizable with its large nose, two blue smudges where the eyes are, and sharp chin softened with smeared paint. The floppy hat is gone. Taking its place are the talons of a falcon, gripping a branch of my dark hair. The bird is painted precisely, perfectly in focus. Its one chocolate eye, staring from the canvas at me from its turned head, is alert as the bird spreads its steel-coloured wings to take off. Its beak mirrors the nose on the face below but is sharp-edged, piercing. What surprises me most about the portrait is the beatific smile on my face, a look I believe I haven't possessed for a long time. I am unperturbed by this bird on my head, content with wherever I am.

"Do I really look like that?"

"Sometimes, yes."

I hug her. When she leaves to return to her tent I walk partway with her, not wanting the illusion of our union to end. The moon hasn't risen yet. Venus and Jupiter are up there. A barred owl couple calls to each other in an otherwise quiet forest. *Who cooks for you? Who cooks for you-u-u?* We kiss goodnight for the last time, and as I turn for home, Thunder's steps reverberate on the ground as she runs by me and through the open door. She is my cat now. I stop. The stars are brighter than usual, the air cool, no breeze. Peaceful and silent. Lina has stopped to look up as well. She calls back to me.

"See that V of stars by Leo?"

I do.

"It's calling to you."

I hear it.

"It's telling you that you belong here."

I know it is.

"You know I love you, don't you?" she calls.

All I can do is nod. At times like this I am learning to have faith in my ability to become a monk. I climb into my bunk and open the small window behind my head. I am in my sleeping bag, tucked inside four blankets, while outside the owls call. *Who cooks for you? Who cooks for you-u-u?*

October 25.

The painting leaning against the wall startles me when I wake. That falcon takes me back. The anniversary of a death is like the point that a snail shell coils around year after year as it grows. The point becomes more distant, enfolded deeper within layers of living and forgetfulness, but it's always there at the centre of everything. You spiral through life, coming each year to the date where memory plays out those long-distant events, and more than likely you still don't understand. You continue to digest memory, trying to understand what happened so you can forget it. At least that's the way it is for me.

Most of the time I live a well-bounded life, striving to con-strain change and make each day like the preceding one. That's how I maintain the illusion of stability and security I so desperately seek in this chaotic world. But then today comes along, Lina leaves, probably for good, and that illusion is revealed as a fraud. I am separated from routine, floating in the present. There is no such thing as stability.

It is time for me to let go.

Chucko's piece-of-crap car stutters to a halt on the road and doors open and slam shut. There is laughter. I consider not getting up. Lina taps on the cabin door and opens it. Thunder jumps from the bed to greet her. Lina speaks quietly to her and scratches her ear.

She comes to the bed and kisses me. I am gripping my cheek with my teeth so that I almost draw blood. We walk together to the road and put her pack in the back seat. I try not to look at Chucko.

"Will you see Art?" I say.

"We'll go by the hospital on our way through town."

The love she and I shared this summer was like that ball I used to shoot against the garage door back home. There was a moment when time stopped, when we both recognized that love existed, and then it was gone. She asked me to marry her; I was afraid. After that instant, our trajectory took us away from that door, into new territory. The love was gone.

She hugs me and gets in beside Chucko. Then the engine turns over and the yellow car moves away from me. They sputter along Lily Lake Road and go up the little hill at the end of my property. She is turned around in the passenger seat to wave to me through the rear window and then the taillights disappear from sight between the two banks of trees.

39

New York City

Rachel stood in front of her bedroom mirror, a red lipstick in her hand, colouring her lips. She buttoned her green silk blouse.

"He's going to jump your bones as soon as you walk through the door," Benny said.

"The way you cock-tease him I wouldn't doubt it."

Benny laughed and got off the bed from where she was watching Rachel dress in front of the mirror for her date with Leroy. Benny reached around her waist and hugged her from behind. Rachel turned her head and kissed Benny.

"Do you mind me going to see him?" Rachel said.

"He's a good guy."

"Please come with me."

"It's you he wants to see."

Rachel took her wallet out of the top drawer of her dresser and put it in her back pocket.

"I'll see you later." They kissed again. Rachel was at the door.

"Rachel?"

She turned around.

"You're a good friend," Benny said. "I'll miss you."

"I won't be late coming home."

After Rachel left the apartment, Benny found a pair of scissors in the kitchen and chopped her hair ragged. Then she dyed it black like Rachel's. She phoned United and used her credit card to buy a one-way ticket to Seattle out of Newark for the next day, to throw people off her trail. She sat down at Rachel's desk and wrote a letter to Leroy:

> *My dear friend,*
>
> *This is the way the world ends. At least for us. It's not the end I had in mind. You've been a good friend and you deserve better than what you got from me. I'm sorry I lied to you. Rachel knows about my genetic disorder. Ask her. Maybe then you'll understand why I never loved you like you deserve. Maybe not. I think you two would be good together.*
>
> *I'm leaving. I've done what I needed to do. It's been heartening to have such a cheerleader as you this past year. Kick ass in Gabe's lab.*
>
> *love,*
> *Ben*

She would mail it on the way to Penn Station. On another scrap of paper she wrote, *I can't keep running. I have to stop.* She folded it and wrote *Rachel* on it. She ruffled through Rachel's drawers and found her passport beneath her underwear. She left the note for Rachel where the passport had been and went to the bathroom mirror to compare her new look with the photo in the passport. She thought it would do. She opened the medicine cabinet and found a travel sewing kit. She put it, along with the passport, in her backpack.

She hesitated at the door, wanting more of a goodbye than she had time for. Better to stop thought and, she hoped, feeling and get on with her journey.

At Penn Station she caught a bus to Newark airport, then had a cab take her to the Port Newark terminal on the waterfront. She waited until the driver was out of sight and walked to the offices of Maersk. They had a container ship leaving that night, bound for Göteborg via Halifax, to deliver empty containers that were to be refilled with lumber and returned to the States. Maersk took on the occasional passenger willing to pay for the luxury of a cabin smelling of bleach and paint, both of which were meant to cover up the scent of vomit, urine, and diesel that pervaded the ship. She bought passage with them to Göteborg and was told to come back at six to board.

She went down to the waterfront, an industrial wasteland that looked over Newark Bay into Bayonne, hoping to catch a glimpse of the city she was leaving. She couldn't see it. Clouds had covered the sun at her back, but the sky was a deep blue near the horizon to the east, where she was headed. A light wind brought the smell of sea water, diesel exhaust, and a complex mixture of industrial chemicals to her.

At six she boarded the ship and went to her cabin to stow her backpack before returning to the deck to watch their progress out of the harbour. The clouds had made their way over Newark and it was drizzling. A tug piloted them through the Kill Van Kull and into Upper Bay. Off the port side in the distance was the Statue of Liberty and the Manhattan skyline. The tug pulled the ship slowly through the Narrows and under the Verrazano-Narrows Bridge. In place of the huffing and pounding feet she and Rachel had heard the previous November was the whirr of cars and trucks crossing into Brooklyn. Then came the myriad streets of Staten Island on the ship's starboard and Coney Island and lower Brooklyn on her port side and they were beyond the New York she knew. The tug left them at Ambrose Seabuoy and the ship continued east, then north, on its way to Halifax.

The foaming water of the ship's wake was creamy like the head on a pint of stout, leaving a trail in the black that could have stretched all the way back, under the Verrazano-Narrows Bridge, to the island that had been her home. It wasn't too late for her to follow it back to her neighbourhood pub and sit with a beer in front of her. Benny tried to focus on one spot and to allow the foam to pass through it, but her eyes kept drifting toward the stern as if they could find what had been lost.

The water seemed to be inviting her home, to let go and sink into its embrace. What was preventing her from dropping into its arms, allowing it to swallow her? If someone wanted to drown, if she chose to jump over the rail into the cold, cold water, it wouldn't be hard at all. It would be easy to climb over the low railing. She imagined the water's pressure, like hands cradling her on all sides. She wouldn't have to fight. She could rest in the water, like one lost in a winter storm lying in the snow and giving in to the desire for delicious sleep.

The breeze bit into her and she knew she was wrong. Jumping would be easy, being in the water would not be.

The sea was cold, and that cold would hammer spikes into her hands and feet. Her extremities would be the first to feel it as blood was diverted to her trunk to keep her core temperature from falling. Her lips would become two blue lines within minutes and she would fight it all the way. Then her legs and arms would grow listless. She would struggle right to the end, Isaac wrestling with the angel in the desert. She would want her heart to stop before she slipped under. She gripped the railing for protection—from what? From herself?

Benny shuddered and left the deck of the ship with its stacks of rusty containers standing rigid like sentries in the drizzle and wind. At the commissary she bought a sandwich. A slice of cheese and a limp leaf of lettuce glued with mayonnaise and margarine to two slices of white bread. She wanted a cup of tea but turned away when she saw the pile of Styrofoam cups. The feel of the squeaky plastic against her fingertips and lips would take any enjoyment out of it. She took her sandwich and found a seat. One of the Filipino crew, shorter than she was and looking not much more than a teenager, smiled at her as he smoked a cigarette.

40

Forest Garden

Lina's been gone five days. I have a doctor's appointment for a test I need done. So I bike down the hill to the hospital to see Art.

"Can't you explain this genetic mumbo-jumbo so an ignoramus can understand it?" Art says from his hospital bed.

"You're a far shot from ignorant, Art."

"Pish."

I'm getting to the part of the story that worries me. I don't know how Art is going to respond when I tell him. It makes me nervous to dive in, so I'm procrastinating by overwhelming him with technical details. However, my concern is premature. Before I find out how he'll react, Art detonates a bomb of his own.

"That's enough about Benny for today," he says. "I'm tired. How have you been while I've been eating all these delicious hospital meals?"

"I'm blue about Lina leaving me."

He says something under his breath I can't make out.

"What'd you say?"

"I said," he continues, raising his voice, "that you don't deserve her."

He's never been overly polite, but it seems that his ankle wound has made him surly.

"What are you talking about? I was nothing but good to her."

"Son, you don't know beans from bananas," he says. "It's not about who leaves who. It's about having faith in your woman."

He and I have become close over the past two years, but this time my mood is dark enough that I am not going to placate him. We're like two bull moose in the fall. I ask what he knows about it.

"I've been married to the same woman for fifty-nine years. I know Lina too. She's honest about who she is. She never tried to mask who she is or how she loves. Like I say, she deserves to be trusted."

"She lived with you for a couple of months and grew flowers. You didn't love her and have her break your heart."

He looks at me as if he has something to say and is weighing whether to say it.

"What?"

"Louise would understand. She knew I was always faithful to her even with my roving eye. She knew I wouldn't leave her. But we're dealt a hand and we have to play it or go home. I've always chosen to play it."

"I have no idea what you're talking about."

"No, I don't suppose you'd care to." It is so quiet I can hear him breathing. "Ah, well, it's river under the bridge. She's gone off with another man, hasn't she, leaving both of us behind."

"Thanks for reminding me."

He lies there thinking, deciding whether to continue. Then he says it. He says it and he might as well have got out of the bed and whacked me upside the head with his crutch.

"You don't know what you had. I missed her touch after she found you. She's so gentle for someone as strong as she is."

I can barely hear my own voice. "What?"

He doesn't say another word. He turns to the window and looks out at the bare branches of the maple. I could hurt him, say something that he'll feel. Yet all I see is a hobbled stranger in a bed. I get up and leave the room, not looking back, and bike home up the mountain.

Maybe I've been a fool telling him Benny's story. In any case, there are parts of it he doesn't need to know.

41

At Sea

Benny spent the next two days in her cabin. The smell of oil paint and diesel were stuck in her nose. She could taste the fumes. The last night, as the ship approached land, Benny sewed a pocket on the inside of Leroy's sweater and put Rachel's passport in it. Then she sewed the pocket shut and pulled on the sweater. Her clothes were on the chair at the foot of her bunk. Her journal lay closed on the pillow where she'd tossed it. The door clicked shut behind her as she made her way to the deck. There was a twenty-foot walkway with a railing on the port side of the ship. The stars glittered above a dark mass of land in the distance.

This is what he must have felt right before he died.

She shivered and wrapped her arms around herself. The door opened at the other end of the deck. It was the crewman she had met. He was the only person she'd talked to since boarding the ship. She walked toward him, landing one foot ahead of the other, the soles of her shoes slapping against the bumpy metal of the deck. As they passed he touched his hat brim and looked into Benny's eyes. She kept walking, turned to look at him, put one hand on the rail, and vaulted into the sea.

When she hit the water, the cold gave her a headache, sharp and throbbing. Her hands went to her face, but soon she couldn't feel them. When she surfaced the crewman was shouting for help, then there were more people shouting. An alarm bell sounded, six short rings followed by a long one. Then, broadcast in a rich baritone for all the ship to hear, a disembodied voice called, "Emergency stations, emergency stations. Man overboard."

A beacon above the bridge flashed on and off. A searchlight scanned the choppy darkness of the sea.

The waves lapped against her, threatening to take what breath she had left. As she was raised on a wave, a Zodiac was being lowered over the ship's side. It sped away from the ship followed by a searchlight. She descended into the trough, and by the time she had been lifted once again, she was turned around and the ship was not in sight. She caught the searchlight combing the surface out of her peripheral vision. She saw the ship once more and then all that was left was the lapping of water against itself.

42

Forest Garden

I have avoided Art since he told me about him and Lina. He has left the hospital and gone home. Jen says his ankle wound is not healing well and he has aged quickly. My anger remains—at him? At Lina?—I hardly know. I decide to go to him nevertheless. We have unfinished business.

When I arrive, he tells me that he's been up all night with incredible pain. He hasn't been eating much. I catch him grimacing as he gets up from his chair on the way to the bathroom.

"You better take me back to the hospital."

"What is it?"

"My ankle."

He lifts his pant leg. His ankle is the colour of boiled lobster guts.

I've never seen it, but the word **gangrene** is written in bold letters in front of me. I retch. Obviously the antibiotics are no longer working. I help him up and put my arm under his to hold him. We hobble to his pickup and I drive him back to Soldier's Memorial. The emergency room resident is the doctor who did my test the last time I was here. She winks at me as if to acknowledge that we're complicit in a secret, then complains to us that she's exhausted from being in her thirty-seventh straight hour of work. We ease him into a wheelchair. She squats to examine his ankle and foot.

"This does not look good, Mr. Mosher," she says, aiming for nonchalant but hitting way wide of the mark. "What happened to his shunt?" She throws me a wide-eyed look.

"What shunt?" I say.

"It's almost gone."

"It broke," Art says.

"When did this happen?"

"After my last visit here."

The polystyrene shunt delivering the antibiotic cocktail to his leg is almost disintegrated. The doctor pulls on it and it snaps easily. She orders more blood work and waits for the results. Then she tells me to go home and come back tomorrow.

The morning is cold as I head down the mountain to see him. When I enter the room he's propped up in his bed, another IV tube taped to the back of his hand. He smiles when he sees me and waves me in with his other hand.

"They tell me I've got an infection. Ha. The antibiotics aren't working."

"What are they doing about it?"

"Take a look if you want." He points to the chart at the foot of his bed.

I look at the chart. He has an MRSA infection. "Possibly vancomycin-res." He has vancomycin, linezolid, tetracycline, and trimethoprim dripping into his arm. They might as well nuke him at this point.

"And these tubes keep breaking."

The dizziness comes over me quickly. The blood drains from my face and arms as if it's leaking out my shoes onto the floor. I need to sit down. Art has a feeble smile.

"Aw, don't start crying." He laughs. "I ain't dead yet."

"Sorry. Give me a sec." I leave the room. As soon as I'm in the hall I break down, cupping a palm over my mouth to stifle the sobs. Art has an infection with a *Pseudomonas* strain that's eating the PETE tubing. I breathe deeply and return, forcing a wan smile as I go through the door.

"I need you to visit Louise," he says.

"I will."

"I like to think that she remembers," he tells me. "That the words and memories are still in there even if she can't get them out. There's a nurse at the home that told me she can still see a spark in Louise's eyes. Visit her."

"I will."

There is nobody left who really knew Art as a young man. I used to assume that death was easier for old people to accept. I believed that the pain for an eighty-year-old whose wife has all but died would be muted by all those years, one more piece of evidence that he, too, would soon be gone. But maybe it's more devastating for him to be alone, to have the only person who knew what he was like sixty years before as a boy disappear.

We sit quietly. Then he says, "Cut to the blasted chase, will ya? We don't have much more time."

—

His eyes are closed.

"Are you awake?"

They open. "Keep talking. Please."

I've been dreading this, but I can't hold out any longer. One, two, three, and then I'm running along the dock. I jump.

"When Benny was nineteen she discovered something about herself."

Art grimly nods.

The familiar abdominal pains returned when she was a junior at Lowell. This time though they didn't subside. She lay in the fetal position on her bed for days, moaning. She went to the clinic on campus. The doctor on duty was an older man. He palpated her abdomen. He told her there was a lot of mono going around campus and asked if she'd been more tired than usual. He then palpated under her ribcage, trying to determine if her liver was enlarged. It tickled at first, but then she winced and gasped.

"Your liver seems fine. I doubt it's mono. Do you have painful periods?"

She told him she had never menstruated. The doctor took his hand off Benny's abdomen and stood back from the table. He referred her to the campus gynecologist, who in turn referred her to a reproductive endocrinologist. A week later, Dr. Wilson guided Benny into his office, closed the door, and motioned for her to sit down. He asked her to disrobe. She jumped when he put his cold hand on one of her breasts and massaged it. That was only the start. By the time he was finished, he was able to write in her file:

Small breasts with little palpable breast tissue.
External genitalia appear normal. Vulva of normal
appearance. Clitoris slightly enlarged. Vagina of
normal length. Cervix present as determined by
rectal palpation.

He told her he wanted to run tests to rule out some things. An abdominal X-ray and blood work to look at her hormone levels. And he scraped the inside of her cheek to perform a karyotype of her chromosomes. Ten days later she went in for the results.

He explained that they had expected to see a fuzzy ball of chromatin in every cell, which all females have. They didn't see any fuzzy ball. They looked at the chromosomes themselves. She had one X chromosome and one Y chromosome.

Art opens his eyes. "What'd she say?"

"'That means I'm a boy, doesn't it?'"

Art whistles.

"The doctor told her that, technically, she was male. 'But you were raised a girl,' he said. 'People think of you as a woman and you look like one. Genetically, you may be male, but physiologically and socially you're female.'"

I can hear Art's breathing, laboured, rattling.

"The doctor let that sink in and then he told her what it meant for her health. Her X-rays showed a bone age of someone much younger, as well as signs of osteoporosis in her skull, spine, feet, and hands. But despite having a Y chromosome, she had developed as a female, with female genitals. She had something called gonadal dysgenesis."

"What'd she do?"

He said that there was good news and bad news. She didn't

have ovaries and that's why she wasn't producing estrogen. That explained the osteoporosis. The good news according to him was that hormone replacement therapy would correct that. She'd have to give herself a shot of estrogen every day.

"I'd hate to hear the bad news," Art says.

"He said her undeveloped gonads were likely to become cancerous and needed to be removed. So they made two small incisions in Benny's abdomen and cut out her streak gonads."

I stand up. I reach for my shirt and begin to lift it. His eyes grow wide.

"Here and here," I say, pointing to the two scars.

♀/♂

As soon as I jumped I knew it was over. My Rubicon, the cliff, the death sigh. It was the shock of the cold that changed me and made me what I am now. Like an oyster, my sex was changed by the cold water. I struggled for life. I was surrounded by frigid water, gasping for breath as wave after wave buffeted me. I didn't much care. I had been struggling all my life.

The moment she ended, just as Benny hit that cold, cold water, was the moment my life began. I have not forgotten what came before — how could I? — but I am no longer her. I am me.

Arrival. Is there ever such a pure thing? Isn't the journey, indeed all life, a constant coming and going like the tides out of which I emerged, reborn? My father had been born in Nova Scotia and here I was, coming home.

43

Forest Garden

I stand by his bed, with my shirt lifted to reveal my scars, waiting for his response.

"You?"

I nod. I'm waiting for a slap, harsh words, rejection. I try to be prepared, but it's going to kill me if he bites. He's all the family I have left. I listen to the tick of the wall clock and the sound of a television in a room down the hall. I pull my shirt down.

Once I was in the water, the shore seemed a lot farther away. I swam to a place where I could climb out. I was lucky to find a spot with smooth rocks that gradually rose out of the sea. I later found out this was Herring Cove. I took off the sweater and left it above the high tide mark in the open where someone might find it. I walked, then jogged, in an attempt to warm up.

—

In the hospital after the surgery I came out of the murk. I pushed off, hoping for the surface. I was made of stone and my muscles ached as I struggled to rise up. The first thing I heard was Dr. Wilson's voice.

"...gonads were calcified," he said. "Fortunately, there was no evidence of... We removed her fallopian tubes, to be sure. She has a hypoplastic uterus..."

Words were fluttering out of his mouth, falling to the floor around my bed. I couldn't see who he was talking to.

"...not completely developed... only three centimetres long. She'll never have children."

It was that "only three centimetres long" that made it concrete for me. I began to cry, imagining the baby I'd never have trying to wriggle inside something the size of a fava bean.

When I came up and could comprehend what he was saying, he told me what he thought was more good news. My genitals appeared quite normal and with hormone replacement I would be able to have regular periods. I would never ovulate but—and I remember thinking I was mishearing this—he said I should be able to "function adequately sexually."

Later an endocrinologist prescribed female hormones to replace those my body wasn't making. I began taking estrogen and progesterone and the changes were rapid. I had regular periods every month. My cycle was always twenty-eight days long. I had been skinny when I began jabbing a 21-gauge needle into my hip every morning. The hormones gave me boobs, raised my voice, and changed the hair on my body.

—

A thousand years later, Art reaches for my hand. He takes it in his huge mitt and rubs my fingers under his calloused palm. He motions for me to sit on the edge of his bed.

"I was working in my yard one day," he says, "slaughtering chickens, when two young fellas come up the driveway. I could tell something was up because Lucy snarled and ran up to them with her hackles up."

"Like she did with me."

"She always knows when someone fishy is coming." He grins. "They're both wearing white shirts, starched and pure as snow, with little black ties. Neat haircuts. I figured they was selling something. After our hellos the shorter one says, 'Have you heard the good news? The world is a wicked place.' Old Shorty did all the talking. 'Have you noticed how there's more violence, more wars and pestilence, and bad neighbourly feeling in the world in these modern times?' I smiled. 'You call that good news?' 'Well the good news is, the Lord sees fit to bless us sinners anyway.' I put up my hand. 'Hold on a second. Look over there.' I pointed to the bay. The sun was sparkling on the water as it set. 'Ain't that a beautiful sight?' He started to sputter again, like a rusty old lawnmower complaining, but I stopped him. 'This world's a miracle. We don't need no saving. And I sure as hell don't need yours.' Then I lifted my axe, walloped the head clean off that chicken, and watched blood spurt all over those clean white shirts."

I laugh through my tears. He stops talking and closes his eyes. His breath rasps, in, out, in, out.

"Son, the whole mess is buggered up and perfect just the way it is. We're all buggered and perfect. You included."

44

Forest Garden

I could say it this way: my consent feels like leaving home; God's grace feels like coming home; the struggle to be faithful to a call feels like being outside in the weather.
  —*An Accidental Monk*, Marylee Mitcham

It's early morning. Still dark. A gentle rain falls. Ping! Ping! on the metal roof. I'm propped against the wall with the light from a candle illuminating my book's pages. *Middlemarch* again. I've always loved Dorothea and her idealism. I root her on, hoping this time she'll make her vision manifest. But, unlike my mother, I don't identify with her. I know how to get shit done. Instead I think I'm like Casaubon, with his key to all mythologies. He had a longing to create one thing to justify his existence. I wanted to create something of value. A cleaner world, a small garden, a home.

Each night I have to make the choice between staying burrowed in blankets, hoping I can stay warm, or getting up to stoke the fire. Thunder decides she wants to go out. She is scratching on the door. Polar air wraps around my legs when I drop my bare feet on the plywood floor. I open the door and say a little prayer that the coyotes won't get her. She stands in the open doorway, tail twitching, smelling the night air. When she feels comfortable enough to leave, she bolts off the door stoop, onto the rock that is my step, and along the path. I return to bed, rolling up in my yellow and black blanket, rubbing my feet together to try to get them warm.

I miss the warmth of Lina's body in my bed. Since I stopped taking estrogen I've lost a layer of insulating fat and can't keep my feet warm. What haunts me is the way she affected all my senses. The pungent, arousing smell under her arms, her ticklishness when I nosed in there. The soft roundness of her body, the fullness of her breasts, of her belly. The way she tasted, of brine, wild, unfathomable. The smooth skin on the top of her feet and on her back. The curve of her neck, her tapered fingers. It's all gone when I open my eyes, the way I can no longer see her tent from my cabin window when I wake up.

I created all right. The patriarchs in the Sinai, or whoever told the story of Genesis for the first time, must have been tired of seeing women creating, generation upon generation, miracle after miracle, and what did those men make? Diddly-squat. They grew barley, made wine, beat each other over the head with clubs, or formed the constellations into a hunter or a lion. Big fucking deal. So they made up the story of a creator who is the ultimate man, creating a creature in his own image out of dust and spit. Then the man falls asleep, loses a rib, and Eve is born. Everywhere around them the evidence insisted that the male always came from the female.

It's the only way it could happen, but they decided to turn things upside down. It's the only way it could happen then and the only way it happens now.

The story I have been telling Art, my creation myth, is almost finished. Whether it's true or not, I can't tell. By force of repetition we come to believe the stories we relate, as a child can have a memory planted in his mind by hearing a tale repeated by his parents.

I know now what being faithful to a call means and where it leads. It means being an exile, erasing your previous life, living alone in the woods. It leads to conversing with ghosts.

The karyotype they did on me suggested, visually at least, that the Y chromosome Dad gave me is intact. But I suspected otherwise. Something had happened to it between Dad's body and mine. Scientists had discovered a gene called the sex-determining region of the Y chromosome. SRY. It's on the distal part of the short arm of the Y chromosome. When it's introduced into female mice they develop male genitals. Male mice with mutated Y chromosomes appear female. I guessed that my SRY was damaged, and Leroy's sequencing proved this.

All fetuses are female by default unless they get a signal to become male. The SRY gene is that signal, directing a fetus to develop testes instead of ovaries. If SRY is damaged or missing, the fetus remains female even if it's XY. SRY by itself is capable of transforming a female embryo into a male. Or when it's mutated, doing nothing of the sort.

I could never have had ovaries, fallopian tubes, or a normal uterus.

If my SRY gene hadn't had that transversion mutation, my embryonic gonads would have developed into testes, they would have produced testosterone, there would have been development of Wolffian ducts, and I would have had male genitals. As it is, my gonads remained primordial and will never make eggs or sperm. Gonadal dysgenesis. Swyer syndrome. One nucleotide changed and I wound up with a vagina and a small uterus by default. I looked like a girl, so they raised me as a girl. I never have felt like a girl.

Being forced into this false dichotomy did not work. My parents raised me as a girl because I looked like one. But I never felt like a girl any more than I now feel like a boy. Once I had the choice I chose this—to live as a man to everyone but Lina and now Art—because it is expedient. I was able to stop the injections, which I hated, and I changed my identity in case the bacteria I released are ever traced to who I had been in New York.

I became obsessed with gender research the winter I spent in Halifax. I learned that to pass as a female in the 1964 Olympics, athletes were given a digital exam to prove that they had a vagina and no penis. I would pass this test. By 1968, athletes had buccal smears taken, looking for two X chromosomes. After the Olympics that year, a few athletes competing as females were found to lack a second X chromosome. There were others who had XYY or XXX. They were counselled to avoid embarrassment by feigning injury and withdrawing from competition. Their athletic careers were over. The test had the illusion of being failsafe, since it was believed that all females have two, and only two, X chromosomes.

My hero that winter was a Polish sprinter, Ewa Klobukowska. She failed the test, was stripped of her Olympic medals and world record, and was barred from competing at the international level because she was XXY. Despite her female habitus, she was judged male due to that Y chromosome.

To minds that crave binary order, and the simplicity of the male–female dichotomy, the study of gender can lead to despair. They say that women with Y chromosomes and men with two Xs are abnormal. But *normal* is just a word that gets thrown around when we try to make sense of biology.

A few years after the 1968 Olympics, Klobukowska became the first man in history to give birth.

*

I'm flipping through AM stations, passing over pop songs and the near-ubiquitous fundamentalist rants. According to the pastor from the Assembly of the Righteous, syndicated out of Philadelphia, Jesus will only return once the last tree standing is cut down. Apparently, in addition to homophobia and misogyny, Jesus approves of clear-cutting. The preacher also sees the loss of plastic as a sign of God's wrath, and Armageddon around the corner. Preachers have grown even more confident about the impending Rapture with the latest stock market collapse, the difficulty of transporting goods without plastic containers, the lack of potable water in cities in the Northeast, and the blackouts. I find a news station coming out of Boston, crackling up the coast to my little radio. The lead piece involves the genetically modified bacterium responsible for the original loss of plastic. Long thought to have originated in a lab in New York, it has, they say, been traced instead to a Japanese pharmaceutical company. The US government is currently preparing a lawsuit against the company, as well as the Japanese government, claiming damages of $4 trillion. Japan's bankrupt already.

Here, food may be a problem, but at least we still have drinkable water and trees for fuel.

*

The last time I saw Art I asked him if he knew how we were related. I told him my grandfather had been Stuart Mosher and that, after he died, my grandmother and father had moved to Williamstown in western Massachusetts.

"Stuart was my second cousin. Lived in Port George as a kid. He was a few years older than me. He moved into town to work at the lumber yard. Poor sap was killed when he was twenty-seven at Dieppe. His woman was pregnant at the time."

With my father.

*

Scratching at the door wakes me again. It's Saturday morning and the sky is beginning to blue. There are only coals left in the wood stove. I hop across the cold floor in bare feet to let Thunder in where there is warmth, security, and sleep for her. I pick her up, loving the feel and perfumed smell of her cold fur. She jumps from my arms and leaps onto the bed, curls up, and looks at me. I put on cold rubber boots and go out into the garden. The pumpkin leaves lie withered and dry, revealing the orange fruit they fed all summer. The tomatoes, miraculous and lush considering the thin soil they came from, are long gone.

I take the path to the depression of grasses where Lina's tent was. The thin fingernail of moon is hovering over the spruce silhouettes in the blueing sky. Earthshine completes its circle. By tomorrow the moon will disappear for a few days. I watch the steam rise from my stream of piss as I squat. Frost covers the ground and sparkles in the air. The songbirds are all gone, the Vs of geese have headed south. The only tree with leaves is the lone beech in the garden. It hoards its dry russet leaves like an old miser counting his pennies. More than once I've been startled by footsteps as I smoke on the low wall and have turned to meet whoever is coming, only to see the small beech rustling in the breeze.

Orion is high in the sky. I've learned to associate those ten stars with the coming of winter and the killing of deer. For some of my neighbours a buck in the freezer means the difference between having enough meat for the winter and going hungry. It is too early yet for the pond in my woods to be frozen, but I look forward to the new year, when I can skate again in the woods.

I blow on the coals in the wood stove and they glow. They are hot enough that the pieces of cedar shingle I use as kindling catch quickly. I put more wood on top of them, close the door, and climb, shivering, back into bed. I light a candle by my head. The wood screeches and pops. I won't be able to sleep until the cabin is warm again. As I wait, I reach beside the bed for a letter Lina sent me from somewhere on the road in Alberta. Though I doubt she scented it on purpose, some of her rubbed off on it. I hold the paper up to my nose and breathe her in. It brings her back into my cabin as if I had returned from having sex with her in the woods and her scent was on my coat, my hands.

One Monday in the Dalhousie library, when the sun had set too early on a January afternoon and the snow piled up, I came across a clinical report of a woman who found out when she was forty-two that she had a Y chromosome. "She was married in 1954 and has functioned satisfactorily as a wife." Did they mean she gratified her husband sexually? Was she gratified sexually? It was a cryptic comment shouting at me across the decades. As I looked at my reflection in the darkened window I wondered if a normal life might be possible.

The letter relates Lina's daily activities. Places they've been, things they've seen. Her words make no sense. They use the same alphabet as the love letters she used to write to me but now they're flightless. They are like a robin lying beneath the window that stopped its flight, wing broken and fluttering, blood oozing from its beak. Was I too much of a freak for her?

There's something else I still can't understand. Why does this world provide us with everything we need to live, then bend itself on our destruction? The trend toward chaos not only destroys us, it obliterates any record of us once we're gone. Our bodies, the letters and photographs we cherish, and even our memories disappear. I try to keep the lost and the dead alive by saying their names on my living lips, but even these memories become shapeless with excessive handling. They are shards of shattered bottles, sunk to the bottom of the sea, rolled smooth by the ceaseless motion of the tides. They are sea glass, collected from a beach and put in a bottle on the sill of a sunny window to gather dust.

I see a woman in town, a stranger, and the perfume I smell, her frown and weary-eyed burden, are more real to me than the memories of my father. Yet I am compelled to talk about my dad and tell Benny's story because when they fade what does that say about *my* life?

I have sought the answers and yet the mystery remains. Linnaeus has been no help. The nuthatch clinging to the tree is not distinct from the jay higher up in the branches, nor from the bark of the tree itself. And Newton's view of things is not quite right either: the universe is not a pool table where things can be controlled and understood, but a curved foreverness where strange things happen to light and matter. It is a place that does not care for an individual and his sorrow.

The cabin becomes warm and I float, as if rising on a thermal to circle in the sky above. The wind has picked up and blows branches against the metal roof. The bats in the ridge of the roof are scrabbling around, anxious to get outside but unable to fly in this weather.

You're stabbed with a poison-tipped foil after all that thrust and parry, all that love and effort and pain, and you have nothing more to say. You lie in pain in a hospital bed and are jabbed with a morphine-filled needle after all that love and effort and suffering, and you have nothing left to say. You fall in a lake and water fills your mouth, your lungs, and you have nothing left to say. The rest is silence.

For those left behind that silence is insistent, impossible to ignore, like bats in the ceiling and the arms of trees scratching against your roof.

45

Forest Garden

The end of the year is a quiet time, when hauling water and splitting some firewood is all the work a day requires. I am left to read and do any minor repairs that arise. This morning I am working on my roof under a grey sky, with a brisk wind climbing the slope from the bay, flying through the forest, and cresting the mountain. A section of my Selkirk chimney blew loose in the night and I can't relight the fire before I fix it. By late afternoon I'm finished. I light a fire in the stove and anticipate the warmth as the smoke goes the direction it is intended to. The cold of last night won't be repeated.

I sit on my low stone wall after the sun is below the spruce trees. The wind has died down. What a peaceful time of day. *Entre chien et loup*. I press shreds of tobacco into a rolling paper. The fall rye we planted as a cover crop is a few inches tall and green. The oat straw blanketing the garlic is golden. Blue jays and crows come by to make a racket all around me, keeping me company. I lick the edge of the thin paper, roll it shut, and put the cigarette between my lips. The struck match mingles sulphur with the smoke on my throat. I relish it as it fills my lungs. It's on this wall that their lives come to me.

All those who followed me here. They come to me as their breath, exhaled all those years ago. I breathe them in—their carbon dioxide, their memories, ideas, conversations—and incorporate it all, filtering it through this traitorous body. My father, Leroy, Rachel. When I blow out, the smoke disperses in its own time in the still, cold air. It is my story, moving out of me, a part of me no longer, going out into the world.

I go inside and sit on my bed. My feet are warming under the blanket and Thunder is curled between my knees, resting for her nighttime prowl. The fire crackles and the orange light from it glows on the wall opposite in the dimming afternoon light. Other than the pops of the firewood and the purring of the cat, all is quiet in garden and forest. Then I hear a voice, coming toward the cabin, yelling. Martin bursts through my door out of breath.

"The cops just phoned me. They're looking for you."

"What for?"

He's shaking his head. "Get your coat on and hurry up."

I want to run. Art must have told them it was me and they're coming to lock me up.

"What did they say?"

"To meet them at my place. Come on."

He runs ahead while I walk, trying to decide if I should be going at all. Martin turns to shout.

"Ben, they said Art is hurt."

And then I am running, the soles of my shoes grabbing gravel. When we get to his back door Jenifer meets us and hugs me. I want her to tell me, but what I see in her eyes tells me all I need to know.

An RCMP car pulls into the driveway. An officer opens the door and strides to the house. We all go inside.

"Are you a relative of Arthur Mosher?"

"Yes."

"I'm afraid he's dead."

They're all looking at me. There's a ringing in my ears.

"He shot his wife, then himself."

He relates the story, seeming to regret having to say it aloud. Art had somehow dragged himself and his festering leg to the rest home in Bridgetown. He went straight to Louise's room and closed the door. The nurses heard three shots. When the police arrived both of them were dead. Louise had been shot in the heart and in the forehead. The back of Art's head was gone. His fingers still gripped the gun.

"What gun?" I ask the cop.

"His service revolver from the war. Enfield. Why do you ask?"

So he finally pulled the trigger.

"I don't know," I say.

"We've been to his place," the cop continues. "We found this on his kitchen table." He passes a piece of paper to me. I take it and am startled to see my name at the top. Underneath, in his neat hand:

> *I can't bear to think of her there without anyone*
> *to come see her. I know my time is running out. It*
> *doesn't matter if I die now or in a few months. But*
> *it does matter if she's rotting there alone with nobody*
> *to visit her. This is the only honourable way to go.*
> *I'm sorry your left to pick up the pieces. Your a good*
> *listener to an old mans stories. Don't waste your time*
> *crying over your past or me. I had a good life. And*

*don't waste any more time over Lina. She's gone and
you should find yourself a good woman like the one
I have.*
    — Art

I'm not proud of my first thought. Finally, someone kills
himself and has the grace to leave me a note.

*

It is time to vanquish my ghosts. I don't count Art among
them. One day I may be angry at him for doing what he did,
but I'm not now. I have no regrets about my friendship with
him. His death feels less like a betrayal or an abandonment
than a true goodbye.

First, my father. I was angry that he disappeared from my
life and I was angry that he became an alcoholic. I learned
to live with both of those disappointments and almost accept
them because of all the good memories. I could never forgive
him for killing himself. I guess I believed he had so my anger
could be justified.

I have another doctor's appointment to get the results of
my Pap smear. I walk into Middleton, past the big dairy farm,
smelling sweet and fetid like a stagnant pond. Ranged beside
one of the corrugated metal barns are the marshmallows of
haylage, wrapped in white plastic, shredded in places where
the sun and, possibly, my recombinant microbes have begun
their work. Another fifteen minutes and I'm in town. The
remnants of a grocery bag flap in the crooked fingers of a
maple tree. It is a contemporary prayer flag, tattered by sun

and wind. Above it, so still that I haven't noticed it until I am almost at the tree, is a crow. She has been watching me, and when she sees that I see her she caws once, then pushes off to fly away from town.

The liquor store smells of the musty funk of unrinsed returns. I find a mickey with the familiar yellow and red Gordon's label. I need that label to make this memory trip right. By the cash are the little airline-sized bottles labelled "Stocking Stuffers," aimed at the heart of pain that is Christmas morning for many of us. The middle-aged woman at the cash has the creases and husky voice of a lifelong smoker. *Go on, smoke*, I think. It's not like there's anything pure for us to breathe anymore. She has a sore on her cheek that glistens with some yellowish pus. She puts my bottle in a big plastic bag with *Nova Scotia Liquor Commission* plastered on both sides. She sees me eyeing it, thinks I'm worried it will split on the way home.

"These are the new ones that won't fall apart. They came in yesterday."

I don't complain about the plastic. Everyone has more pressing personal concerns than the state of the natural world. They don't want me reminding them of it.

"Merry Christmas," she says to the counter.

I'm tired of the fight. There's a cost for the constant sense of guilt we feel for what we've wrought. I look at the bag. My distress—anger, frustration, sadness—is one result of having lived in this mad world. At least I didn't bring a child into it. I imagine if I had a child he would ask me why we pollute so much. The only truthful answer would be because it is convenient to do so.

Down the street to the SaveEasy. There's not much there

this time of year. Canned soup, apples, magazines. I pass the tabloids looking for something to read. There's Melvin Leach on the cover of *Time*, again. He's dressed in a Superman cape, with an asinine smirk on his face. "The Superscientist Who Saved the World." I put down my basket and flip through, looking for the article. He claims to have created a means to stop the rampaging bacteria that are wreaking havoc around the globe. Nowhere in the article does it point to his lab as the origin of the problem. Apparently, he's looked at as a pioneer of what is now called genetically engineered environmentalism. Good for him.

Then, along Main Street to Soldier's Memorial, where I see the resident, who informs me that I might have dysplasia and that it will take another week to get further lab results. I laugh because what else is a guy with a cervix supposed to do?

Hell, we need more labels for all of us out here.

I fill a glass half full with gin and top it with tonic water. I sit in my chair with my feet resting on the edge of the wood stove looking out at the snow-covered garden. Stalks of kale, tomato stakes, and the short beech tree jut out of the snow. I down my drink.

A little knowledge is a dangerous thing. It's something my virology prof at Cornell used to say to us. She saw that whenever her students came across a novel piece of evidence they were likely to apply it to every circumstance. It was that way with my father's death. I was a geneticist, studying the molecular mechanisms of disease. At Lowell, after his death, I had looked in my *Merck* for something, anything, that would explain his behaviour. When I looked under *tremors* the first listing was *alcoholism*. But under that, halfway down the page, was another. Angry outbursts, sloppy gait, and moodiness. Depression, myoclonic jerks, facial grimacing, and irritability. I was convinced then that he hadn't been an alcoholic. He had Huntington's disease. Attributing his tremors, his angry outbursts, and his mood swings to a genetic disease absolved the man I adored—my hero—of responsibility.

A little knowledge is a dangerous thing. And some little pieces of knowledge are so dangerous we choose to ignore them.

I get up and pour myself another drink. Then another. I take a sip of the third one, am overcome with fatigue and dizziness, and lie on my bunk.

I wake not knowing where I am. It all seems wrong. It's dark and I smell cigar smoke. My head is pounding and I'm feverish. My hair is wet with sweat, my back soaked and sticking to the sheets. I don't want to move. The room is pulsating like a heart, seeming to get bigger, then smaller. At the foot of the bed is a figure whose silhouette I can only see when he moves in front of the window. I am afraid of the quiet and want some sound to intrude, even my own voice.

"Is that you?"

Your heartache is not unique, he says. Everyone has suffered. Some people lose their father young. Some lose their mother young.

"I didn't lose you. You killed yourself."

It's not that simple. I'm not speaking only of my death. I'm speaking of our disconnection from that which nurtures us.

"I didn't say it was simple."

And you're not living as if it's simple. We all experience heartbreak, betrayals, loss. We tell stories to each other to make sense of that suffering. You believe that you're done with grief. It's not done with you.

He stands there for a long time.

You'll find love, he says, love that matters and feels like home. But only after you've let me go. Let them all go.

I say nothing, and then he's gone.

I start up in bed, gasping for breath in the darkness. I am puffing like a steam engine, disoriented, tangled in the sheet. I had been running the 26.2 miles from Lowell to our house in Newton on the day my father died but my feet were leaden and I couldn't move them. Once I catch my breath, I flop down, facing the wall. Then someone is rubbing my back, soothing me. I lie there, not frightened at all by that hand.

"Dad?" I whisper. There is no answer.

I have the urge to talk to him about things I don't even know how to bring up with the living. So I do, in a whisper, afraid that my voice will break the spell.

"Did it all happen? Remember casting our lines from the canoe in Moosehead Lake, hoping to catch pike? Just the two of us, best friends spending an easy afternoon together. I loved having you to myself, like in the old days when we were driving for days through New England."

I try to get the words out, but they fill my mouth, leaving little room for breath. I am so tired. I have to know whether he committed suicide. He did drown. But he didn't leave me a note, and the coroner reported that his blood alcohol level indicated he had been drinking heavily. Perhaps he meant to drown and got drunk to give him the courage to do it. Perhaps he slipped and it was a mistake. Either way, his drinking wasn't an accident, and that was what killed him.

The tapping of a woodpecker on the tin roof wakes me. The hand on my back is gone. The smell of cigar smoke is gone. What continues to confound are the skates he left on my bed before he died.

My third drink, the one I poured before falling asleep, sits nearly full on the floor by the chair. I can smell the juniper berries and I remember. I get up, take the glass to the door, open it, and pour the gin and tonic out. It separates into droplets that, by the time they reach the snow below, are no more than a mist.

Christmas morning. I wake from a dream of my death. A blanket is wrapped around my arms and over my head. I am struggling, unable to breathe. I squirm and my wings are free. I shake my tail feathers and leap from the branch. Up, up and circling the treetops, snow glistening on spruce boughs in the bright sun.

One day soon I will take the train to Montreal. Leroy's name was in *The Globe and Mail* this morning. He recently published work on the genetics of colon cancer that should make screening easier. I wrote to his lab at McGill and got a response from him immediately. He wrote about his efforts in the lab and told me that he and Rachel had married before leaving New York. He invited me to visit them — they have a daughter — but I can't face that right now. He said my "escape," as he called it, worked well. The RCMP had phoned Rachel to say her passport had been found, along with Leroy's sweater, on the rocks by Herring Cove by a woman walking her retriever. He also wrote:

> *We had no idea why you put $37,000 into Rachel's account. We were sure you were dead, but then you asked Rachel to send you that money to the bank in Toronto and we thought we'd find you. I looked in telephone directories, online. Nothing. You did a good job of erasing yourself.*
>
> *It's ironic that your work in L's lab forced the development of biodegradable plastics. They're still finding ways to swamp us in the shit. There's a landfill outside the city here that uses microbes like yours, and I read last week that an Australian environmental organization is hoping to collect the plastic in ocean gyres in nets, bring it ashore, and digest it to CO_2 and H_2O. It all seems too little, too late to me, but you never know.*

He said that American authorities had been led to Leach when DNA analysis of the bacteria revealed an engineered plasmid with cassettes that could only have come from his lab. Leach was able to convince them that it was Benny, describing me as a rogue element in his lab. That I stole Rachel's passport to get across the border convinced them, and when the FBI went looking for me, the trail ended on the container ship. They had to assume that I drowned off the coast of Nova Scotia.

It is dark in the cabin by five o'clock. Dark and cold. The fire has gone out. I light a candle. I speak with the dead. They haunt me because they *are* me. I climb into the rafters of this tiny cabin and pull down the boxes of letters and photos I have stored. As if happiness can be hoarded for lean nights. The two days I am most concerned with don't exist.

It is time to bury yesterday. Tomorrow will look after itself.

I open the wood stove door and handle each letter. I remember what is in every one. Letters from Katharine. Lay them on top of the cold ashes. A card from my mother when I left home for the first time, to go to summer camp. She was sad and wrote that she'd miss me. The few from my father that I've cherished. More from Lina.

I strike a match and touch it to the pile.

In my hands is the photo of my dad laughing as he holds me over Crystal Lake. I am wearing the blue bathing suit with the frilly skirt that I adored. He looks so happy. I had trusted him to protect me. I throw it into the fire. The flames change the colour of his face and erase his smile.

I close the door when it's all in the fire. Once the fire dies down I take the ashes from the wood stove and put them in a bowl. I unscrew the cap of the gin bottle and smell the juniper. I take a small sip, enough to coat my tongue, and hold it there. I put on my rubber boots and a sweater and go out into the cold. The stars are magnificent. I find the oak Lina and I planted on my birthday. I sprinkle the ashes around its stem, then pour the remaining gin on top of them. This oak has been through a lot. Back in my cabin I blow out the candle and go to bed.

I am through with the past.

I have remembered my shortcomings, and my father's, remembered how I loved him and was loved by him, and in so doing I have attempted to resurrect a time that once was. I have longed to be enveloped in the living I knew in New York, not because it was all that much fun, but because it is my past. And that past is forever linked to the past that came before it, back to a time when I was a kid and life was harmless and I was loved. What I am left with is a visit from the past. And a visit is nothing more than a little death.

Ghosts inhabit this world.

The End

I know that we are going to destroy the world that holds us. We are savages, treating the Earth like a toilet, fouling our own nest. We all seem to agree on that now. Our heads have been in the sand since I was a little girl, when we first realized how good we had it and how we were screwing it all up. We knew what we were wreaking and it scared us, most of all because we couldn't see any way of stopping it. So we stick our heads in the sand. The ostrich does this not to become invisible to its foe; it wants to avoid seeing what's coming for it.

What I created will not stop our destruction of the world. What I am doing here at Forest Garden will not make a difference either, but I have no choice. I acted in New York because I cared, and I have to act now because it matters to me still. The world will continue to change, probably for the worse, but it remains a beautiful place to be. And there is hope, people hold on to hope, even the most pessimistic. Leroy and Rachel see, like the rest of us, where we're headed, yet they chose to have a child. They must believe that we can right our wrongs or why would they have done that?

I look out my window onto a sunny morning. It snowed yesterday and all the night too, and the sunlight on the snow is brighter, but in a different way, than on a summer day. It's hard to be pessimistic on a morning with that sun, the snow still clean, and the birds gliding in the light. Why not love this morning? I stretch. The bay continues to empty and refill twice each day in sync with the moon.

A crow flies overhead. Black, sleek, it reminds me of Lina. It looks down, its beak pointing to the ground. It's the birds that give me heart to continue. Birds keep doing what they do, colourful and tenacious, while the world burns.

I stoke the fire I had left to die out and lie down on my bunk. Leroy's premonition came partly true. We both live in Canada. My skates are hanging from a nail on the wall. "We make things happen by believing they will," he once said to me. "We dream where we're headed, and one day, as if entering that dream, we arrive there."

I'm the one in the cabin in the woods, alone on a peaceful sunny morning. I jump from the bunk, lace up my boots, put my coat on, grab the skates from the nail on the wall as well as my shovel, and leave the cabin. I walk deep into the forest beside coyote tracks in the snow along the woods road. The tracks come to a pile of rabbit pellets and a rabbit track crossing it perpendicular to the road. The coyote tracks veer off to follow the trail of the rabbit heading into the woods.

The pond is solid and covered with snow. Its edge is rimmed with spruce laden with snow and with the skeletons of maples, highlighted by the white that rests along their stiff branches. I lace up my skates and begin to shovel the ice clear. It becomes the shape of a rink in a fairy tale, all curves and blips and narrow bottlenecks between trees that lead into open spaces. The shovelling warms me up and I throw my coat on the snowbank I just made. I rest my bare palms on my sweater, feeling the comfort of wool and the solid flesh of my healthy body, and look up at the sky. It is blue as only a sky in January can be blue, outlining the spires of the trees that pierce it. I thank the sky, and the sun that casts shadows of branches on the snow and ice, and the cold air that fills my lungs.

We won't survive. That's no reason to stop trying though, no reason to stop caring. There's nothing else we can do.

I begin to skate, feeling the smooth ice beneath my blades. Some things won't be lost.

SOLUTIONS IN ENVIRONMENTAL MICROBIOLOGY, May ___, p. 2122-2123
0037-1254/37/$03.00.9

Creation and Characterization of a Polyethylene Terephthalate-Digesting Mutant of *Pseudomonas aeruginosa*

Benita R. Mosher, Jonathan Yovkov, Melvin A. Leach*

Department of Microbiology, Cornell University Medical College, New York, New York

Received 6 December ___ /Accepted 12 February ___

Polyethylene terephthalate (PETE), like many petroleum-based polymers, has a half-life of natural degradation exceeding millennia. We report here the creation and selective cultivation of mutant strains of *P. aeruginosa* capable of survival on media containing PETE as the sole source of carbon. These strains apparently cleave PETE in liquid culture, resulting in ethylene glycol as well as other, as yet unknown, short-chain organic compounds. Preliminary analysis of the enzymatic function suggests a novel esterase activity.

Polyethylene terephthalate (PETE) is a condensation polymer resulting from the transesterification of dimethyl terephthalate and ethylene glycol, with methanol as a by-product (Fig. 1). It is one of the most important synthetic polymers and is used in the manufacture of bottles to contain soda and water, food containers, and other liquid containers.

Given its near ubiquity, stability once discarded, and the failure of recycling programs to capture more than 20 per cent of manufactured containers[3], a means of eliminating this waste product from landfills, ditches, and the waterways of the world is essential. There has been a report of a strain of *Pseudomonas* that eats high-density polyethylene[1] but this has not been confirmed

As part of our ongoing pursuit of sustainable solutions to this problem, we have engineered and/or selected for strains of *P. aeruginosa*[6] and *S. aureus*[2] that are capable of exploiting carbon held within the long-chain polymers that make up various plastics.

We found these strains to be minimally effective in degrading synthetic polymers in liquid culture. Wanting to expand on this work and, hopefully, to discover strains capable of rapidly and efficiently digesting plastics, we used mutagens to create cells with altered properties. These techniques were accompanied by screening and selective pressure to unequivocally identify mutants with the enhanced characteristics.

Through random mutagenesis and selection, we have created a strain of *P. aeruginosa* capable of rapidly degrading PETE in vitro into ethylene glycol and terephthalate.

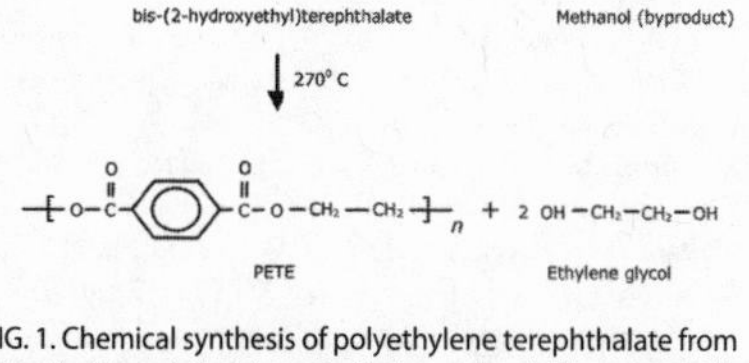

MATERIALS AND METHODS

Organism. *Pseudomonas aeruginosa* strain K212 (5) was the wild-type strain used in this study. It was treated with mutagens, followed by selection, resulting in two PETE-digesting strains: BRM92 and BRM106.

Culture conditions. Single colonies of randomly mutated cells of *P. aeruginosa* K212 were grown in 2X LB medium containing 100 µg/ml carbenicillin and 35 µg/ml tetracycline in 100 ml Erlenmeyer flasks. Cells were spun, washed 3X in distilled water, and resuspended in distilled water containing minimal broth with 100 µg/ml of PETE as the only source of carbon. These liquid cultures were incubated at 300C, observing for cell growth. Cultures not exhibiting any turbidity were discarded after seven days.

Chemicals. Ethyl methanesulfonate (EMS) was purchased from Blako Chemical Co. (St. Louis, MO). Acridine was purchased from McNeil &

FIG. 1. Chemical synthesis of polyethylene terephthalate from dimethyl terephthalate and ethylene glycol. The enzymatic breakdown, presumed to be via esterase function in the mutant strains BRM92 and BRM106, releases ethylene glycol and other short-chain compounds yet to be identified.

* Corresponding author. Mailing address: Department of Molecular Biology and Genetics, Cornell University Medical College, 1300 York Avenue, New York, NY 10021.

Sons Industries (Cleveland, OH). γ-rays were applied using cobalt-60 supplied by Atomic Energy of Canada Ltd. (Chalk River, ON). A circular film of PETE (diameter 65 mm and approximately 750 mg) was obtained from DuPont. Mutagenesis. Liquid cultures of strain K212 were subjected to mutagenesis with each of the agents listed above. They were then grown in minimal broth with PETE. Incubations. 1 ml samples of mutated cells of strain K212 growing in minimal broth with PETE as the sole source of carbon were analyzed using reversed-phaed HPLC. The presence of ethylene glycol was used as a preliminary indication that PETE was being degraded. Those liquid cultures containing significant concentrations of ethylene glycol (>30 mol/L)were subjected to column chromatography.

Detection of PETE-degrading activity using reversed-phase high performance liquid chromatography (HPLC). The liquid cultures were analyzed in a Varian ProStar HPLC system. The polar mobile phase used trifluoroacetic acid as an eluent. The eluent had a flow rate of 0.7 ml/min. The column temperature was kept at 32°C.

Random mutagenesis and selection of P. aeruginosa K212. Two cultures of mutagenized K212 grew in minimal liquid media containing PETE as the sole source of carbon. Strain BRM92 resulted from mutagenesis with EMS and strain BRM106 resulted from mutagenesis with gamma rays. Fig. 1 shows the growth profiles of the wild-type and two mutant strains.

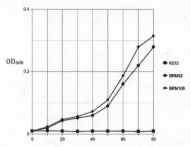

FIG. 2. Growth of *P. aeruginosa* strains in minimal liquid medium containing PETE. Strains K212, BRM92, and BRM106 were precultured at 30°C for 2 days in 2X LB medium, triple washed with distilled water, and inoculated into fresh minimal medium with PETE as the sole source of carbon. Cultivation was continued under the same conditions for 80 hours. Cell densities were measured by optical density at 600 nm.

Characterization of strains BRM92 and BRM106. Lysates of the two mutated strains showed significant degradation products of PETE (Fig. 2). A large peak corresponds to ethylene

glycol, one of the expected products of PETE digestion. A smaller significant peak represents terephthalate. There are many other, smaller, peaks representing products that have not yet been analyzed.

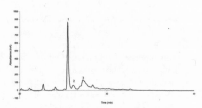

FIG. 3. Chromatogram of PETE degradation products. A lysate of strain BM92 was incubated with PETE for 4 hours at 32°C. Peak 1 is ethylene glycol. Peaks 2 is an unknown degradation products to be analyzed. Peak 3 corresponds to terephthalate.

In this paper we report the creation of two strains of *P. aeruginosa* capable of growth on medium containing a synthetic compound previously impervious to biological attack. The strains rapidly degrade PETE in vitro into ethylene glycol and terephthalate.

This is a significant find because of the potential to utilize such strains in the degradation of waste products currently disposed of in landfills.

It will be interesting to determine the genetic alteration behind the supposed enzymatic changes that allow these bacterial strains to digest a xenobiotic compound.

ACKNOWLEDGEMENTS
We thank Gabriel Nawthorn and Leroy Timmins for critical reading of the manuscript.

REFERENCES
1. Entwistle, J., Townsend, P., Daltrey, R., and K. Moon. 1976. Strain of Pseudomonas aeruginosa capable of eating vinyl LPs also digests high-density polyethylene. J. Irreprod. Res. 48:38-41.
2. Foss, T.L. and M.A. Leach. ____. Selection of strains of S. aureus for ability to exploit the carbon in polyethylene. J. Biochem. Fund. 27:215-222.
3. Burn, S.M. 1991. Social psychology and the stimulation of recycling behaviors: The block leader approach. J. Appl. Soc. Psych. 21:611-629.
4. McNeil L., and M. A. Leach. ____. Purification and characterization of an extracellular manganese peroxidase from Pseudomonas aeruginosa. Microbiol. Symp. 57:62-69.
5. McNeil L., Foss, T.L. and M.A. Leach. ____. Selection for strains of P. aeruginosa competent at utilizing long-chain polymers as a source of carbon. J. Biochem. Fund. 25:356-361.

Acknowledgements

All of the characters in our dreams—all the lakes, guns, beasts, and other strange stuff—are aspects of ourselves. We inhabit our dreams in various guises, wearing the cloak of an old girlfriend, a crow flying overhead, or the wood stove that heats our cabin. This book is one such dream.

Books and quotes

The Oppenheimer quote at the beginning is from Joyce Nelson's *The Perfect Machine: TV in the Nuclear Age*, 1987, published by Between the Lines, Toronto.

The Wendell Berry poem is from his *A Timbered Choir: The Sabbath Poems 1979-1997*. Permission to quote granted by Counterpoint Press.

An Accidental Monk is a wonderful book by Marylee Mitcham (1976, published by St. Anthony Messenger Press) that buoyed me through a winter in the woods in Nova Scotia. She gave me permission to quote from it. Her blog is at anaccidentalmonk. blogspot.com.

Darkness Visible is William Styron's memoir chronicling his depression. It helped me realize that the pain of losing a parent at a young age can lead to depression. I knew it was debilitating; I continue to see the myriad ways in which that manifests.

People

I am grateful to my editor, Bethany Gibson, for her diligent assistance. I am especially thankful that she championed my novel to the folks at Goose Lane and convinced them to take a chance on it, and on me. She good-naturedly read draft after draft, never seeming to tire of my questions. Thanks, friend.

Thanks to the many who were willing to read and provide comments on early versions of this book. They include Ben Gallagher, Sarah Selecky, Bill Kowalski, Heather Jessup, Eric Philpott, Greg Georgas, Patrick Murphy, Chai Duncan, Erin Robinsong, Ann Macklem, Julie Paul, Angela Klaassen, Annie Bray, and Mavis Spencer.

I have such gratitude for the generosity of Crane Stockey, who hosted me in his boat house on the Northwest Arm. That time along to write was luxurious, peaceful, and inspirational.

The Writers' Federation of Nova Scotia is a wonderful organization. It was their Atlantic Writing Competition that gave me a boost when I needed it. Thank you especially to Nate, Sue, and Susan.

I have been in good hands ever since Susanne Alexander and everyone else at the Goose said yes. Thanks for treating me so well and with such enthusiasm.

Thanks to the Wired Monk Writers Group—Dina Desveaux, Chris Benjamin, and Simon Vigneault.

The Nova Scotia Department of Communities, Culture &

Heritage has been generous with their support of two Creation Grants during the completion of the manuscript.

For two of the many older men who have mentored me: Con Enright, for teaching me to garden, and Bob Philips, for sharing his stories. The writing of fiction is a way of raising the dead.

Thanks to the owners and baristas of The Trident Booksellers and Café in Halifax, who provided a peaceful respite from city life, pots of Dragon Phoenix Pearl, and an uplifted environment in which to read *The New Yorker* and write. Their efforts to awaken us to the plight of the environment are an inspiration.

Thanks to Helen Brown for the joy, work, and struggle of life in Halifax; on Hornby Island; and, especially, at Forest Garden. Without that, at least half of this story wouldn't be.

To my neighbours on the North Mountain, who were nothing but polite, helpful, and supportive as we hacked, swatted, dug, sawed, and nailed our way onto that piece of land.

To my siblings, John, Jill, and Alexa; to Hazel; thanks for supporting me and caring about me and sharing so much.

To my loving, devoted parents. Despite their flaws, they were and are heroic. It is heroism based in simple things: home-cooked meals, tucking children in nightly, keeping a garden, and month-long camping trips to experience the natural beauty of our continent. The consistency and commitment that good parenting requires are more difficult to maintain than writing a book or probably anything else. They were and are very good at it.

To Annie and Ruth, for keeping me company.